THE LEGENDS OF

MOSS RIDGE

SIMONE E. OWS

 FriesenPress

Suite 300 - 990 Fort St
Victoria, BC, V8V 3K2
Canada

www.friesenpress.com

ISBN
978-1-5255-8620-0 (Hardcover)
978-1-5255-8619-4 (Paperback)
978-1-5255-8621-7 (eBook)

1. JUVENILE FICTION, FANTASY & MAGIC

Distributed to the trade by The Ingram Book Company

Cathy—

I am ever so grateful that you've chosen an interest in my story telling and will share this wonderous adventure with me. May the journey bring you endless smiles.

This book is dedicated to the memories of Angela Smith, David DeWolfe, Tina Composano and Meron Lomas. Without their encouragement, I would not have stayed on track for as long as I have. I would also like to thank my husband, my friends and our families for their support, and Sandy Rusic and Trina Washington, who have remained a captive audience to all my crazy and wild ideas.

Simone E. Ouy
2021

A Tale of Westfield County

Legends are made by the stories that are told,
passed down through the ages
to the young from the old.
This one's about an alien race
of monsters and mutants
in a magical place.
There's vengeance sworn
and heroes born
with battles yet to be won.
A town that's scared
as no-one will be spared
by the evil that is done.
It's said that a leader
will rise to the call
to free the people
and bring peace for them all.
So justice won't be needed
for a villain already condemned.
One wish will change the entire outcome.
The leader, the Golden Gem.

PROLOGUE

"Dad?" Zareb called out.

Khalon raised a hand from underneath his aircraft's gas capsule. "I'm here!" He waved. "And since you're passing by it, hand me the micandul please." The instrument broke down coloured gems into carbon fuel much more quickly than heating the gems at high temperatures.

Zareb picked up the tool and stopped for a moment to admire the aircraft's translucent wings that rippled in iridescent colours extending out from the metal frame. Even though he had joined the Az-Yen fleet two years ago, the beauty of the aircraft still gave him goosebumps.

"What's on your mind?" Khalon asked, taking the flat metal device out of his son's hand and placing it inside the capsule.

"When I turn thirteen, will my sister be ready for the truth?"

"I'm hoping so," Khalon replied, standing up and throwing his gloves on his work bench. He looked into the boy's face and smiled sadly. Zareb had his mother's hazel eyes and freckles, as did his sister. It was a constant reminder of how much he missed the two of them.

Zareb let out a sigh. "You're thinking about Mom again, aren't you?"

"Yes," Khalon responded.

"That's okay. Sometimes I do too."

"You do understand why we must wait for your birthdays to arrive, right?"

"I do," Zareb answered, "but sometimes I just wish the rules could change."

Khalon nodded grimly.

"I'm not *that* different, am I?" Zareb asked.

"No, neither one of you is. It's not your physical appearance the Elders are concerned with. It's your bloodline. I've told you this before. You and your sister are of mixed races."

"I know," Zareb said reluctantly, then added, "she has all the powers."

Khalon wrapped an arm around Zareb. "There's no need for envy. Your abilities are just as extraordinary."

"I guess," Zareb said, "but it's not the same."

"Well, you have something that your sister will never have."

"What's that?"

"A world record for being the youngest astronaut."

The boy chuckled and playfully pushed his Dad away from him. "Twelve isn't *that* young!"

Khalon laughed. "It is by *human* standards."

CHAPTER ONE

1981

All he did was blink … and suddenly, Murphy's world was unrecognizable.

He didn't remember how he got there, or even why, but his baffled expression reflected back at him as he stared into hundreds of glass fragments strewn across a gravel floor. Murphy rubbed his tired eyes, trying to focus, and hoped that the throbbing in his head was not a brain tumour causing a hallucination. He needed some fresh air to clear his head. But as soon as he moved forward, he lost his balance and fell to his knees. Judging by the pins and needles tingling down his thighs, he had been crouching for a long period of time. What was he hiding from? Murphy squinted from the rainbows bouncing off of the glass as he searched through the pockets of bright light for something to trigger his memory. At first he didn't see anything that was helpful, but then he noticed a silver object lying next to his foot. It was a metal cuff linked to heavy chains and attached to a rock wall.

Murphy picked it up and felt the weight of it. Whoever had put him in the stone chamber wanted to make sure he stayed. He twisted his calf to assess the damage to his ankle and saw that the pant leg was torn. He lifted part of the hem and swallowed down his fear. There was a lot of blood, enough to cause a cardiac arrest, but thankfully it had crusted over. Somehow he must have used the shards of glass to free himself, but to his astonishment, there were no cuts or bruises on his hands. Satisfied that he didn't have any life-threatening injuries, and grunting from the stiffness in his legs, Murphy pushed himself up to a standing position.

This, of course, was the wrong thing to do.

A skittering noise had his head whipping in all directions. He couldn't locate the sound so he stepped quietly out of his safe zone, listening intently for movement. He passed under a solid archway chiseled in the same rock as the chamber. *This has to be a cave, or maybe some kind of underground army bunker,* he figured as he dragged his feet to an open area. It was an identical room to the one he had been held hostage in, but darker. As he waited for his eyes to adjust, a hissing noise brought his body to attention and he backed up into the rock wall.

Within inches of his right ear, a frigid breath escaped the lips of the unknown figure whispering, "Watch your back, child. There are plenty of monsters lurking about." Then to prove its point, it ground its teeth together. Murphy jerked his head away from the creature and it snarled, chomping its jaws. Murphy ducked, and it missed biting his head off by inches.

Then Murphy saw it.

It was a hideous monster, and it was held captive with the same type of chains secured to the rock wall as Murphy's. The thing was a hybrid mix of Neanderthal, bird and insect, and it strained against the shackles, thrusting its black claws out and thrashing the air. The more Murphy backed away, the stronger its determination to free itself became.

It screeched, and Murphy covered his ears at the deafening sound. Was it hurt? He didn't want to stick around to find out the answer. Murphy only cared about putting as much distance between himself and the creature as possible. His stomach churned with a sickening lurch as he observed wet liquid ooze from the creature's belly and gather like globs of tar underneath its monstrous legs. The dark, inky liquid rolled toward him, almost reaching his shoes before he jumped out of the way. Was it bleeding because of its attempts to break loose of its bonds? *But when blood spills, it spreads. It doesn't merge together and form little balls of—*

Oh man, I think those are centipedes!

Whatever that thick substance was, it was bubbling and forming a disgusting row of squirming, multi-legged maggots with human features, gasping for air. The creature didn't seem to mind that the bugs were crawling up its torso and swarming into a mass of pulsating lines that latched onto its back and tail. It stretched, raising its gaunt, feathered limbs to expose a pale chest and wrinkled skin that hung like wings ready to flap into action. It rounded its back and seemed to delight in the fact that it was being eaten alive. Murphy gagged, watching with a morbid curiosity as the bugs dug their way into the creature's body. The holes they dug widened, splitting and tearing what was left of the creature's skin. Within moments, spiny appendages too numerous to count broke through on either side of the creature's waist and touched the ground with feet made of talons.

Murphy turned and ran. But no matter how hard he pushed forward, he couldn't get ahead. The creature had a hold of him. Its grip was strong, but Murphy's will to live was stronger, and he pulled out of its grasp. It screeched in anger, glaring at him with hollowed eyes.

Murphy took a careful step back, then bolted out of the room. He had made it as far as the entrance when a sudden explosion knocked him off his feet. He rolled onto his knees, throwing his arms over his head to protect against the crumbling rock that tumbled down the wall as the tremors continued.

BOOM! BOOM! BOOM!

Murphy tried to stand on the gritty surface but his feet slid apart as the ground shook and he lost his balance as one leg slipped over a ledge and dangled in the open air. He scrambled over to the security of the wall, feeling the intense heat rise from the deep cavity. He listened to the pebbles fall like rain over the slope towards the red glowing ribbons that flowed freely down below. His heart was racing as he leaned over to peek around the arched doorway, unaware he was holding his breath. He saw the creature throw itself against the wall over and over again causing shock waves that reverberated throughout the cave. Stones showered down from the metal plate that secured its leash. It pulled on the chain and the bolts loosened, but the links would not break free. Murphy's air ran out and he gasped. It whipped its head in his direction and went berserk, clawing at its own neck in an effort to pull the circular fastener over its head, but its jaw was too large. The creature's tail whipped violently up and down, sending a spray of slick black goo across Murphy's face. With lightning speed that he didn't know he had, Murphy wiped off the bug-infested crud with his t-shirt and threw it away. He definitely did not want that stuff to take him as a host.

The creature managed to crawl partially up the wall and made a daring leap in his direction. But the chains held and it dropped in mid-air, landing with a thud that sent up a flurry of grey feathers. Despite his circumstance, Murphy grinned. The creature could not fly.

Howling in pain, it opened its mouth, revealing a set of very sharp teeth. Then, in a peculiar gesture, it pointed its clawed finger directly at Murphy and waved it back and forth, as if it was scolding an unruly child. It laughed. Murphy didn't find anything funny about it. His smile faded as panic washed over him.

There were no exits, except for the one the creature was guarding. The only way Murphy would be able to escape was if the creature keeled over and died.

Murphy wished for a miracle, but he wasn't expecting it to work.

He froze as the creature tore loose, but when it removed its last shackle, a heap of boulders crashed down upon its body, pinning it. Murphy coughed as the dust covered him in a blanket of black powder.

"Ready or not, here I come ..."

The sinister voice gave Murphy the incentive he needed to move. He shuffled forward blindly, using the wall as a guide, until he found a deep crevice nearby and wedged himself inside. He squeezed his eyes shut, knowing he wouldn't win this game, but crossed his fingers anyhow.

...

Murphy woke up to a painful burn running down his thigh. He rubbed the area and his hand passed over something prickly. He lifted his knee to get a better look, and to his horror, a clawed hairy limb poked through the tear in his pants where his left leg should have been. *This cannot be happening!* He whimpered, shaking the limb in hopes that it would fall off, but it remained in place and moved when he willed it too. He gingerly set his new leg on the ground, and the claw dug into the gravel as if it was made of chunky peanut butter.

"Now you have a part of me to hold onto," the creature jeered.

Murphy raised his pale blue eyes and defiantly glared back at the monster. "You're not real!" he snapped. "You can't—"

"Can't I?" the creature snarled. "You *are* the creator," it reasoned.

Murphy grunted with frustration. "If I started this, then I could end it too!" he shouted, feeling a bit bolder and convincing himself that he actually had that power. "I command you not to hurt me!"

The creature smirked, crawling toward him. Murphy shuffled backwards, smacking his head against a low ceiling of chipped stone. He was trapped and sank to the ground, pleading for the creature to spare his life.

It moved in closer, savouring the tension.

Murphy began to hyperventilate. He rested his head against the wall as tiny white stars danced in his vision. Part of him wanted to fall into the depths of unconsciousness, but the thought of having another leg amputated persuaded him to stay alert.

Just give up, he thought. No one was coming to rescue him anyway. Then an inner voice reached out to him and asked, *So what's your next move? Will you run or stand your ground? Are you a cheetah, or ...* Murphy knew without a doubt that he was more like a chipmunk.

He used every ounce of energy he had to pull himself up, but his useless insect appendage splayed out and wouldn't bend properly.

This leg is really starting to bug me!

The creature used Murphy's distraction to its full advantage and slipped away into the shadows. Murphy crawled over to the ledge, peering down at the flickering lights that snaked its way along the deep cavity. Sweat beaded on his forehead as he watched it churn. He heard a skittering noise and looked up just as the creature landed on top of him. As it attempted to sink its needle-like teeth into his neck, Murphy slid closer to the edge. He bucked, throwing the creature off, and it fell onto its back, thrashing about to turn itself over.

This was the moment Murphy had hoped for. He wanted to push the creature's body toward the edge, but its tail whipped back and forth, preventing any moves he tried to make.

The creature was relentless. It rolled onto its legs, then bolted toward Murphy like a wasp that just had its home disturbed. Murphy was already on the other side of the cavity when the creature caught up to him. He didn't even bother turning around. He could feel the claws slicing through the air as it tried to cut his skin. How could he outrun a creature that had twenty legs and built-in cleats for feet? *This creature would put an Olympian to shame,* he thought.

Murphy darted around a pile of rocks, picking up a few and hurling them toward the creature. But in his attempt to slow it down, he slipped on the loose stones and slid over the edge. He gripped the jagged rock and dug his feet into the wall, stopping his descent with the help of his insect claw.

Sweat dripped across his brow. Murphy's hands were tiring. Where was the creature? Did it leave? His answer came when he saw the creature looking down at him. A moment later, there was a sound of scraping rock. It was dragging a boulder the size of Mount Everest to the edge. With the strength of five thousand men, it picked up the massive rock, ready to fling it over and crush Murphy. But the ledge it was standing on cracked, and as it dropped the rock, the ground collapsed. Dirt and stones washed over Murphy like a tidal wave. The creature screeched, thrusting its legs out in all directions, scrambling to find something to hold onto, but it lost its fight against gravity.

Murphy watched as it plunged into the watery grave. Reds and golds illuminated the cavity as it swallowed the creature whole and then he realized that it wasn't a sea of swirling colours he was staring at but of molten lava. When he was certain that the creature wasn't going to return, he pulled himself up and rolled onto his back. Lying there exhausted, he listened to the sizzling and popping sounds bubbling up from the sea of fire. The putrid aroma wafted into his nose.

He told himself that this was just a dream.

A very bad dream …

…

Something *definitely* was burning. Murphy woke up gasping and almost hacked up a lung breathing in the smoke-filled air. He rubbed his eyes to clear his blurred vision and sat straight up in bed. There was a hazy fog trailing up to his room and a surge of panic made his heart race. Was the house on fire? He tried to recall the safety tips he had learned in school while forcing his legs into a pair of balled-up sweatpants he had thrown on the floor, and was startled when he heard his mother's distressed voice.

"No! Stop!" she cried out.

Murphy ran into the hallway, where he found her waving a towel at the end of the stairs, trying to prevent the smoke alarm from blaring its warning.

He blew out a sigh of relief and sat down at the kitchen table.

"Your waffles are ready," she said, plunking down a plate full of black disks stacked on top of one another.

Murphy picked up his fork to examine the charcoal bits and made a face.

"Don't you dare say a word if you have nothing nice to say," his mother grumbled, irritated by her own lack of cooking skills.

Murphy's dad smirked. He was leaning against the counter with a bowl of cereal in his hand.

Murphy's breakfast smelled as awful as it looked. He poked at the unrecognizable mound. It crunched as his knife punctured the first layer, breaking it in two. He poured half a bottle of syrup on them to drown out the taste and swirled a piece into the liquid pooling at the bottom of his plate. Then he shoved the small sliver into his mouth and got as far as chewing it once before spitting it out.

"Well, at least *mine* can't be incinerated," his dad teased, sliding his box of cereal in front of his son.

His mom flung water at his dad with her soapy dishcloth.

"And ..." he added, drying off his chin, "it's fortified with whole grains, which means *lots* of fibre."

"Gee, that sounds a whole lot better!" Murphy commented sarcastically. He stuck his tongue out as he scanned the healthy ingredients. Where was the sugar?

His mom took his plate away and handed him a spoon. "I suppose you'd rather make your own breakfast," she said, sulking. Murphy thought of a

PB and J sandwich, but kept quiet for fear that he'd hurt her feelings if he suggested it.

"Sure, he could. Right, buddy? All he needs to get started is a handful of raisins ..."

Murphy sighed and gave in, grabbing the skim milk.

"Look at the *power* in those bran clusters!" his dad stated with too much enthusiasm.

Murphy poured the cereal and looked into his bowl. What he saw appeared to be more like dried up rabbit turds than something that could give him super-strength.

"Guaranteed to make your hair grow too! See that?" Murphy's dad bent over to point out a few strands poking up from his thinning hair. Murphy shook his head, clearing his thoughts of looking like a bald Yeti as he aged. "Plus," his dad added, "the bulk keeps you regular. You don't want your plumbing to be backed up."

Murphy set his spoon down, unable to respond. He was trying to think of a reasonable explanation as to why his dad was acting so strangely. Maybe he had taken too many of his vitamins all at once and they got lodged in his throat, cutting off the vital oxygen that caused *sane* behaviour. Most *normal* fathers just sat at the table with a hot drink in one hand and a newspaper in the other and grumble about things that need to get done with no time to do them. But his dad went out of his way to be weird. *He* had to hobble around the table with his chest thrust out, pounding his fists back and forth like an ape. He looked even more ridiculous when he tried forcing air into his upper lip, resulting in milk bubbles coming out of his nostrils. Murphy couldn't stop laughing as his dad blew his nose into a tissue. Then his dad joined in, and they were both in stitches until his mom cleared her throat.

"Wade, let him eat what he wants. It's too early for your jokes. Honey, there are cherry turnovers in the freezer if you'd rather have those."

"Oh, that'll start him off well, Jules." Murphy's dad smacked his lips, exaggerating. "Mm-mm, very nutritious."

"Well, it's a lot more appealing than those soggy nuggets *you're* eating. Blah!" his mother declared. "Besides, there *is* real fruit in the pastry. That counts as healthy."

"*Healthy* is what makes up this fantastic package," Murphy's dad responded, winking at his mother.

She tugged at his tie. "Does being messy come with this parcel too?" His dad looked down at her while she blotted his collar.

Murphy left the room before their flirtatious behaviour got worse. But before he went, he hauled out the orange juice and shook it. He drank it straight from the carton, and then gagged. It was sour. He took the stairs two by two, scrambling into the bathroom to spit out the foul taste.

"Hey, buddy!" his dad called up, "aren't you supposed to be at school in ten minutes?"

Surprised, Murphy poked his head into his room and saw the time. *Yikes!* He changed into a pair of jeans and whipped his arms into a black and red checkered top as he gargled with mouthwash. "I'll have to skip breakfast today, Mom. I'm late!"

He caught her reaction when he rushed past her and cringed. *Uh-oh,* he thought, *I'm in trouble.* He knew that look. It was the one where she pointed a finger and gave him a warning.

"You're this close," she advised, showing him an inch between her index finger and thumb, "from being scratched off my good list."

"Mom! I have to go!" Murphy responded and swung his backpack over his shoulder. He was about to reach for the door handle when his mom yelled out, *"Murphy Carter Robinson!"*

He froze in place.

She met him at the door, offering a bag full of apple slices. "Take this," she said. "I don't want your principal calling me to say you've fainted from hunger. Or worse yet, Child Welfare knocking at our door and claiming that I don't feed you!"

Murphy rolled his eyes. At least she didn't add that he might die of malnutrition. His mother was so dramatic. *Six more years,* he told himself, *and then I'll be eighteen.* His mom would no longer have to fret. And he'd have the freedom to go anywhere as he pleased without her covering him in bubble wrap.

Unfortunately, Murphy knew he'd acquired the same pessimistic gene. His middle name should have been "Cautious" instead, because he had a real dislike for taking risks, especially if the outcome was unknown.

And surprises he hated even more. So he was completely baffled that his regular morning routine had slipped away from him so quickly. But then he recalled the power outage yesterday and figured that he must have forgotten to reset his alarm in the evening.

Of course, he thought, *that's just my luck. Bad luck, that is.*

It's true that Murphy despised being left with his defenses down and he was usually very careful about everything that he did. He actually enjoyed the everyday monotony of life as a seventh-grade student. He went to school, came home and played baseball with his friends. It was predictable, but safe, and he *liked* being safe. But today wasn't going to be an ordinary day, he was sure of it.

At least he could rely on the month of October to be the same every day. It was always gloomy, cloaked in dreary grey, and this Thursday's overcast wasn't any different. The endless rain was pummeling down upon the classroom windows, making them almost impossible to see through. But it was much more difficult to focus inside, as the students sat in darkness wondering what just happened to the lights.

Mr. Harris, the janitor, came by to each classroom and distributed several flashlights, explaining that it would be a while before the power was restored. Apparently, the heavy rainfall overnight caused some water damage to the main generator, resulting in this morning's electrical problems. A lot of cheering followed as students anticipated the cancellation of class, but the short burst of joy was shattered when the principal, Mr. Phelps, stopped by to announce that all lessens were to continue until further notice.

The hydro flickered on and off about a hundred times during the first hour, making it feel like the lightning had found its way into the room. But by 9:55, the dilemma was solved.

Mrs. Sheldon, the teacher, was awfully quiet during the commotion and it struck Murphy as odd that she wasn't her usual self. He thought that she would have made a joke to ease the tension and change the mood. But instead, oddly, she just stared outside, as if she was expecting something to happen. He looked over at his best friend, Jason, who shrugged, looking as dumbfounded as Murphy felt.

His friend Chloe tapped Murphy from behind and whispered, "Do you know what's going on?"

Murphy shook his head. "I've got no idea."

"Are we getting any lessons today? Or can we go home?" Duncan asked, breaking the silence.

Mrs. Sheldon seemed to snap out of her trance. "Oh! My apologies. I was thinking about one of my adventures and I suppose I got wrapped up in my own thoughts. I am so sorry, class."

"What was it about?" a student asked.

"What was *what* about?"

"Going senile," Duncan murmured under his breath.

"Your adventure," the student replied, giving Duncan a dirty look. "Aren't you going to share your story with us?"

Mrs. Sheldon smiled at the young girl. "Perhaps another day," she offered, lifting a stack of Xeroxed papers off her desk and handing them to a student in the front row. "Please pass these down."

Chloe had the unsettled feeling that something was wrong, and she wasn't the only one. Mrs. Sheldon loved talking about her past experiences. Her motto was "Explore exciting opportunities as often as you can." She wasn't nearly as jovial as she usually was, nor as energetic. She seemed tired, anxious and preoccupied. She fidgeted with the gold chain around her neck. It was a piece of jewelry she always wore. From the chain hung an old-fashioned key. Apparently, it was very precious to her. Students and colleagues alike had asked her about it, wanting to know the secrets of its origin and its purpose, but Mrs. Sheldon had always kept that information to herself.

Dark clouds rumbled in the distance and a flash of brilliant light illuminated the sky, casting an eerie glow on the pavement. Water droplets clung to the windows, distorting Murphy's view as he watched the storm gradually lose its intensity. Jason lifted out of his seat and nudged Chloe. He jerked his chin toward the playground, and she followed his gaze.

There was something fleshy and strange crawling toward the swing set. Murphy saw it too. A moment later, the wind picked up and another round of torrential rain fell, distorting the objects.

"What *was* that?" Jason asked Chloe.

"Maybe a cat?" she replied.

Jason didn't think so, but Chloe was the expert on animals.

A loud bang made everyone in the class turn their attention to the window. It was too dark to see what had hit the glass, but it glowed for a moment before it slid down to the ground.

"Was that a bird?" a student asked, concerned.

Mrs. Sheldon quickly walked over to the window and pulled the drapes closed. "I believe it was," she replied, "but it's gone now."

She was just about to address the class when a resounding clap of thunder suddenly shook the room. Mrs. Sheldon jumped, muttering something under her breath, and Duncan snickered at her reaction.

Murphy's tension grew. Mrs. Sheldon didn't seem the type to be afraid of much. After all, she'd travelled the world by herself since her husband passed away. She had seen many things while collecting treasures, good and bad, and she'd never mentioned being nervous in any of those situations.

Another bolt of lightning slashed through the sky, striking the side of the building and triggering the fire alarm. Mrs. Sheldon ushered her students to the exit, and they joined the others outside at the designated safe zone. She spoke briefly with Mr. Toth, the gym teacher, and then took off like a bullet into the parking lot.

Chloe and Murphy wondered where she was going in such a hurry. But Jason was more interested in the playground and wanted to know what that *thing* really was. Duncan slipped through the throng of students to do a little investigating of his own. For some strange reason, he knew Mrs. Sheldon had fibbed about the bird. He was shocked to find blood smeared on the window pane, but there wasn't anything lying dead under the window.

"Duncan Fisher!" Mr. Toth called out, raising his voice over the approaching sirens. "Please return to your group immediately!"

Murphy wiped away a clump of wet, coppery hair plastered to his forehead and grumbled. He hated his straight hair and wished he had an umbrella. Chloe seemed to be struggling with the same problem, except hers had sprung to life with an agenda all its own. She smoothed out the curls with her fingers and Murphy watched with amusement as Duncan stared at her.

Jason squeezed into the space between Murphy and Chloe. "Lover boy is staring at you again," he reported, turning her around to face the back of the line. Murphy chuckled and Chloe rolled her eyes, pretending to look the other way. But Jason caught on. He laughed and jumped in front of her. "Caught you looking!" Chloe giggled and her face darkened into a blush.

As random flurries cascaded down, blanketing the soggy grass, Jason tilted his head back and stuck his tongue out, wanting to taste the first snowfall of the season.

"We can go back to class now," Murphy said, seeing Mrs. Sheldon jog up to Mr. Toth before joining them. As they approached the back doors, pellets of ice the size of peas attacked them with their frigid sting.

"Hurry now!" Mrs. Sheldon urged, looking back toward the parking lot and smiling. Murphy wasn't sure what that reaction was all about, but he knew something had changed. Mrs. Sheldon's mood had suddenly shifted, and she was back to her old self again. Strangely, as she passed through the school entrance, the sun came out.

"This has been the most peculiar morning," she said. "It reminds me of a time when I was young. The weather had suddenly turned nasty..."

Mrs. Sheldon's enthusiasm rubbed off, and the students were thrilled to hear another animated story of mystery and magic. Her imagination was amazing. She could describe a scene so vividly that her students had dedicated a wall strictly for the pictures they drew about her voyages on the sea and of the dangers that she encountered in faraway lands.

"And the waves came crashing down, filling the boat with too much water. I had to act fast before it sank, so I turned it over. And as I clung to the side, a flying beast with a wing span this large"—she splayed her arms to simulate the length—"swooped down from the sky and attacked me. It grabbed my hair and pulled me out of the water, but I fought back, and I forced it to use its own strong wings to carry me to the shore..."

"What did the beast look like?" a student asked.

"Black beady eyes and claws ..." She paused a moment, as if realizing that her tale was frightening some of her students. "It was as hideous as any monster in a bad dream."

Murphy shivered, remembering his nightmare.

Chloe leaned forward and whispered, "Do you ever think that Mrs. Sheldon's bizarre stories are more than just fiction?"

Murphy nodded. "All the time," he replied, sliding out of his seat as the recess bell rang.

Their teacher knew things that no one else did. She gave hints with subtle clues and used those examples to teach her lessons. Out of curiosity, Chloe, Murphy and Jason had investigated some of her stories, and they'd turned out to be true events. It was as if she could go back to the past and relive a part of history, or fast-forward to the future. She was like a fortune teller in a time machine. Chloe wondered if Mrs. Sheldon had psychic abilities.

The buzz of excitement grew louder as each student walked into the classroom and passed by the display of artifacts on the teacher's desk. There was a menagerie of items, including a dragon statue, a witch's hat, a flying saucer, a water globe with a mermaid inside and a silver flute.

Once the class settled, Mrs. Sheldon began writing words on the black board: *mythology*, *fairy tales* and *folklore*. "Close your eyes for a moment, please," she said, "and think of a story that gave you a feeling of joy, sadness or even fear."

Jason peeked as the room went silent. Mrs. Sheldon, who hadn't turned around yet, was fastening a string behind each ear. She asked everyone to open their eyes as she faced the class. She wore a mask that had one eye protruding in the middle of the face. The jaw hung down lower than her neck and the mouth was filled with giant, marshmallow-sized teeth. She laughed as she pulled it off and raised it above her head.

"Can anyone tell me what creature this mask represents?"

Murphy raised his hand. "A Cyclops."

"Very good," she replied, tapping the first word on the board. "What other creature has an appendage growing from its crown and has magical powers?"

Chloe looked over at Jason and tried to suppress a giggle as he pressed his hand against his forehead and stuck out his index finger.

"Jason?"

"Unicorns."

"That's right," she responded, circling the next word on the list. "Each of these examples has been used to help answer the questions that plagued a certain era."

16

"Could we get to the *real* stories?" Duncan commented. "I want to hear about unsolved crimes, not this fantasy nonsense."

"Do you know for sure that it is all nonsense? What if I told the class that I have seen one?"

"Then I'd ask for proof."

"Sometimes, there isn't any to give. Take the story of Adam and Eve, for instance; many Christian followers believe that there was a garden of Eden, yet there is no evidence of its existence except for the written words in the Bible." She shrugged. "Perhaps folklore will interest you, as there is some truth behind the stories."

Mrs. Sheldon grabbed her history book and sat on the corner of her desk. "Please open your textbooks to page ninety-four."

Chloe flipped to the page. It read, *Urban Legends.*

"Mrs. Sheldon?" A student asked. "What did the unicorn look like?"

Duncan rolled his eyes.

"I was about your age when I first met the animal," Mrs. Sheldon said. "It was small and sandy-coloured, with a thick horn that curled into a halo..."

Mrs. Sheldon explained how it had miraculously healed a friend of hers. They had been playing a game in the woods when Ellie tripped upon a tree root and fell, injuring both her wrists. She begged Mrs. Sheldon to find help, as she was in too much pain to move. But Mrs. Sheldon lost her way. Then she saw a light penetrating through the trees and ran toward it, hoping to find someone nearby. As she got closer, she witnessed the animal hurtling through a tree trunk that was split in half. Its backside was invisible, giving the appearance that it was balancing on its two front legs. It turned its head toward her and bleated. Relying on her intuition, Mrs. Sheldon sensed that she had to follow it. The animal led her back to her friend, and it lowered its head to allow Ellie to touch its horn. When she did, Mrs. Sheldon saw Ellie's bones knit together and the swelling disappear. After removing her hands from the horn, Ellie told Mrs. Sheldon that the animal's name was Grothen, and he had given her the ability to understand and communicate with all the animals in the world.

Mrs. Sheldon peered up at the clock and walked over to the table. "For the remainder of the morning, I'd like all of you to read the poem I've handed out and the first two pages of chapter six, then create your own story using one of the narratives posted on the board. I have some examples here," she said, picking up the dragon figurine, "if anyone needs some inspiration."

Chloe looked down at the paper Mrs. Sheldon had given them. It was about a local superstition titled: *A Westfield County Tale.* In the 1800s there had been a nanny wrongly accused of using witchcraft to kill the children that were in her care. She was sent to an asylum and her only child was taken away. She cursed the people of Westfield, promising to destroy their lives as they had hers. There were many diseases that year, and the death toll rose. Then children started disappearing from their homes, never to be found.

The whole class was familiar with the story. Every October they were reminded. Some community members believed that the curse still remained, and took their families on vacation in October to avoid potential tragedy. Chloe recalled an incident last year when a sixteen-year-old girl vanished from her front porch in broad daylight. Although the police had reported that the girl ran away, the fear was real nonetheless. *So, was it just a teenager that went rogue?* Chloe wondered, *or was it a sinister act meant to copy the crimes from long ago?*

CHAPTER TWO

Chloe paced along the fence impatiently, waiting for Murphy to return from lunch. When he arrived, she bolted toward him at top speed. He saw her coming and braced for the impact, knowing she'd topple him over if he didn't plant his feet firmly enough.

"Mrs. Sheldon," Chloe puffed. "She's gone! Something happened to her!"

"What do you mean? Is she hurt? Is she in the hospital?"

"No, I mean … I'm not sure. But I *do* know that she's not home because her car is still in the parking lot."

Murphy shrugged, unconcerned. "She probably just went for a long walk."

Chloe shook her head.

"Out having lunch with another teacher? They have to eat too."

Chloe sighed impatiently.

"Dentist appointment?"

"Would you hush for a moment so I can explain why I'm worried?"

Murphy pretended to button up his lips.

"Mrs. Sheldon carries her purse everywhere she goes, right?"

Murphy nodded, not saying a word.

"Well, it's still on her desk." Chloe grabbed his wrist and yanked him forward. "Come on," she said. "We need to find her."

Murphy resisted, pulling his arm out of her grasp. "What's the big deal? She's probably inside the school somewhere."

"Mr. Phelps and all the teachers have been looking and they can't find her. There was a meeting during lunch and she didn't show up."

"Maybe she forgot." Murphy suggested, knowing how lame that sounded. Mrs. Sheldon never forgot important dates, and she was always on time. "Did they check the ladies' washroom?"

Chloe gave Murphy a look, as if he was an idiot.

"What?" he replied defensively. "She could have the runs."

Chloe crossed her arms. "Duncan told me—"

"Hold on—*Duncan* told you all this?"

"Yeah, he was outside the office when he overheard …"

"Well, that makes sense," Murphy commented.

"Stop rolling your eyes! Listen, he's telling the truth because—"

"Come on, Chloe. Wake up and smell the petunias." He tried to knock on her head but she swiped his fist away.

"It's *coffee*, not petunias, goof ball."

Murphy made a face. "Yuck. I hate the smell of coffee."

Chloe chuckled. "That's because your mom burns everything."

Murphy laughed. "True."

"Okay," Chloe continued, "if Duncan was lying, then tell me where she'd go without taking her purse. And why she didn't let Mr. Phelps know?"

Chloe had a point.

"Like I said, maybe she ate something that made her sick and she's still on the toilet."

"Ugh! I swear, Murphy, you have poop for brains."

He laughed, but she didn't. "All right!" Murphy said. "Sheesh. I was just kidding!"

"What if something happened to her?" Chloe remarked, fiddling nervously with the ornate metal band around her wrist.

Murphy agreed that it was unusual, but he was still skeptical. "So, Duncan must be on a first-name basis with the staff then," he remarked to change the subject. He didn't like to think that Mrs. Sheldon was losing her marbles. "That would impress *me* if he wanted *my* attention."

"Who cares!" Chloe snapped, clearly irritated. "Duncan was alone when I passed by him in the hallway. He was sitting outside the office serving part of his detention. He wasn't *schmoozing* with any of the teachers," she grumbled under her breath, commenting on Murphy's hint about Duncan's infatuation with her. She thought it was all in Murphy's head.

"What did he do this time? Steal some poor kid's lunch money?"

"I didn't ask. I was only inside to drop off papers. The office needed a record of my recent doctor's visit."

"So, you *do* have cooties?"

"No, goofball, I had an allergy test done and I'm allergic to feathers, *and* the obnoxious boy in front of me."

"Nothing contagious? You won't foam at the mouth?"

Chloe started clenching her fists, and that was Murphy's cue to stop, or else he'd be sore for the next few days.

"Grow up." Chloe moved away from him in a huff, flicking her black hair off her shoulders.

Murphy trailed behind Chloe, making sure to keep his distance. He didn't want to agitate her more. He knew that when she had made up her mind, that was it. Case closed. She was very stubborn.

Murphy was jolted from his thoughts as two girls ran past him, squealing with delight over something exciting. He hadn't realized that his classmates had already gone inside.

"You can stop obsessing, Murphy, I'm over it."

"So I'm off the hook?"

"An apology would be nice."

"For what? I didn't say anything that wasn't true, *and* I don't obsess," he remarked.

"Oh, yes you do," she replied. "If you can't be right, you mope." She watched his reaction and laughed. "You're too easy, Robinson." She motioned toward the side doors. "We'd better hustle."

"Yeah, or we'll end up in detention with your *lover boy*," Murphy teased, leaning away from her. "Ow!" he said, rubbing his arm.

Something caught Chloe's attention. "Go on ahead," she urged. "I won't be long."

"What's the matter? Where are you going?" Murphy quizzed her.

"Shh! Keep your voice down. I think I just saw Mrs. Sheldon," she whispered and pointed to the cars.

Murphy followed her.

The school bell rang and they dashed over to the chain-link fence that separated the schoolyard from the parking lot. Mrs. Sheldon was squatting between two vehicles, hiding. She motioned for them to come closer and to keep their heads down. Who was she trying to avoid?

Mrs. Sheldon said, "I know you have questions, and you'll get those answers soon. But right now I need you to listen. Can I count on both of you to keep a secret?"

Chloe nodded but Murphy hesitated. "Does this mean that we can't tell Jason?" he asked.

Mrs. Sheldon smiled. "You may inform Jason, but no one else." She handed Murphy an envelope. "Please deliver this to Mr. Phelps. It will explain my sudden absence."

"So you won't be teaching class this afternoon?" Murphy asked.

"No," she replied as her eyes traced the sky. "I'm afraid not." She watched as heat lightning flickered across pale grey clouds like firecrackers, and frowned. "I am needed elsewhere and must leave immediately." She stood, peeking over the hood of an Oldsmobile.

"Is there anything else?" Chloe asked.

Mrs. Sheldon nodded. "In late August," she said, addressing Chloe, "you happened to walk by Mr. Moss's yard and noticed that my car was parked in his driveway. You came around the back and approached me while I was planting flowers. You had asked me what I was doing, and I answered that every year on the anniversary of Mr. Moss's death, I return to pay my respects and renew my pledge to him that I will find the truth behind his untimely passing. Do you remember what I showed you?"

Chloe chewed on her bottom lip, trying to think back. She shook her head. "Sorry."

"That's okay," Mrs. Sheldon replied. "Perhaps this will jog your memory." She took both hands and lifted the chain around her neck, placing the mysterious key into Chloe's palm.

Chloe stared at her hand. Then she looked up. "The treasure," she recalled. "You buried something valuable and its hidden underneath the birdbath."

Mrs. Sheldon nodded. "Guard the key and keep it safe."

"I promise. Is this to unlock it?"

"You'll know soon enough," Mrs. Sheldon responded. "That's why I chose you."

"What if—"

Murphy nudged Chloe and pointed up. She followed his gaze to a white glow that hovered above their teacher.

"I must go now," Mrs. Sheldon said, moving to the rear of the car. "Be careful," she advised. "There are powerful things in this world, and not all of them are friendly."

She disappeared.

Murphy turned to Chloe. "What *things*?"

Chloe shrugged. "All I know is that she warned us about something."

"Yeah, and it sounded *really* bad."

Chloe agreed, wondering what kind of trouble they were getting into.

"Did you see her leave?" Murphy asked. "Because I didn't. It's like she was sucked into another dimension! I bet she's an alien!"

"I'm still wondering why she picked us," Chloe replied. "Why are we so important?"

"Hey! Check this out!" The passenger window of the Oldsmobile had frosted over, displaying a message.

NEED YOUR HELP FIND TREASURE

Chloe ran her thumbnail across the words, scraping away the evidence.

Murphy said, "Do think Mrs. Sheldon could be Westfield's baby snatcher?"

Chloe's mouth dropped open. "Murphy! How could you *think* that?"

"How about a spy? Or maybe she's a police officer working undercover."

"Could be," Chloe said, walking briskly to the doors. "We can figure it out later. But first we need to get to class."

...

"Stop it," Chloe scolded. "You're going to get us in trouble."

Murphy turned around in his seat and scribbled a few sentences on paper, then flung it behind him.

"I can't reach it," she whispered. "It's under your chair."

Murphy bent down to retrieve the note but it was wedged under the chair leg. He pulled and it tore in half. A pair of brown, polished shoes stepped into his view, and he cringed.

The teacher placed his geometry book upon Murphy's desk. "Mr. Robinson, would you care to explain why your letter is more important than my lesson?"

"Not really, sir."

"Perhaps the class would like to hear what your note has to say," Mr. Toth remarked. He was replacing Mrs. Sheldon for the afternoon as Mr. Phelps was unable to find a substitute teacher in such a short time. "Go on," he urged.

All eyes turned on Murphy and the room became very quiet.

Murphy swallowed, took a deep breath and blurted out "Call me so I know what our next move is. We should meet behind the bleachers—it's more private." Murphy had to admit that once he read the words out loud, it sounded differently than he'd meant it to.

Duncan snorted. "Try again, Romeo."

Chloe groaned, hiding her face in her hands as the room erupted in a frenzy of whispering voices.

Jason cupped a hand over his mouth, laughing so hard he started to hiccup.

Mr. Toth's moustache curled up as he grinned. "Do you have anything to add, Miss Baker or Mr. Tremblay?"

Chloe and Jason shook their heads.

"Good," Mr. Toth said, adding a formula beside the trapezoid picture drawn on the chalkboard. "Then I'll continue."

Jason turned to Murphy and puckered his lips, creating squeaky kissing noises. Mr. Toth glanced over his shoulder and Jason immediately stopped.

"If there are any other interruptions, we will remain here until we're finished. That applies to Friday as well since I'll be teaching here again tomorrow."

As the class vented their complaints, Duncan cracked his knuckles and scowled at Murphy. Murphy pretended not to see him. *Just great*, he thought. *Now he'll really have an excuse to pummel me after school.*

WHACK! Chloe backhanded Murphy across the side of his head—not hard enough to hurt, but enough to show him she wasn't happy.

The rest of the afternoon was a blur. Murphy's eyes glazed over as shapes and numbers faded into the background. He was so tired, and math was so boring. His mother nagged him constantly about applying more energy to the subject, telling him that if he gave it as much time as he did his creativity, he wouldn't have difficulty solving the calculations.

Murphy liked to think that there was more to life than numbers. If he chose to, he could accomplish many things, including playing sports. He proved that by showing off his batting skills during a baseball game. He practised a lot to correct his swing. Last year, his team, the Mighty Oaks, won the championship. His dad took time off work to watch him play the last game of the season.

Murphy could remember the scene like it was yesterday. The bases had been loaded. Everything had depended on him. He'd hit a homer and gave his team their victory. His dad had dressed up for the occasion and surprised everyone with his outfit. He wasn't wearing a shirt and tie; it was more of a costume, with a bull's head and the team's jersey stretched over his own shirt. Everyone had wondered what he was up to.

"Dad," Murphy had asked, "why are you dressed like a buffalo?"

"Technically, I'm supposed to be an ox."

"Okay," Murphy said, confused. "Why?"

"The Mighty Ox," his dad replied. "Get it?"

Murphy had been thrilled to have his dad witness his best game, but at that moment he'd wished his dad had stayed home. "It's the Mighty *Oaks*, Dad. You know, like the big trees that have acorns?"

"Ah, that makes sense. Now I know why I was getting those questioning stares."

Murphy smiled to himself. *Poor dad. He tried.*

Mrs. Sheldon had coached the team. Not only was Mrs. Sheldon the best coach ever, but she was also great at teaching. Unfortunately, Mr. Toth was not. He was assigning homework for the evening. Murphy jotted down the list in his binder and yawned.

"Sir, Mrs. Sheldon doesn't give us work to do on holidays," Duncan commented.

"Well, Mr. Fisher, need I point out that I am not Mrs. Sheldon. And while Saturday *is* Halloween, it's not a holiday, nor is Friday for that matter."

"It should be," Duncan grumbled, shoving his chair away from his desk and crossing his arms. Mr. Toth ignored him.

Jason shook his head, disgusted with his classmate's reaction. He felt that Duncan got off easy because his dad was a lawyer. He'd even bet that if Duncan were older, he'd find him in jail somewhere. Jason wished Mrs. Sheldon was present. She had a knack for keeping Duncan in line. He hoped she was okay.

Florence Sheldon looked very young for her age but she was not a frail lady. She had a husky build with broad shoulders, and arms that would give his brother envy. Her fair skin was dotted with a million freckles, giving her a ruddy complexion that spread right up into her hairline of frizzy golden curls. She wore neon blue glasses but Jason doubted that she needed them. She seemed to see everything quite clearly, even the nasty gestures Duncan hid under his desk.

Jason was getting fidgety in his seat and was eager to talk with his friends, so when the school bell rang, he was on Chloe's heels demanding answers.

...

Reedman's Park was a favourite place for locals to hang out. It had a huge picnic area with enough space to hold several baseball diamonds, and an amphitheatre that gave Westfield County's musicians a place to have concerts. This included Jason's nineteen-year-old brother Gabe and his band, The Deezal Weeds. His bandmates nicknamed Gabe "Diesel" because he worked for a gas station.

It didn't take Murphy long to reach the park. He locked his bike at the bleachers and clambered up onto the largest maple tree adjacent to the stage. From the high vantage point, he was able to see his friends coming from a block away. Chloe was wobbling back and forth on her bike, trying to keep a steady pace with Jason while her puppy, Buckles, took lead of the pack, pulling on his leash. Buckles came over to the tree to greet Murphy with his tongue sticking out, panting. His tail wagged enthusiastically as he let out a friendly yelp. Murphy swung from the lowest branch and jumped to the ground.

"How ya doin', little guy?" Murphy said, rubbing the puppy's belly as he wiggled on his back.

Jason squatted, lowering his hand to scratch under Buckles' chin. The puppy quickly rolled over and jumped onto his lap, gnawing playfully on the fingers closest to him. "Ugh. He's slobbering again," Jason commented, wiping drool onto his jeans.

"I can't help it if he thinks you need a bath," Chloe remarked with a smirk.

Murphy laughed as he watched her puppy tug on Jason's shoelaces.

"Aw, now I'm going to have slimy runners!"

Chloe giggled as Jason made a show of slipping and falling onto the grass, giving Buckles full reign to jump all over him.

"Why did you name him Buckles?" he asked.

"He was chewing on a leather belt when I spotted him at the pet store. By the time I persuaded my mom to adopt him, he only had the clip in his mouth. He dropped it at my feet when the clerk opened the dog pen." Chloe bent down and ruffled the puppy's ears. "You're so smart, aren't you," she cooed. Then Chloe eyed Jason. "Watch out, he might pee on you if you get him too excited."

"AH! Take him! I think he already did!" Jason replied.

"Just in time," Murphy remarked, pointing out the puddle.

"That's a good boy," Chloe said, patting Buckles on his rump while she wrapped the leash around her bike handle. They all laughed when Buckles raised his leg again just to have more praise.

Chloe and Murphy filled Jason in on Mrs. Sheldon's situation, and after a brief discussion, they narrowed down their options. There was no doubt that Mrs. Sheldon's hasty exit meant she was running from someone, and that whatever she was involved in was bad enough for her to relinquish her key. They agreed that the only link was the treasure, and that in order for them to help her, they needed more clues than just her stories.

So, they decided to split up. Chloe graciously took the most boring job: researching at the library. With all the newspaper clippings on microfilm, she hoped to find some past events that might explain some of the strange tales that Mrs. Sheldon liked to tell and possibly uncover why she still believes that Mr. Moss's death was suspicious. Chloe wondered why her teacher would choose to hide things that are precious to her in his yard and not her own. Was there a connection? Does Mrs. Sheldon know more than what she claims? Could it be that she has evidence to support murder?

Jason chose to start with Mrs. Sheldon's neighbours, claiming that between him, Chloe and Murphy, he was the most irresistible. He knew that Mrs. Sheldon always participated in the annual autumn Bulbs to Blossoms Festival on Mr. Moss's land. It took place out on the ridge where the women would throw lily bulbs from the cliff that overlooked the valley below. The event gave Lily Valley its name. It was said that if one's bulb flowered in the spring it would bring them luck. Of course, no one could be sure which lily belonged to whom, but the idea of receiving good fortune remained. Jason hoped that one of Mrs. Sheldon's friends might know something about her disappearance, especially if they had heard or seen something unusual.

Murphy's job was to bring a drawing of the key to the local nursing home and ask around in case anyone knew its historical background.

They chose to meet in the park at 7:30 p.m. Chloe reluctantly agreed not to bring Buckles that evening or the following day, though she made a good argument that he could dig faster than any one of them.

...

Chloe knocked softly on her mother's bedroom door. "Mom?"

Her mother hastily wiped the tears rolling down her cheeks. "I'm fine," she said, motioning for her daughter to come in.

Chloe sat next to her on the bed and picked up the photo album resting open on her mother's lap. "Why do you do this to yourself?" Chloe demanded, but kept her voice low. She jumped up and slammed the book shut with both hands. "It just makes you sad!"

Her mother sighed heavily. "You'll understand when you get older."

"I get older every year!" Chloe argued, "And I *still* don't get it. You said he'd come back, but he hasn't been around since I was in diap—" She immediately stopped. Her mother was shaking as she buried her face into both hands and wept. "I'm sorry." Chloe sniffed. "I know how much you miss him."

Chloe's mother pulled her closer. "Don't you miss him?"

Chloe dropped her arms. "Not really," she replied. "I don't remember him. I was too little." She twirled the bracelet around her wrist. It had been a gift from her father when she was born.

Her mother reached over to the bedside table, but Chloe rushed in and closed the drawer she opened.

"Please don't take those pills," Chloe pleaded. "Last time, you were out cold for two hours!"

Her mother tugged at the drawer. "I'm not getting any medication. I threw those out."

Chloe folded her arms. "Then what are you getting?"

"It's for you, not me. I have something for you."

Chloe spun her bracelet as she backed away. "Don't need it."

Her mother massaged her temples and sighed. "Hear me out, okay?"

Chloe nodded, sitting back down.

Her mother handed Chloe an envelope. "I was supposed give this to you on your birthday, but it's probably best that you open it now."

"Who's it from?"

"Your father."

Chloe froze, dropping the envelope. She stared at her name written on the front in black ink.

Her mother put an arm around her. "I know right now you don't care, but your answers are in this letter." She picked it up from the floor. "I just wish you had more interest in your father's—"

"What for?" Chloe interrupted angrily. She crumpled the envelope inside her clenched fist. "He's gone, Mom, so why should I waste my time when he hasn't had the decency to spare a moment of his?" She shoved the photo album under the bed, knowing that her mother would retrieve it later.

"I'll admit he hasn't been around you physically, but he *has* been watching over you."

"How?" Chloe asked, skeptical. "Is he dead? Is he the ghost roaming Moss Ridge?"

Her mother raised a finger as a warning. "Don't you use that tone with me, young lady."

Frustrated, Chloe tossed the scrunched paper into the wastebasket and stormed out of the room. She went to her room, slammed the door shut and locked it.

A little while later, her mother knocked. Chloe didn't answer.

"Chloe, please open up."

Chloe dragged her feet on the carpet to go open the door. Then she ran to her bed and flopped on it, hiding her face in a mountain of pillows.

Her mother rubbed her back. "Can I show you something that might make you feel better?" Chloe lifted her head and rolled over, scooting to one side to give her mother room to lie down.

Her mother threaded her fingers through her daughter's and brought their hands closer to their faces. "Your bracelet is like a crystal ball," she started, admiring the beauty of the intricate metalwork. "This teardrop," she confided, tapping the yellow crystal, "gives your father a way to see you at all times, day and night."

Chloe snorted. "As if."

"I know it's hard to believe, but I am not fibbing."

"So it's magical?"

Her mother loosened her grip and stood up, placing the wrinkled letter on the bed. "I'm going to give you your space. You need time to absorb this."

Chloe spun the gold mesh strap around to look at the yellow jewel more carefully. It had dark orange veining with speckles of brown and black scattered along the edges. The jewel was set in the middle of five wiry stands of gold shaped into triangular tips. They connected to a flat disc made of onyx. Five tiny clasps secured the jewel and gold strands to the disc's inner rim.

Chloe rubbed her finger over the gem, wishing silently that her mother's statement was true. Then suddenly, the jewel flashed, and the orange webbing rippled under the surface. Chloe felt a warmth spreading around her wrist and gasped as it continued up to her elbow. She watched with curiosity as her blood vessels swelled, raising her skin to form lines. She touched her forearm and the pattern seemed to vanish along with the heat. It left her itchy, and she scratched until dark marks appeared.

Stuffing another pillow under her head, she patted the mattress and located the letter. She ripped it open.

Chloe,

I know that you believe I have been absent in your life, but that is simply not true. I have loved you from the moment you were placed in my arms and continue to do so from afar. Each year I have watched you grow, and you have made me proud of the person you've become.

Please understand that I did not want to leave you and your mother. I had no choice. In order to keep you safe, I must keep my distance. There are rules that I have broken. My people forbid relations with races other than our own. I'm terribly sorry that I have caused so much pain.

Your thirteenth birthday marks a significant change. Celebrate the unique gifts you have with people who you trust. I hope that when I see you again, you will find it in your heart to forgive me.

Dad

Chloe folded the letter and tucked it under her pillow. *Is he really returning at some point?* She sighed, rolling off the bed and murmuring, "I won't hold my breath over it."

...

Chloe set the projector onto the small table provided and switched it on. She slid her reel onto the spindle, carefully unravelling the end of the film to pass it through the intake roller, knowing that the flimsy strip was as fragile as photo negatives from a camera. Newspaper clippings moved across the glass plate, reflecting the tiny words onto a white screen in front of her. Her hand remained on the knob as she adjusted the size, unsure where to start. Articles of simpler times raced forward as she scrolled to find something that would catch her eye. Then, one of the headlines made her backtrack. It read:

Local Man's Death: Accident or Suicide?

According to the article, several witnesses had spotted Mr. Moss flying his handmade aircraft over the Valley but lost sight of him when he'd banked too low. Shortly after, there had been a massive explosion.

Chloe continued to read through the related news clips.

Police Baffled by Lack of Evidence in Moss Case.

The article said that Mr. Moss's body was never found and only a mirror was recovered from the blast. Speculation had grown that he and his family were plagued by misfortunes because a witch had once resided on that land and therefore the property was evil.

Next there was a small insert from a history buff explaining the events that had created Lily Valley. A meteor formed the bowl-shaped depression, and all the homes nearby were built upon the space rock fragments. One legendary tale spoke of a foreign substance that had leached into the water that once flowed upon the Valley floor, giving the first humans immortality.

Chloe removed the film and put in another one, dating back almost a century.

Anticipation Builds as Bridge Construction Begins.

She scrolled rapidly through the old text, finding nothing of importance and set aside the older articles to focus on more recent news.

Wheeler House For Sale

Chloe tipped her chair back and whistled as she counted the zeros. The mansion's price tag was a hefty one and would explain why the place remained unsold. *Who has that kind of money around here?* A relative who wished to remain anonymous had made the listing. Disgusted, Chloe pulled out the film and fastened the last roll. This one had many articles that caught her eye. The first excerpt Chloe recognized was a court case her mother had been involved in. Several victims had come forward to join in a class action lawsuit against the aging psychiatrist that treated his former patients with experimental and often dangerous medications. Her mom had been among the witnesses to stand trial and he was finally forced to leave his practice. She shuddered, recalling her mom's strange behaviour, and scrolled down to the next section.

Westfield's Only Psychiatrist retires; Son to Take Over Business.

Chloe skimmed over the details that announced, "New patients are welcome to visit renovated office."

She scoffed at the lie and turned to the Obituaries but found the death announcements very sad. So many children had lost their lives at such a young age, but the Wheeler family had the most tragedies.

Another snippet with the title: Is October 31 Cursed? was interesting. A list of names identified faces that Chloe had only ever known through the newspaper. The disappearances had no pattern. There were infants that had vanished from their cribs, children as young as four that had been taken from the safety of their yards and teenagers that had left without warning. Each of them had different backgrounds.

Chloe rubbed her eyes. She had been looking at the screen for a long time and needed a break. As she stood to turn off the machine, she just happened to notice a highlighted name: *Sheldon.*

Woman Given Medal for Saving Child's Life.

Huh, Chloe thought. *So Mrs. Sheldon isn't just a super person, but a local hero as well …*

...

Willow Crest was a renovated old brick building that had been a mental hospital in the late 1800s. In the foyer, it proudly displayed black and white pictures of days gone by. A plaque above the collage read: *Spruce Haven Asylum and its patients.*

The massive oak doors were heavy. Murphy pushed his way into the lobby, and immediately the strong scent of Pine Sol assaulted him.

"Can I help you?" the receptionist asked from behind her desk.

"Um, yeah. I called earlier. My name's Murphy."

"Ah yes, you're here to work on a school project." She wheeled her chair back and grabbed a paper. "You'll need to fill your name out here," she pointed out, "as visitor."

Murphy scribbled his signature. "Thanks."

"Donna," the receptionist called. A portly nurse walked toward them. "Can you escort this young man upstairs to the lounge, please?" Then she smiled at him. "There may be some people in the TV room that could help with your questions."

Donna pressed the button to close the elevator as Murphy stood awkwardly beside her, staring at the metal door. She hesitated as shouts came from beyond the doors, growing louder and more combative. "I'll be right back," Donna promised. She calmly walked over to the agitated man, and told his nurse, "I'll take him up for you."

The other woman rolled her eyes. "He's all yours."

"This is Dr. Joel Bradford," Donna told Murphy, wheeling the man into the elevator. "He's one of our oldest residents and the wisest among the bunch."

Joel grumbled but accepted her compliment with a nod.

Murphy waved but kept his distance. Donna encouraged him to strike up a conversation with Joel, but Murphy was reluctant. Joel kept looking at him as if he was his next meal. His eyes were eager and ravenous.

Then Murphy realized it was the paper the doctor was staring at.

"Whatcha got there, boy?" Joel asked. "Looks like a drawing of a key."

"It is," Murphy replied, holding it out in front of him. "I was hoping that someone here might be able to recognize it."

Joel squinted and pressed his face closer. "I remember this one. It has secrets."

Murphy's heart jumped into his throat when a loud chime signaled that they had reached the fourth floor. Donna wheeled Joel out and Murphy followed them into a room with a couch, a card table and a few lounge chairs.

"I'll leave the two of you alone, if that's okay," Donna said. She saw Murphy's panicked expression. "You'll be fine," she reassured him, "his bark is worse than his bite." Murphy smiled wryly at her ironic statement.

"Hey!" Joel protested. "Where are you going? You can't just leave me here with him. He's not a nurse!"

Donna squatted beside his wheelchair and looked up at Murphy. "Don't you mind this one, dear," she said while adjusting Joel's pant legs. "He may seem crusty on the outside, but he's all pudding inside." Donna chuckled at her own joke and handed Murphy and Joel each a cookie from a dessert tray that another staff member passed around. "I'll be back in thirty minutes to check on both of you."

Joel waited until the nurse was out of hearing range to speak. "So, where's the real key? I'll tell you all about it if you bring it to me."

"I can't do that, sir. It's not mine. I don't have it."

"Then who does?" Joel demanded, raising his voice.

"A friend."

Joel pounded his fist against the armrest of his wheelchair. "That key should me mine! I was so close to having it in my possession!" He pointed his arthritic finger at Murphy. "Did your friend tell you the power it holds?"

Murphy shook his head.

"I can show you what it does," Joel responded in a sickly sweet voice.

"I told you, I don't have—"

"LIAR!" Joel yelled. "Who put you up to this? Did *she*?"

"You mean Donna?" Murphy asked. "No, she—"

"Not the nurse, you imbecile! The witch!"

"Huh?"

"That's it!" Joel insisted. "You're one of her slaves sent to drive me mad, aren't you?"

Murphy didn't say it, but he sure wanted to tell Joel that he was already there.

"Oh, shush now," a lady chided from behind Murphy. She startled both of them, as no one else had been in the room a moment ago.

"Who's that?" Joel inquired brusquely.

The lady ignored him. "It's time to take your pills."

Murphy watched her blonde ponytail sway back and forth as she whirled Joel around and rudely walked away with him.

Murphy slid into the nearest chair, puzzled by the old doctor's comments. *Was he supposed to inherit the key? Did his family lose it, and Mrs. Sheldon just happened to find it?* His mind raced as he bolted up from his seat and began wandering the halls for answers.

"He's in room 415," a male attendant told him. "Down the hall to your left, just past the nursing station."

Murphy thanked him. As soon as he rounded the corner, he knew something was wrong. Donna scurried past him, excusing herself as she delegated tasks to the attendants rushing by.

"Call an ambulance, his heart stopped again!"

Murphy inched forward and peeked into the room. Joel was sprawled on the floor, unresponsive, and Donna began CPR on him.

"I'm sorry, but you'll have to leave this area," A tall woman advised, blocking the doorway.

"Is he going to be okay?" Murphy asked.

The tall woman looked back and sighed. "I really don't know. Are you a relative?"

"No, I just met him."

"Well, I hope your day gets better than mine," she remarked, moving aside as the paramedics approached with a stretcher. The door was open just enough for Murphy to peek through and witness the medical staff kneeling over Joel's ashen body, shocking him with paddles.

"We've got a pulse!"

Joel took a haggard breath and said, "She tried killing me again."

The paramedics laid Joel onto the stretcher and strapped him in. "Sir, we are transferring you to the hospital."

Murphy shuffled out of the way as they moved their patient. He overheard one of them say, "I swear this guy has nine lives."

Murphy followed the stretcher out to the waiting ambulance.

"Can you tell me your name?" a paramedic asked Joel.

"I'll tell you my name when you bring me back to my room," he said.

"Can't do that, sir. You've had cardiac arrest and we need to keep you monitored."

"That place won't protect me. She'll be waiting."

"Who will? Your family?"

"My family's dead and I'll be next if you don't listen to me. My heart did not fail—I was electrocuted."

The doors to the ambulance closed.

CHAPTER THREE

"**M**om, are all the stories about Moss Ridge true?" Murphy asked.
"Yes, I suppose. But time has a way of twisting the facts … Why?"
Murphy shrugged. "Just curious."

His mother raised her eyebrows. "I hope you're not going on a wild goose chase in search of the lost caves."

"Aha!" Murphy responded. "So you do know more than you're letting on. Come on, spill."

"Honey, people have been telling those tales throughout the ages and no one has found a magical door that opens to a room full of treasures."

"Then why did a man at Willow Crest tell me that the key has mysterious powers?"

"What key are you talking about? And why on earth were you at the nursing home?"

"The seniors are old, so I thought they'd know more about ancient stuff than we do."

"And was your visit worthwhile?"

"Almost, but then Joel, I mean Dr. Bradford—"

"Excuse me?" his mother questioned, raising her voice with alarm. "No," she muttered, "that can't be." She shook her head, as if clearing disturbing memories. "He'd be well over a hundred by now."

"He looked it."

"Stay away from him. He's dangerous."

"Do you know him?" Murphy asked.

"I know what he's capable of," his mother said. "Let's leave it as that."

...

"I found out that Mrs. Sheldon's neighbours like to gossip," Jason stated as he trudged up the last step to join Murphy and Chloe at the top of the bleachers.

"We already knew that," they chorused.

"Bet you don't know this scoop! But first, I need to sit. Those grandmas sure know how to feed a quest. I'm stuffed!"

Murphy took a step back and placed his hand over his chest. "No way! You? Full?"

Jason pushed his stomach out and rubbed it. "Uh-huh, so much food! I had cheese and crackers, then some kind of mushy fruit on ice cream, powered doughnuts, Oreo cookies and a slice of lemon meringue pie—"

"All right! Enough said. You're making Chloe drool." Murphy chuckled.

"What a Hoover!" Chloe added. Jason sucked in air, mimicking the sound of a vacuum cleaner.

Murphy cleared his throat and gestured for Jason to continue. "Could we get on with this?"

"Sure," Jason replied. "Dorothy lives next door to Mrs. Sheldon and they've been friends for over thirty years. She claims to have heard things. *Unusual things.*"

"For instance?" Murphy asked impatiently.

"Well, for one, Mrs. Sheldon likes to talk to herself. I'm talking full-fledged conversations in her backyard with no one around."

Chloe and Murphy spoke simultaneously. "That's strange."

"So, Dorothy confronted her one morning and asked who she was talking to. Mrs. Sheldon told her she was only meditating. But why in a different language?"

"What kind?" Chloe asked. "Like French?"

"No, she's never heard the language before."

"That's all?" Chloe wasn't impressed. Dorothy seemed like a nosy neighbour that had eavesdropped on a woman simply repeating a mantra in her own quiet surroundings.

Jason shook his head. "There's more ... Gladys, the lady that lives behind Mrs. Sheldon, said she saw two glowing bubbles hovering close to her house. She thought it might have been burglars with flashlights and would have called the police, but Mrs. Sheldon opened her bedroom window and the lights floated inside like they were invited in."

"Was Mrs. Sheldon alone in her house at the time?" Chloe asked.

"Don't know," Jason said. "But there's a couple that lives down the street that mentioned they've seen her walking over to Mr. Moss's home at midnight and disappearing into the woods."

Murphy knew something wasn't right when he caught Chloe spinning her bracelet.

Jason grinned. "Oh, did I mention that she only goes out during thunderstorms?"

...

Jason raked his fingers through his wind-blown hair, trying to smooth the dark chestnut strands back into place. He gave Chloe a sideways glance, blowing at a piece of hair that hung over his eye.

"Are you ready?" he asked.

"I've been ready since class ended," she replied. "TGIF."

"Then let's go."

Chloe pushed the tall, formidable gate with her shoulder. The wrought iron screeched with resentment as it swung open. Murphy crossed his fingers and gripped the shovel's handle tightly in his other hand. He followed Chloe and Jason along the fence that stretched the length of the long driveway, its iron bars failing to hold back the wild growth invading the side yard from the open field beside it. A meagre pathway made of flagstone led the way between the side of the house and the garage where the pavement ended. Murphy batted away the weeds with the blunt part of the shovel's blade as he trudged through the dead grass that had grown over the stones, listening to it crunch beneath his shoes. Chloe suddenly stepped off the path and turned towards the house, disappearing as she took a short cut to the back yard.

Murphy rounded the corner and stopped midway, dreading going any further as a sun bleached monument with an angel perched on top blocked his way. *Oh no, not here … please, please be wrong. I do NOT want to unearth a …* "Are you sure?" he asked looking up at the statue's face. The weather had worn down its features making it appear weary as if it was a tremendous chore to protect the yard. Murphy's legs trembled as he passed it by, feeling the scrutiny of its eyes on him. He hated cemeteries.

"Yes," Chloe answered, sprinting towards an area of elevated land where a pair of stone benches sat in a semi-circle on a raised surface of coloured tile. A natural gap in the trees offered a spectacular view of the ridge and open sky. "Oh no! Where is it?" She ran to the clump of autumn flowers bordering the sitting area and spun around. Murphy saw Jason point to something and Chloe pressed a hand over her heart, relieved to find that the birdbath wasn't missing, it had just been knocked over. She kneeled, parting the crowded mounds of white Chrysanthemums to find the depression left by the base. "This is it," she said with certainty.

"Are you absolutely sure this is the *exact* spot?" Murphy questioned a second time leaning over her. "I don't see anything that marks the spot."

Her hazel eyes flared with annoyance. "Yes, I'm sure."

"What's the matter, Robinson, got something against dead people?" Jason teased.

"Me? No, just double checking," Murphy replied staring at a crucifix jutting out from a lopsided tombstone in the field. It was a little too close for his comfort.

But Jason didn't buy it. "Nobody is going to crawl out of the ground and grab you, if that's what you're worried about," he reassured Murphy. "What could go wrong anyhow?"

Murphy grimaced. That was one question he didn't want answered. He sometimes envied Jason because he seemed to remain calm in any situation and had an instinct to protect those he cared about from any harm. Murphy would have been happy just to have his carefree attitude.

"Did your mom say anything about the shovel?" Chloe asked.

"Yeah, she wanted to know if we were planning to use it for something illegal." Murphy rolled his eyes. "Can you imagine robbing a convenience store and holding up a spade?"

Jason laughed, taking the shovel out of Murphy's hand. "It'd be my weapon of choice." He pretended to lash out. "Stick 'em up or I'll bury you in gummy worms!"

Chloe giggled. "Definitely *not* scary."

Jason chuckled as he placed his foot on the shovel's step and threw his weight into a bounce that drove the tip into the solid ground. Chloe lifted the flowers out as he dug deeper but the only thing they found was an empty peanut shell. "Try here," she remarked, pointing next to the hole. "I'm positive it's in this area."

It was late afternoon and the temperature rose to a sweltering heat wave. Murphy could feel it rising from the mound they were standing on. In fact, the mound grew larger as fresh dirt was added each time Jason dug another hole. And there were more than a few. Murphy felt a twinge of guilt that Jason was doing all the labour and offered to dig the last two holes. His palms sweat as he lowered the head of the shovel into the shallow pit, resting his chin on the handle for a five-minute break. A gentle breeze from the east gave them some reprieve from the humidity, but it also carried the stench of skunk. Chloe hopped off the mound and walked cautiously over to the trees dotting the border of a private asphalt runway that curved from the back of the garage and ran through the empty lot for almost a kilometer. Part of Mr. Moss's property, the neglected land was used to fly his aircraft. She searched along the crumbling strip and wild brush, finding the source of the bad smell. She waved them over, indicating it was safe. The skunk was dead and wouldn't be attacking them with its reeking spray. Murphy held his breath, refusing to look at the decaying animal.

Of course, being an animal lover, Chloe insisted that they give the poor thing a proper burial. It wasn't enough for her to know that it died in an actual cemetery. She wanted to find a suitable space amongst the tombstones.

"It's the right thing to do," she said, then added, "I'd do it for you."

"Yeah? Well, I'm not a skunk, am I?" Murphy commented. He glared at Jason, anticipating a sarcastic remark. "Don't even think about it, funny guy."

Jason wondered if the Moss or Wheeler family had been members of a strange cult. It was difficult to imagine that a family would bury their kin in their own backyard. *But kinda cool,* he thought. "Hey guys, check this out!" he shouted, urging Murphy and Chloe over to the lopsided tombstone with the cross. "Look at the dates—they're ancient!"

Chloe rubbed her hand over one of the larger stones, wiping off years of dirt. "Leonard Wheeler," she revealed, "born in 1820, died in 1889."

"Wow, he was only ..." Jason started counting backwards.

"Sixty-nine," Chloe answered.

Murphy thought of his dad suddenly. He'd be that old in thirty years.

"He died of heart failure," she added. "I remember reading it during my research. His wife, Martha, lived to the age of seventy-four. She died of pneumonia."

"And that's why you were nominated to do the research at the library," Jason remarked, his dimples showing as he smiled broadly.

"Actually, *I* volunteered because I knew neither one of you wanted to do it."

"'Cause you're better at it," Jason replied, kneeling between the next two gravestones. He traced the chiseled letters. "I think these smaller stones are for kids. See the dates? Earnest was only seventeen and Ada was stillborn."

Chloe moved in closer. "I think he died in one of the old mines up near Vesper's Pass." She shuddered, recalling the description of falling rocks crushing the men inside.

"Do you know what happened to Bernard? This says he died of head trauma. I wonder how."

Chloe shook her head. "I'm not too sure, but I think it was some kind of accident."

"Here's a girl named May," Jason stated. "1874 to 1888. She died of—"

"Asphyxiation," Chloe recalled.

"That means *suffocation*, right?" Jason asked and she nodded.

"There's one over here," Murphy called out, walking a bit farther down the trail of headstones. "Grace Wheeler. Died of diphtheria in 1886." He added for Jason's benefit, "I think that was some kind of disease."

"How sad," Chloe said. "I'm surprised Mrs. Wheeler didn't die of a broken heart, losing so many of her children."

"These two are from the Moss family," Murphy said.

"Judith *Wheeler* Moss," Chloe corrected, reading the epitaph. "Beloved wife and mother, died of natural causes in 1952. Her husband, Gordon B. Moss, died a year later from kidney disease."

"Mr. Moss's parents," Jason stated. "Which means *his* grave has got to be here too."

He darted to the field of overgrown grass. "Stay where you are. If he's in here, I'll find him."

The weeds were almost as tall as his five-foot eight frame, and as he parted the leafy stems, they snapped back into place as if to swallow him.

Murphy moved away from the tombstones, trying to locate Jason, and stumbled backward as his heel caught a rock peeking up from the ground.

Except, it wasn't a rock. It was a metal plaque. He had found the graves of Fred Moss, his wife Eleanor and his sister, Helen. The unusual inscription read: *Never far from home.*

"I wonder what that means," Chloe remarked. Murphy thought he knew. "Don't you find it odd that there's no birth or death information?" she asked.

Murphy shrugged, following her back to the sitting area. "Not if someone thinks they're still alive."

"So, should we tell him?" Chloe asked.

"Let's hold off a few more minutes," Murphy suggested, leaping onto the stone bench to get a better view of the field. The sun was lower in the sky and he had to shield his eyes from the blinding rays. Chloe joined him, squinting as she shifted over to the opposite side. She nudged Murphy with her elbow and jerked her chin towards the trees. They watched as Jason waded through the tall grass with zeal, heading towards a populated area of evergreens and red maple. Many of them were cut down to provide a clear walkway adjacent to the field that continued to the northeast end of the property. A little more than halfway from Jason's position stood a row of stone pillars with light posts marking the dangerous drop from the rocky cliff with signs and a steel gate that cut across the asphalt for security. "You're going the wrong way!" She yelled out, cupping her hands over her mouth to amplify her warning. But Jason didn't react. It was probably because he was too busy looking for something that wasn't there, Chloe thought. She jumped down and sat next to Murphy, willing to wait a little longer. "He's going to be so disappointed," Chloe said.

...

Jason thought he heard Chloe calling his name. He turned to respond and saw the grass moving. "I'm coming," he said. But no one responded. He only heard the sound of scurrying footsteps getting closer. He sprung into the air and caught a glimpse of his friends lounging around the sitting area.

So if they're over there, then who or what is in the field with me?

Suddenly, a boy crawled out of the grass and frantically got to his feet. He scrambled past Jason without a second glance.

"Hey!" Jason shouted. But the boy continued to run. Jason sprinted after him, ploughing through the grass as it whipped his face and stung his cheeks. "Wait!"

The boy darted back and forth like a scared buck, hopping nimbly over the bushes at the end of the yard and tearing into the woods.

Jason stopped a moment to catch his breath. The boy huddled inside a hollowed-out tree.

Jason approached slowly, saying, "I'm not going to hurt you." The kid was thin and frail. His clothes were hanging off of him. Jason slid his foot forward and took another step.

"No! Stay back!" the boy warned, keeping his voice low. "She'll see you!"

"Who?" Jason asked and spun around, but they were alone. "I don't see—"

A cool mist swirled at his feet, snaking its way up his legs and clinging to him as he stepped back.

"Ahh! The witch!" the boy wailed, bounding toward Jason. The mist gathered into a dense dark cloud and shot forward like tendrils of smoke. It wrapped around the boy's waist and he struggled to free himself. He stretched out a hand for Jason to grab, but the rope-like mist held him tight and dragged him back toward the woods.

"Help me!" the boy cried, digging his bare heels into the soft earth.

Jason dove for the boy, but the grey anomaly lifted him away before he could reach him. Jason dropped into the field of grass, his body slamming to the ground with a thud, knocking the wind out of his lungs.

By the time Jason was able to stand, the boy had crystallized. He was encased in a frozen tomb of crackling ice, with fear petrified on his face. Jason's brown eyes widened as he touched the cold, solid mass. His fingers felt the chill and he backed away, staring helplessly at the boy statue.

"Jason?" Chloe called.

"Yeah," he said. It was all he could muster as he peeled his eyes away from the woods.

In a matter of seconds, the boy's frozen body was hauled into the darkness, vanishing just as Chloe and Murphy stepped into the clearing.

"Hey, we found the—" Murphy stopped and followed Jason's gaze, hoping it hadn't been a ghost that caught his attention. "What's wrong?"

Jason shook his head. "I can't be sure, but …"

Chloe assumed that Jason was troubled by his failure to track down Mr. Moss's grave. "It's okay," Chloe replied, trying to encourage him. "We found the plot. It *was* easy to miss."

Something's not right, Murphy thought. *Jason's too quiet.*

They walked back through the cemetery in silence. Then Jason said, "Did you guys see anyone passing by back there?"

"No, why?" Chloe asked.

Jason looked back at the trees and his face paled.

"Jason?" Murphy moved to block his view. "Are you feeling okay?"

"Yeah, I guess," Jason responded, rubbing his eyes. He gave them a lop-sided smile and the colouring in his cheeks returned. Shrugging off his concern, he patted Murphy's shoulder. "Did you find anything else?"

Murphy rolled his eyes and said, "Yeah, the treasure spot, *finally.*"

"Well, I *was* close," Chloe remarked defensively, then added, "It's under the tiles. I noticed that most of them were faded from the sun except for one spot. It's darker and the same round shape as the base of the birdbath. I'll bet my allowance that it's there."

"You don't get an allowance," Murphy noted.

Jason laughed, "Come on, we have a hole to dig, or at least *another* one," he teased.

"Hey, that's not fair!" Chloe said pinching her nose. The area still had a foul odour lingering in the air. "Doesn't this smell remind you of anything?"

Murphy shrugged, waiting for the answer just so he could hear her nasal voice again.

"*Eau de toilet*?" Jason replied, deliberately pronouncing the word incorrectly with a French accent.

Chloe laughed. "No, but close. Murphy's feet!"

"The guy's locker room is worse," Jason added.

"Aw, gross."

Murphy quickened his pace, turning around as he passed Jason, "I'll start removing the tiles." He didn't want to waste anymore daylight time. The sun was just above the field now, balancing on the tips of the tallest weeds. He knew dusk would come soon enough and he didn't want to be around when it did.

Murphy dug frantically. Finally, the shovel hit something. *Thump!*

Jason got on his knees and used his hands to scoop out the loose dirt. Chloe dug her nails into the sides of the hole, prying the hard object loose. "I got it!"

She proudly held it up like it was a prized trophy, but it was just a wooden box. There was nothing fancy about it. It didn't even have a lock on it.

"Open it, Chloe!" Jason urged, barely containing his excitement.

Chloe flipped the box upside down to study it, but Jason swiftly grabbed it out of her hands and pried the lid off. He unwrapped the cloth that was tucked inside and shook out the contents, letting them drop to the bottom of the box.

"What *are* these?" Jason prodded them with a knuckle. "They look like shriveled onions."

"I think they might be tulip bulbs," Murphy suggested.

"Flowers?" Jason huffed. "*That's* the treasure?" He threw the box back into the hole, not bothering to hide his disappointment.

Murphy stared at the wooden container and wondered.

Mrs. Sheldon went to a lot of trouble to tell us about her secret. What was so special about these bulbs? She must have had a reason to want us to find them, but why? He reached in and retrieved the box, shoving its contents into the back pocket of his jeans before returning the container to the hole. He had a feeling that this was their first clue.

Jason left his two friends to finish filling up the holes and ambled his way through a thicket of trees growing along the other side of the house. He searched the endless shadows, wondering if his imagination got the better of him today, then walked back towards the house. He leaned against the wall, taking care not to touch the egg yolks splattered across the brick and waited for Murphy and Chloe to join him.

Murphy stuck to Chloe's side as he dragged his shovel behind them, making as much noise as possible to scare away any fanged critters lurking in the woods as they approached Jason on the west side of the house. "I bet ten bucks that Duncan and his cousin were the ones who made this mess," Murphy commented, kicking two soda cans that had been dumped on the path. He picked them up, along with a twisted empty box of candy.

"Definitely," Jason agreed, knowing that the grape drink and chocolate covered almonds are Duncan's favourite snacks. He was disgusted with the yellow goo streaming down the wall like tears.

Murphy heard something and tilted his head to listen. It sounded like claws scraping against a window pane. The noise caught Chloe's attention too and she shivered, rubbing her arms to warm them. Jason rounded the corner first and saw that the noise had come from a branch caught on the door handle on the front porch. Murphy sighed with relief. He tossed the litter onto a pile of leaves gathered at the bottom step and noticed how much the exterior of the house had deteriorated. At one time, it had been the most extravagant dwelling in town.

Mr. Moss had inherited the home from his late grandfather Leonard Wheeler. He was the mayor in the 1800s, and had helped to shape the growth and prosperity of Westfield. It was well known that he had money. "Moderate and simple" weren't part of his vocabulary, and building a mansion on a ridge with a backyard the size of an airport proved it.

But now, the home was just neglected and old. Murphy looked up at the colonial pillars, standing like sentries and guarding a palace that was crumbling away. It was a pitiful reminder that nothing lasts forever, and that even all the coin in the world hadn't been enough to protect Mr. Moss's sibling.

Everyone knew the story. Judith was the only child that had survived the hardships of that era. She and her husband had had two children, Fredrick and Helen. For years, the Moss home had been the epitome of happiness. But that had changed when they lost their daughter. Helen was only eight years old. She'd been warned about going into the woods alone and knew not to venture too far, but something had lured her past the safety of the yard and she'd never returned. Mr. Moss took ownership when he married and named the ridge using his surname as a moniker. Like his ancestors before him, the home had provided a joyous retreat, and he carried on that tradition … until his wife, Eleanor, vanished.

Many legends surrounded Westfield County. The hauntings on Mr. Moss's property were common stories. Many believed that Fredrick was the ghost searching among the trees for his missing wife.

Goosebumps ran down Murphy's spine. He no longer wanted to be there, and hoped that if Mr. Moss *was* haunting the place, he'd understand why they were in his yard. He did not want to become another victim to the property's mysterious clutch of death; there was enough people buried there. He tried to convince himself that a ghost wouldn't harm him or his friends, but failed when he recalled that Mr. Moss needed a reality check and digging on his land without permission could spark some anger.

Rumours had spread that Mr. Moss's personality changed dramatically after authorities informed him that they were discontinuing their investigation into Eleanor's disappearance and filing the report as a cold case. Fredrick never gave up, and pursued his own detective work, eager to find clues that others may have overlooked.

To help find answers, he built a machine that could propel him in the air to search the woods from up above. Neighbours had questioned his sanity as he gathered pieces of metal from the junk yard. He became so obsessed with his creation that he rarely stepped outside, and eventually stopped talking to his daughter. She left Westfield, got married and raised a son in the big city. Disaster struck before Mr. Moss was able to mend their relationship, so he never got a chance to meet his grandchild.

He'd designed the aircraft off a canoe. It had two large trailer wheels attached to the back and a smaller one in the front. The window was made of a simple clear plastic, bent into shape to form a half-dome covering the pilot's seat. The steering had a complex system of levers that were secured to the rudder and wings. There were gigantic, accordion-style fans that swished back and forth horizontally, creating the movement to propel the machine forward. They were made of a thin, black parachute material overlapping each connecting joint to resemble the construction of an umbrella. Below this were two smaller wings created from scrap metal.

Each had its own helium tank welded onto the tip to help with levitation, while the motor from a go-cart gave the machine the speed needed to soar off the edge of the ridge.

The weather on the day he circled the valley shifted drastically from clear skies to dark clouds within minutes, and strong winds had prevented him from landing. He had fought to keep his aircraft steady as he dipped dangerously low. Several people claimed to see a lightning bolt strike the wing, causing the aircraft to tip sideways, ricocheting off the ridge and cartwheeling to the earth. They lost sight of the aircraft as it careened down the slope, but stated that there had been an explosion. Police speculated that Mr. Moss had purposely lost control of the machine. It was the only possible answer, as there had been nothing left of the accident to go by.

Murphy didn't believe Mr. Moss had been self-destructive. He'd been too determined to just give up his quest and end his life. *But why fool the whole town? And if he survived,* Murphy thought, *where did he go?*

The For Sale sign posted on the front lawn creaked as the breeze swung it back and forth, then it suddenly dropped, pulling the rusted chains off their brackets and making an awful clatter as the links fell one by one to the ground. Murphy was sure this was an omen. Something bad was about to happen.

He suddenly felt alone and realized he had wandered ahead. Murphy leaned his shovel against the advertising post then turned back to join his friends, pulling out the cloth from his pocket and unwrapping it along the way. He rolled the bulbs around in his palm, wondering what made them so special, when a gust of wind seized the fabric. It launched in the air as if catapulted, soaring over his friends.

"Grab it!" he yelled, chasing after it.

Jason tried catching it in mid-air, but it swirled up beyond his grasp and floated toward the backyard. It tumbled over the grass and finally came to a stop as it snagged onto a thorny bush. Chloe plucked it off.

"Look!" she said as the boys gathered around her. "There's writing on it."

The script was faded and too difficult to decipher under the diminishing light.

"Is it in English?" Jason asked.

"What did you think it was written in, goblin lingo?" Chloe replied, giving the fabric back to Murphy.

"Har, har!" Jason answered, sticking out his tongue.

"Very mature, Mr. Tremblay!" Chloe chided, then smeared her dirty hands on his T-shirt.

Jason picked up one of the gooey eggshells lying crushed in the dirt. "Oh yeah? I'll show you mature." And he flung the broken pieces at Chloe as she ran away squealing.

"You missed me!" She put her thumb on her nose and wiggled her fingers.

Jason quickly gathered up several more pieces. Chloe slid behind a tree, but the meagre protection couldn't save her from the onslaught of slime flung her way.

"Ew!" Chloe shrieked, shaking off something stuck to her pant leg. Jason laughed hysterically.

"Hey guys … guys!" Murphy uttered, trying to break up the squabble. "Shh! Listen …"

It only took a few minutes for them to acknowledge that they weren't the only ones on Mr. Moss's property.

CHAPTER FOUR

Something caught Murphy's eye. It moved swiftly among the maple trees that traced the perimeter of land. "Did you see that?"

Jason's heart raced and he motioned for Chloe to step back.

"We should head back home," Murphy hinted.

"What was that?" Chloe asked, ignoring the suggestion and focusing her attention on the darker patches of open space.

Jason didn't respond.

"You mean ... *who* was that?" Murphy replied.

Jason stared at the faint outline. Its disembodied shape bobbed up and down, floating above the uneven ground. It was white and partially transparent, and too large to be human.

"We should find out what that is," Jason suggested. Though he was apprehensive, he grabbed each of his friends' arms and pulled them toward the unknown apparition.

"Not a chance!" Murphy objected, breaking free of his hold.

"I'm staying right here," Chloe stated, resisting, "didn't you see the glowing eyes? What if it's a wild animal?"

"But you *love* animals," he teased.

"I do. But I prefer tame ones," she responded.

"It's too dangerous," Murphy declared.

"Danger is my middle name."

"Delirious is more like it," Chloe remarked.

"Fine, then I'll leave you two chickens behind and go myself." Jason flapped his arms and clucked, goading them to change their decision. And it worked.

"Okay! We'll come with you!" Chloe said. "Just stop with the bird dance."

"Imitation is the best form of persuasion," Jason responded with satisfaction.

"You mean *flattery*," Chloe corrected him.

"Whatever! Who needs to give compliments when it's more fun enticing you with my charming abilities." He smiled, purposely revealing his dimples.

Chloe looked over at Murphy. "Let's go. before his head explodes."

Just as they stepped into the brush, the figure disappeared.

"Where's the shovel?" Jason whispered, dropping his arm. He was going to take it for their protection until he noticed Murphy didn't have it. Murphy cringed, "Front yard," he replied. Jason shrugged and led the way into the deep, dark woods.

A blood-curdling shriek rattled the stillness in the air. Murphy's hair rose on the back of his neck as the monstrous sound reverberated into the valley.

"Over there!" Chloe pointed out. "It's coming this way!"

They stood motionless as the drama unfolded, each of them with the same expression of bewilderment on their faces.

"What the—?" Jason remarked, unable to finish the sentence.

The apparition transformed into two heads and four legs. It seemed to be tripping and falling in a very erratic manner.

Murphy let out a ragged breath. The impossible became plausible as the ghastly figures were unveiled. Duncan and Stuart were wearing their Halloween outfits—white bed sheets with cut out holes for the eyes. They were running so fast that the costumes fell to the ground and neither one of them went back to pick them up.

Stuart rushed over to meet the three of them head on, seemingly terrified as he tried to get air into his lungs.

Chloe put her hands on her hips. "A little early for those getups, don't you think?" she asked, knowing full well why they were dressed up. "Looks like your plan backfired."

"Next time," Jason chimed in, "have someone do your makeup; boys dressed in togas aren't really scary."

Stuart didn't challenge him as he passed by in an awkward shuffle, holding onto the back of his pants. Murphy wanted to laugh at the fact that Stuart was so spooked he'd crapped himself, but Duncan abruptly gripped his shirt and twisted it.

"If I catch you telling *anyone* about tonight," Duncan warned, "I'll tenderize you like a piece of steak. Got that?"

Jason stepped in. "Leave him alone, Duncan. Perform your freak show somewhere else."

Jason wouldn't budge and Duncan huffed with annoyance. He wasn't used to anyone being unaffected by his intimidation. He glared angrily at Murphy and shoved him out of his way. "For your info," he replied through gritted teeth, "that wasn't us, I swear! There's something in there!" He shone his flashlight toward the trees. "I don't know *what* it was, but it tried to attack us. It was like a gigantic bat with wings as large as ..." He trailed off, seeing the uncaring way Jason had his arms crossed. "Okay, Tremblay, if you're so brave, then why don't you prove me wrong?" He sneered, hoping to get a rise out of Jason, but Jason didn't take the bait.

Chloe pulled at Jason's collar, saying, "Don't do anything dumb. We have a lot to do tomorrow. Besides, Duncan was just leaving, right?"

Duncan lowered his eyes. "Yeah, I'll go, but only after you tell me why the three of you are here."

"It's none of your business," Chloe remarked.

Halfway across the yard, Stuart hollered, "Duncan! Are you comin' or not?"

Duncan grumbled his impatience. But before he stalked off to meet his cousin at the front gate, he addressed Chloe. "You should go too. That beast might still be around."

Duncan's eerie cautionary words sent Murphy a wave of nausea. His dream suddenly surfaced like a geyser boiling over with intense pictures. He felt dizzy, and adjusted his stance to prevent keeling over.

Chloe waved her hand in front of his eyes. "Earth to Mr. Robinson, come in, Robinson."

"Are you okay? You sort of zoned out on us," Jason commented.

"Sure, I'm cool."

"You don't look it, bro. You look like you've just seen a ghost!"

"Hardy, har, har!" Murphy remarked, laughing.

"It's good to have you back," Jason mused.

"I never left."

"Yeah, but you were thinking about it, weren't you?" Chloe added, smirking.

Murphy chuckled. Chloe knew him too well, and he supposed it was due to the few years they had lived together in his home. His mother had offered a place to stay while Ms. Baker recovered from mental and financial stress. Chloe became more like a sister to Murphy, and both their mothers became the best of friends.

"Well," Murphy said, "if Duncan and Stuart wanted to make a lasting impression, that did it for me."

He was about to move when Jason stopped him. "Hold on, Mr. Jitters. That's the whole reason why we should go into the woods—to prove once and for all that either something strange exists in there, or that it's just a bunch of nonsense to scare everyone off the property. Besides, the Fisher Boys are gone now."

"You didn't even flinch when they came toward us, did you?"

"Not an *inch*," Jason said proudly, flexing his arm.

Murphy glanced at Chloe. "What are you doing?" he asked with piqued interest. She was behind Jason, mimicking a body-builder's stance and exaggerating the poses.

"I'm just joining in. I don't want to be left out of this macho moment."

Jason turned around. "Is that so?" he replied, pushing his chest out. "Too much testosterone for you to handle?"

Chloe rolled her eyes.

"She probably has as much as you do," Murphy stated.

"You think so, huh? Well, I bet you've got more *esters-jeans* than Chloe has."

"Esters-what? Is that some type of ladies' fashion?"

"He means *estrogen*." Chloe answered.

"I know—the female hormone thing," Murphy quickly said, feeling uncomfortable.

"Whatever, it's all *girly* stuff anyway," Jason added.

Chloe laughed. "You have the hormone too, Jay."

"No way."

"Yes, way," Chloe and Murphy chimed in together.

"Know-it-all," Jason jested, pushing Chloe into Murphy.

She stuck out her tongue.

Jason watched as the sun faded beyond the horizon. "What time is it?"

Murphy glanced at his watch. "Oh, man! I have eight minutes to get my butt back home before my curfew ends." He didn't want to be grounded for being late. He was looking forward to Gabe's Halloween bash in the park tomorrow.

"The shovel!" Chloe reminded Murphy as he whizzed by and then skidded to a halt, returning a moment later with the tool slung over his shoulder. "Thanks," he said, "Mom would kill me if I didn't bring it home."

...

Murphy hit the alarm button as he pried one eye open. A line of bright yellow welcomed him, and he sprang out of bed with excitement. It was Saturday, and the weather was perfect. Nothing was going to ruin his mood.

He tiptoed down the stairs and swiped a handful of vanilla wafers from the pantry, poured a glass of apple juice and placed his breakfast on the coffee table in the den. Then he bounded up the steps to retrieve the mysterious cloth from his jean's pocket, heading straight to his radio where he had left them. But they weren't there. The bulbs he placed on top of his bedside table stayed in the same spot, but not the pants. He looked everywhere, but couldn't find them. *There's got to be a logical explanation. They don't just get up and walk away.*

He stuffed the cookies in his mouth while he searched the main floor and noticed that the basement door was open. He cringed when he heard the washing machine switch to the rinse cycle.

"Mom, are you down here?" he called out. "Are you doing a load of my clothes?"

His mother, Julie, appeared at the bottom of the steps. "Hi, honey. You're up awfully early. Is everything okay?"

"You didn't happen to take my jeans that were on my radio, did you?"

"I certainly did," she said as she came up the stairs. "They were filthy! What in the world were you doing last night?"

All Murphy could muster at that point was, *"AAAAH!"*

He scurried past his mother to shut the machine off.

"I just put them in, so they won't be ready to wear yet," she stated in an irritated voice.

"Did you check my pockets?"

"No, I didn't … Murphy, what is this all about?"

He lifted the washing machine lid, ignoring her question, and plunged his hand into the cold suds, feeling around for a soggy piece of material. "Found it!" he said, shaking off the water and unfolding it.

His mother crossed her arms and waited. "I expect an answer, young man."

Murphy looked up. "Sorry, Mom. I thought you were sleeping. But I did eat, just not the cereal because there wasn't any milk, only junk food, and I needed this"—he held up the dripping cloth—"so I could read it later, and that's why I went back to my room, but then I couldn't find it and—"

"Whoa, slow down! You're not making sense."

Murphy took a deep breath, ready to repeat his explanation, but his mother shook her head smiling. "Go and grab the hair dryer," she said.

Murphy kissed her on the cheek and ran up the stairs.

"Next time," she hollered out, "if there's anything important that you're storing in your pockets, make sure you take it out before you go to bed. Okay?"

"Okay!"

"And have a carrot muffin. You're going to get scurvy if you don't eat your veggies!"

Yup, he thought, *she's definitely a drama mama.*

…

Sitting under the big maple tree, Murphy repositioned himself more comfortably by stretching out his legs and crossing them. Chloe was lying on her stomach with her chin propped up in her hands, munching on a granola bar, and Jason leaned his back against a mound of leaves he had gathered together. They listened as Murphy repeated the words written on the cloth for the second time:

Beyond the ridge, there is a place
Where water falls but can't be traced.
This sacred ground can be your treasure.
The power it holds cannot be measured.

To seek this gift, plant what you've found
Deep within the Valley's ground.
If you do, you'll soon behold
A magical gift, more precious than gold.

These wonders will show what you can't see,
But challenge awaits you on this journey.
The key to your future is not far behind.
Never say a word of the things you find,
For in the hands of those that don't believe,
Danger will come, and destruction it will leave.
These two different worlds are not same in the least,
One is the Protector, the other is the Beast.

"So … what do you think it means?" Jason asked.

"I have no idea," Murphy responded.

"I might," Chloe declared, "but we'll have to return to Moss Ridge and find a way to get down to the Valley without being noticed. Our first clue tells us to plant the bulbs there."

"Couldn't we just throw them over the edge like everyone else does?" Murphy suggested.

"It says to bury it in the Valley's ground," Chloe pointed out.

"Yeah, I figured that out, genius."

"Then why do you still look confused?" Jason asked.

"I'm not, I was just thinking that this ground probably has the same dirt as Lily Valley. So why go to Mr. Moss's place when we could save ourselves time by planting them here? The bulbs wouldn't know any difference."

Chloe rolled her eyes. "You just don't want to go back because of the big, bad bat-thing."

"Wow! Say that three times without getting your tongue tied," Jason said, elbowing Murphy in the ribs.

"You're not helping."

Jason shrugged. "I thought I was."

"Then could you find out if your parents have a trowel we can use?" Chloe laughed, seeing Jason look at her as if she had three heads. "It's a handheld scoop," she explained, "used for gardening."

"Yeah, I'll get right on that, boss."

Here we go again, Murphy thought. *Chloe has a plan, and when her mind is set on something, there's no stopping her.*

"Do you guys remember Mrs. Sheldon describing a doorway that led to a body of water?" She tapped the poem. "It's all connected. What if her stories are true, and the bulbs will somehow show us a hidden door that the key opens?"

Impressed, both boys nodded their heads, agreeing with her.

It had been during a history lesson, she recalled, when Mrs. Sheldon spoke to the class about an ancient cave with a river flowing through it, and the tribal people that had once lived there. As the years went by, their preservation had been compromised when the entryway that kept them safe and hidden was destroyed. They'd had to move to another discreet location. Mrs. Sheldon taught the class that the underground pools of water were called aquifers, and that the large rocks that hung like giant fangs were referred to as stalactites.

"So, are we gardening in our Halloween outfits?" Jason asked, brushing off the leaves clinging to him as he stood. "Because mine will be really difficult to kneel in."

"Probably not," Chloe responded. "We should find out what's in the woods first. We wouldn't have to stay long, and we can always call the police once we're back home if we need to. That way, we'll still have plenty of time to dress up for the party."

"You do realize," Murphy advised, "that the poem also mentioned that there's a 'Beast' lurking about, right?"

"I know, but there's also a 'Protector.' Did you ever think that this might refer to Mrs. Sheldon?" Chloe reasoned. "What if she was scouring the woods, helping to find the missing kids, and got hurt in the process?" She thought about the microfilm, and the word 'hero' came to mind. "Don't you want to help her?"

"Sure, I do. But I sense that my simple day of fun has now been obliterated ... again."

"One day you'll thank me for this," Chloe said.

"For what? The chance to see up close what an oversize, bone-crunching bat looks like?"

"This could be an opportunity for us to solve the mystery of Westfield's most infamous crimes!"

Jason nodded. "What if this thing is the reason for all of the kidnappings? If we can find it, then we could capture it, and just like that"—he snapped his fingers—"the problem would be gone."

Murphy conjured up an image of adoration from the town. "So, if we *do* go ... then we might be heroes?"

"Okay, dreamer boy. We have absolutely no proof yet, so you can wake up from your nap now," Chloe said.

Murphy jumped to his feet. "Well then, what are we waiting for?"

"Are you wearing last year's outfit?" Jason asked Chloe.

"No, I tore up all the bandages just trying to remove them."

"Too bad. That was a great mummy costume."

"Thanks, but wait until you see this one."

"So, tell us what it is," Murphy replied.

"You first," Chloe said without any real interest. Something ahead had distracted her, and without warning, Chloe sprinted across the park toward the ball diamond, disappearing out of sight as she went around the bleachers at full speed.

Then she screamed.

"Chloe!" Jason ran to the bleachers without hesitation, and Murphy followed close behind.

"What's wrong? Are you okay?" Jason asked. Murphy had never seen him so anxious before.

"My bike, it's gone!" Chloe bellowed, clenching her fists. She looked both ways down the street and stomped her feet, having an outright temper tantrum right there on the road. She came back and picked up the chain, holding it out for Murphy and Jason to see that it had been purposely cut. "Why didn't they take yours too?"

Jason rubbed his forehead and let out a sigh. "I think this will explain why," he said, twirling the lock around his finger. He pulled a scrap piece of paper off his bike and handed it to Chloe. "It's addressed to you."

Uh-oh, Murphy thought as Chloe took the note. He could swear that her face turned red with anger. *She should have a warning label.* "What does it say?" he asked.

"It's from Duncan." She read the hand-scrawled printing out loud:

"Chloe, I know you dug up something important yesterday. I'm willing to make a deal. You'll get your bike back as soon as you give me the note from the box. And I want the original! No copies!"

"Oh, that's just great! How are we supposed to solve anything without the poem?" Murphy blurted out loud.

Jason shook his head. "I don't know. How could he even know about it? Unless he was spying on us in the woods before they got spooked."

Chloe didn't comment, but her body language said it all—she was ticked. Her arms were crossed, and her lips were pursed so tightly that not even a crowbar could pry them open.

"We need to figure out what to do," Jason added. "If we confront him together, no one will get hurt."

Murphy liked the idea. "Yeah, he couldn't take us all on at once."

"So we give the jerk what he wants? No way!" Chloe huffed.

"It's the only way," Jason answered. "If we don't comply with his stupid demands, you won't get your bike back, and if we tell anyone, he'll just make it harder for us at school."

"Jason's right. If we tell our parents and he's punished for it, we're all doomed. He'll have Stuart and all of *his* friends on his side." Murphy shuddered. "We would definitely be outnumbered then."

"What if we asked your brother?" Chloe asked Jason. "Do you think he'd help?"

"Doubt it. He'll be too busy practising with the band."

Chloe's face took on a pathetic pleading look.

"… But we could try," Jason offered.

Chicks, Murphy thought. *They always get their way.*

…

"So … you're being threatened for *this*?" Gabe inquired for the second time. He removed his sunglasses and slid off of the picnic table pushed against the side of the garage. He was sure that he'd heard the story correctly but just couldn't believe it. "I know what Duncan's capable of, but extortion? Wow." He held the fabric in both hands, walking the short distance of his family's backyard, trying to decipher what the hype was all about but couldn't. He pinched the bridge of his nose, holding back a smile. "What would you have me do about it?"

Murphy thought of many things that he'd like Gabe to do, but he kept his opinions to himself. "What if we just make a duplicate for ourselves and give Duncan the original?" he offered as an obvious choice.

"That sounds like a good start. You see, Jay, Murphy knows what to do. Besides, Duncan probably won't understand the note anyhow. *I* don't even understand it."

Chloe spoke up, sounding a bit more hopeful. "Gabe has a point. It took us a while before we figured out *one* of the verses. It'll take Duncan forever to decipher the poem."

"He'd give up eventually," Murphy said, agreeing with her logic.

"Except . . ." Chloe paused, chewing on her lip.

"Go on," Gabe encouraged.

Chloe squatted down and turned her head up toward Gabe. She took the cloth between two fingers and lifted the corner up, focusing on something underneath. A hint of uneasiness crept into her voice as she said, "We might have a hard time reproducing *this* stuff."

"Huh?" Gabe turned the material over.

"It looks like some kind of map," Chloe speculated.

They stared at the lines, rounded humps, dips and flat edges, sketched in faint pencil markings that had faded from the wash. It didn't have any street names or formal directions. It didn't even have a legend. But, oddly enough, Chloe began to see an outline that she recognized. The spot featuring an arrow looked familiar.

"That's Lily Valley!" she said, stabbing a finger onto the marked position. "It *is* a map. A map of Westfield County!"

They easily recognized landmarks made from rudimentary pictures scattered across the page once they understood the abstract images. There were arrows strategically placed among locations they knew, and Chloe pointed out some of them, showing that they lined up perfectly to create several triangular patterns connecting to Moss Ridge. Just as she removed her hand, Chloe's bracelet got caught in a loose thread. Gabe offered to help untangle the material. He took her wrist, sending a zing of delightful shivers up her arm, and that's when she noticed that her bracelet had the same symmetrical designs as the map. She blushed when he let go, deciding not to share her discovery yet, as she was too embarrassed to speak.

"Does anybody have an idea what these are for?" Jason asked, tracing the four symbols that were drawn at the bottom. No one knew, but there were plenty of unspoken guesses.

Each triangle had a symbol inside. The first triangle, closest to Moss Ridge, was upside down with two parallel lines running horizontally in the middle. The next one was upright and had a smaller triangle inside of it. The third one, with its tip pointing down, looked like it had the mathematical addition sign, and in the last shape, with its tip pointing up, there was a small dot.

"How can you guys make sense of this?" Gabe held up the cloth, allowing the sunlight to filter through.

"It's a puzzle," Jason offered. "Each time we solve a verse, we get closer to finding out what the 'Big Mystery' is." He used his fingers as quotations to emphasize his point.

Gabe laughed. "And ... what would that be? That you need your big brother to fight your battles? Or is it—"

"No, that's not it, at all," Jason interrupted. "Our teacher was nervous about something. She wanted to keep her location a secret. She said she was called away for an important purpose, and then she vanished, and she hasn't returned. We need to find her—*fast.*"

"We think she may be in some sort of trouble," Chloe admitted.

"She asked for our help," Murphy added.

"Mrs. Sheldon is missing?" Gabe's eyes widened as he leaned against the wall. A sudden rhythmic tap behind the garage window had him opening the side door in a hurry. "Give me five," he said. A fist pushed through the crack and gave a thumbs up gesture. "What exactly did she say before she disappeared?"

Gabe's concern rose as they quickly filled him in on all the events. He turned to Chloe. "Do you still have your dog?"

"Buckles? Yeah, why?"

"Well, he's a hunting dog, isn't he?"

"I don't know," she answered, shaking off her revulsion. "He's still a puppy. I haven't even taught him how to shake a paw yet, so I wouldn't have trained him for something like that." The thought sickened her. "The only thing he'll chase is a squirrel."

Murphy laughed. "He wouldn't even know how to attack. Which *is* too bad, because he'd be a good back up if Duncan gets out of line."

Jason agreed. "He's right, Gabe. There's no killer instinct in him. Zero. Unless you count licking someone to death."

"I didn't mean for you to sic your dog on Duncan," Gabe explained, chuckling. "I meant that he could help you search for Mrs. Sheldon. You know, like picking up her scent from where you saw her last."

Jason grinned. "I kind of prefer the other option better."

Murphy smiled, but it faded quickly. The minute hand was counting down with every tick-tock, and his head throbbed just thinking about what lay ahead. Someone had to remind everyone the seriousness of the situation, and of course, it had to be him. He sighed, resigning himself to the inevitable. "We should go."

"Wait a minute, I've got an idea," Gabe offered as he stepped onto the grass to allow his friend Aaron to pull up onto the driveway with his station wagon. He opened the passenger door and rummaged through the glove box. "If I could take pictures ..." He held up a Polaroid camera.

"Dude, there's no film in it," Aaron commented, grabbing his drumsticks while the glove box was still open.

"That's all right," Murphy remarked, seeing how deflated Gabe looked.

Just then, the garage door opened and Ty walked out. His real name was Terrence, but strangely, he hated the formality of it. "Hark! Ye citizens of Westfield," he uttered in a deep, booming voice. "Your aid has come to abolish the heathen's ransom by offering his Canon."

He was greeted with silence.

"Oh!" Gabe said, trying to give a courteous response.

They finally understood when Ty tossed an object at Jason unexpectedly and it bounced from his fingers into Murphy's grasp. Thankfully, he was right there to catch it, or the compact camera would have been smashed to smithereens.

"Hey, thanks," Jason remarked, placing the camera on a workbench. "But we don't have time to process the film."

Gabe shrugged. "All right, suit yourselves."

Ty walked over to Gabe and plucked the cloth from his hands. He laid it on the bench, smoothing it out. Then he took several pictures at different angles, as if to capture a piece of evidence overlooked from a crime they weren't aware of. Then he lifted his bass guitar strap over his head.

"Should malignant forces keep you from—"

"What Shakespeare over here means," Paul interrupted, stepping out from the shadowy corner of the garage and throwing his thumb in Ty's direction, "is that we've got your backs." Then he added, "Dudes, are we jammin', or are we posing for a photo shoot?"

Ty was swift to react and put his palm over his heart as if shocked. "Blast ye who halts my tongue's desire to speak freely!"

Gabe rolled his eyes, laughing. "I'll bring you the photos when they're developed," he promised, handing the cloth back to Murphy, and then turned away to help Aaron take out one of the amplifiers.

Paul waved. "See you tonight."

"And you'd better be there, Jay," Gabe cautioned. "No brawls of any sort, okay?" He messed up Jason's hair. "I want to be sure that you won't be coming to this party all black and blue."

"I'll be on my best behaviour," Jason replied, tiptoeing while he imitated an angel's halo with his hands circled above his head.

Murphy laughed. "You look more like a goofy ballerina with your skirt too tight."

"If not," Jason added, "I could always be a zombie. Then I wouldn't even need a mask." He stretched his arms out in front of him, moaning and pretending to claw at Chloe's face. She swatted his hand away. "Hey, not so hard!" he exclaimed.

Gabe shot him an irritated look but seemed to decide not to encourage him further. "Go on, get outta here." He lightly booted Jason in the rear.

Aaron watched in amusement. "Looks to me like you don't have to worry about anything. *She* could handle herself just fine."

Chloe smiled smugly. "Why don't we just get dressed now, finish this mess with Duncan and then go to Moss ..." She didn't finish because she saw Murphy cringe.

Wonderful, he thought. *Today I get to face off with a behemoth, sabre-toothed flesh-eater* and *battle a fist-wielding, bike-thieving ogre.* At this point, they should be asking for vet assistance—not the army, but the animal kind. (Although Murphy would have been more at ease if they were accompanied by soldiers.)

"The sooner, the better," Jason concluded.

...

Murphy bent over to slip the tan coloured fur coverings back over his shoes. They had loosened during his walk up the steep climb to Duncan's neighborhood and the white plastic claws were dragging against the pavement, clicking with every step. Chloe giggled as his tail rose in the air and she grabbed the tuft of hair at the tip. Her wild hair didn't even move as she twirled under it, humming a simple tune to the sound of the clacking noise while Jason drummed up some harmony on his metal waist. Murphy spread his arms open and danced as Chloe joined in. The feathers on his wings fluttered as he jived to the beat. Then Chloe started to sneeze, which immediately put a stop to the three-man band's performance.

Chloe slowed down as they reached the top of the hill and gazed at all the beautiful modern homes. She was quick to notice the stares. People dressed in fine clothes watched them pass by through windows decorated in velvet drapes and silk sheers. The area oozed wealth and their Halloween costumes looked completely out of place.

As they strode closer to Duncan's house on Balsam Lane, the houses expanded in size to accommodate three-car garages with monogrammed driveways. Murphy had to admit he was impressed. Aside from being a personal injury lawyer, Duncan's father owned a strip plaza downtown. Mr. Fisher had partnered with his brother years ago to build the commercial units, which included his own law firm business. It was between an insurance broker and a bridal shop. *The money must be raking in,* Murphy thought as they found the address. A reddish-brown stone sat near the entrance with the word "WELCOME" chiseled in calligraphy. Murphy chuckled. *How ironic.*

The Fisher home had red brick on all three levels. It had navy shutters and a door in the same colour. Murphy craned his neck to look up at the circular stained-glass window on the third floor just underneath the pitch of the roof, when he noticed a set of curtains hastily drawing shut on the second level.

Duncan's father opened the door and pushed his sleeves up, revealing a dark tan. He peered at his gold watch. "Aren't you kids supposed to wait until the lampposts go on before you start collecting candy?" He leaned against the door jamb, crossing one muscular leg over the other. His hair was casually pulled back into a stubby tail. His face was clean-shaven minus a patch of hair below his bottom lip, groomed into a pencil line that stopped just under his chin. As he stepped aside to allow Duncan to pass by, the diamond stud he wore gleamed in the sunlight.

"Is there a problem here?" Mr. Fisher asked.

It was easy to see the similarities between them once Duncan stepped out onto the porch. They were both tall, with smooth complexions and sandy blonde hair, bleached at the tips from sun exposure. Duncan preferred a military style for his hair, choosing a crew cut to emphasize his square jaw. It was almost comical to see the two of them standing side by side. One was wearing a black t-shirt with a print of Kiss's *Destroyer* album on it and faded blue jeans too snug to be comfortable. The other was sporting a long-sleeved burgundy V-neck sweater and grey cotton twill pants. Duncan tried to convey his father's flair but somehow it didn't suit him, even dressed in fancy attire.

"No, Pop," Duncan said. "Chloe came here to see me." He grinned, giving her a sly look.

Chloe's eyes narrowed.

"Oh, that's right," Mr. Fisher said, "you needed your bike repaired. Well, you'll be pleased to know that he did a fine job and it's as good as new." He squeezed Duncan's shoulder proudly.

Chloe's mouth dropped open.

Mr. Fisher waited for her to respond, likely assuming she would be grateful and praise his son's good deed.

Murphy nudged Chloe. "Say something."

"Gee, Duncan, what would I have done without you? Thanks so much," she answered through clenched teeth.

Duncan held his comment until his father went back inside. "So what are you guys supposed to be? The Cowardly Lion and the Weirdos of Odd?"

Jason snorted and Chloe huffed, expressing her disapproval. "What?" Jason remarked defensively. "We *do* look a lot like the characters from The Wizard of Oz."

"With the exception of cowardly," Chloe added for Murphy's benefit.

Duncan walked past Chloe's glare and met Murphy on the sidewalk. He opened his palm. "I don't have all day, dork. Give me what I want."

Jason stood beside his best friend and crossed his arms. "Not until Chloe has her bike."

"No, not until *I* have that note," Duncan snapped.

"That's enough!" Chloe yelled, stomping over to Duncan. "Give. Me. My—"

"I will, but first your bodyguard has to leave."

"No deal," she countered and raised a hand to stop Jason in his tracks. He got the message and stepped back.

Duncan hesitated, watching Chloe carefully. "Deals are meant to be broken."

Murphy was getting tired of the bantering. "Here," he said, throwing the folded cloth at him. "*We* don't have all day either."

Duncan gestured with his thumb that the bike was in his back yard.

"What time is it?" Jason asked.

"It's almost 12:40."

Jason's stomach growled. He patted his midriff, creating a hollow clanging noise. "This Tin Man needs oil—or should I say, *half-human needs grub*."

Jason had dressed up as a cyborg. He had on black cargo pants and a long-sleeved T-shirt with grey stripes running down his right arm. He had wires sprouting from his neck, silver paint on half of his face and a foil cap that pointed at the top. His boots were black, and he wore a chest plate made of corrugated cardboard, spray-painted silver with latches glued in place.

"You're more like a garbage man with a pyramid on his head!" Chloe taunted.

He peered at her through a piece of blue plastic secured over his right eye. "Oh, is that so, Miss *Scarecrow*?"

"*I* don't look anything like that." She pointed out the fake stitching along her arms and legs. Her battered clothes were tied with twine at her wrists and ankles, and she had a very large red heart drawn on the front of her chest with long pins sticking out of it. Her hair was tousled and teased, and her make-up gave the illusion that buttons were sewn onto her eyes.

"Do voodoo dolls have stuffed brains too?" Jason jested.

Chloe pulled one of her pins out and chased him with it.

Jason raised his hands up. "Okay! I give up!"

Chloe dropped her arm and tucked the pin back into her costume. By the time she weaved it through, Jason was far enough away from having his arms poked that he boldly japed, "At least *I* don't look like a pin cushion with a bad sewing job!"

Chloe exaggerated a gasp at his playful insult. "You're gonna get it!" she warned.

"Doesn't anyone care to make a comment on *my* outfit?" Murphy sulked.

The play-fighting ended, and Jason pulled Chloe up from the ground.

"Your costume *is* amazing. There's no doubt that you'll win this year," Jason replied. "Although … I'm not quite getting the cat-slash-bird theme."

"I'm supposed to be a griffin."

Chloe chuckled, knowing Jason was clueless about the mythical creature Murphy imitated. She rubbed the beak with her fingers, admiring its smooth curve before stepping back. "The wings look so real!" she praised, wanting to touch them. "I've never seen anything like it!"

"Yeah, you gotta love the beard," Jason said, tugging at his chin. "You're simply *fur-ocious*," he added, batting his eyelashes.

"It's a mane, not some hairy growth I just happened to stick on so I can look more masculine."

Jason laughed. "Okay, your *mane-liness*, I won't argue." Despite his silliness, he marveled at the details. "Your mom must have spent a lot of time on this."

"Yeah," Murphy responded, feeling guilty, "about ten thousand hours' worth."

"One thing is for sure, you'll definitely get noticed. There's no way the judges could pass you by without a second glance."

Murphy smiled. "Good. Then their decision should be easy."

Chloe turned to him. "Not *too* cocky, are you?"

CHAPTER FIVE

"C an we grab some grub on the way?"

"That sounds good. I'm starving," Chloe remarked, as she steered her bike toward a sandwich shop called *Sub-burbs*.

"Ugh! I don't know how you guys can think of food right now," Murphy commented. His stomach was somersaulting like a circus performer. "All you're doing is making yourselves more appetizing for that thing in the woods!"

"It probably won't even go after us. I'm sure it prefers the flavour of *Fish-er* kabobs instead." Jason laughed at his own joke. "Get it? Fish—"

Chloe interrupted, "Yeah, we get your lame joke."

Murphy didn't laugh. He grew more anxious as the minutes ticked by and wondered if they were making a mistake by not telling someone about their plans. People disappeared every year. What if this thing was drawn to their scent and hunted them down? What if they really were gobbled up? *So many things could go wrong*, he thought. And just then, an image popped into his head: his body, held up by the seat of his pants, dangling over the monster's carnivorous mouth. He shuddered, trying to block the taunting words of *tasty and scrumptious morsels* from repeating in his brain.

Murphy stayed outside on guard duty, while Jason and Chloe went inside the shop to order. They both returned with foil-wrapped bundles and he knew immediately that they'd bought cheeseburgers just by the smell of barbecue sauce.

"Are you sure you don't want a bite?" Chloe asked, waving the tempting food under his nose. Murphy shook his head. Better safe than sorry, he figured.

Chloe was grateful she had company returning to the upper floor of her duplex home. As sweet as the elderly landlord was that lived on the main level, she liked to chat and Chloe didn't want to waste time. Plus, Miss. Dawson always smelled like moth balls and sour milk. A stomach turner for sure, especially after eating. She wheeled her bike into the storage room, sliding the door closed, and then ran to catch up with the boys. They had stopped on the side of the road, distracted by two girls that were lying on the sidewalk side by side for their boyfriends to jump over on their skateboards. They were encouraging their boyfriends to raise the ramp higher so the jump would be riskier, and cheered even louder when the boys added another block of wood.

Jason nudged Chloe. "I could see Duncan showing off like that. He'd do all those crazy stunts just to impress you."

Chloe snorted. "Doubt that."

"I'm telling you, Chloe, Duncan's infatuated with you. Trust me on this one."

"Well, that's *not* the way to get my attention." She jerked her chin toward the daredevils. "That's just ludicrous!" Murphy chortled and she whirled around, continuing, "And, if he thinks that I'd sacrifice myself in the name of entertainment just to boost his ego, then he's completely delusional!"

Jason laughed, seeing how this riled her. It was funny how uncomfortable she was about being the subject of Duncan's affection. Jason turned his back and pretended to have a make-out session, using his arms to make it look as if a girl was caressing him.

Chloe lunged, pushing him against a telephone pole. "Serves you right," she said, hearing him grunt.

"I almost *served* you my lunch!" he said. "The next time you want to attack me, make sure I haven't eaten beforehand!"

Chloe covered her mouth. "Sorry."

"You two should be in a comedy show," Murphy commented.

"He likes you, he *loves* you," Jason teased, singing off-key. Chloe tried to slap him, but he blocked her hand with his forearm. "Okay, no more songs!" Jason stated, massaging his arm. "Sheesh, I was only joking!"

"If anything," Murphy responded, "he's persistent."

"Maybe," Chloe said, "but I always win."

Jason and Murphy ignored Chloe's smug expression as they stopped in front of the ornamental gate that separated them from Mr. Moss's property. Murphy took a deep breath. It was twenty-five minutes after one o'clock. There were plenty of daylight hours left.

Jason was the first to enter, giving Murphy a pat on the back as he squeezed by. "It's not going to attack all three of us," he said reassuringly.

"You're probably right. There's safety in larger numbers," Murphy replied.

"Unless it's *really* hungry," Jason added with a devilish grin.

In a single-file line, they followed the narrow dirt trail past the maple trees and thick patches of shrubbery. Murphy's costume slowed their progress, as each branch seemed to snag on the fur. Finally, Jason found the fossilized footprints Duncan and Stuart had made the night before, giving them an easy marker to retrace their steps with.

As the woods grew denser, less light filtered through the trees. Shadows became restless, needing to stretch their limbs against the ground for the last rays of sun as darker figures lurked under heavy foliage. Chloe noted that there weren't any birds. There was no sound at all except for the occasional *ping* coming from Jason's outfit when he hit something. She hummed a little tune and looked back to make sure that Murphy was still behind her.

"I'm still here," he said, dragging his feet, until a flickering white glow caught his attention. He caught up to Chloe. "Did you see that?" He looked to his right, but whatever it was had faded away.

"See what?"

"The light behind the"—Murphy counted the trees in a row— "seventh tree."

"It was probably just a shadow." Jason said reassuringly.

An uneasy feeling of something watching them had Murphy shaking his head. "Shadows don't glow," he responded.

Chloe rolled her eyes. "There's no one else here, Murphy. Just us."

Tell that to my brain, he thought as he tried to quell the paranoia.

"What time is it?" Chloe asked.

"It's almost two," Murphy said. "We've been walking for about half an hour."

Chloe slowed down. "Don't you guys think we should have come across something by now?"

"Yeah," Jason replied, frustrated, "the joke's on us." He wasn't thrilled that they'd wasted part of their day looking for something that didn't exist.

"Duncan's probably laughing at us right now," Murphy remarked. "We should head back."

Jason hesitated as he focused on a large uprooted tree lying on its side, blocking the trail. "Just a little farther, then we can go. The path seems to widen up ahead, and that's where the footprints stop."

They cautiously approached the fallen tree, noticing the skid marks Duncan and Stuart had left in the soft ground. The deep grooves indicated that they had changed direction and left in a hurry.

"It looks like someone or *something* used these trunks as target practice," Jason commented, peering at the scorched bark peeling off the trees around them.

"But we're not in danger, right?" Murphy asked, hoping Jason would agree.

Jason didn't respond. He held his hand out, stopping Chloe as she got closer to him. "Don't move," he ordered under his breath.

She froze in her tracks and whispered, "What's wrong?"

"Not sure," he said and darted out to find cover under the slender, fern-like plants across from them. He signaled for his friends to hide behind the decaying tree stump.

"Get down!" Jason warned, pointing to the top of the trees.

Chloe and Murphy followed his advice, squatting behind the massive trunk.

The colouring drained from Jason's face as he ran back to his friends. He stopped in front of the fallen tree and didn't move, acting as a shield to protect them.

"I think he's in shock. We have to do something," Chloe urged.

Murphy stood, using every ounce of courage he had, and grabbed the back of Jason's shirt, yanking him over the trunk. Jason swung his legs over and tried to sit up, but the weight of his costume prevented him from lifting his torso. He rolled onto his stomach and Murphy supported his arms as he got to his knees.

Jason pulled away from the trunk to tilt his head back. Chloe watched as he searched the highest branches. "There!" she gasped, locating the monster. It was about ten meters away and nestled in a cluster of poplar trees. She turned to Murphy, but he had his eyes squeezed shut.

"Don't move," Jason instructed.

Murphy didn't think he could anyhow. His legs felt like noodles. "Did it see us?" he asked, prying one eye open.

Jason shook his head. "I don't think so."

"We should tell the police and let them handle this," Chloe responded.

Murphy nodded with urgency. "I can't b-b-believe the size of it!" he stuttered. The monster was gargantuan. Its beak was the same size as the tree trunk that it perched in. *Wait a minute,* he thought, *bats don't have beaks ... do they?*

Jason took a deep breath. "Stay here," he said, "I want to get closer. But if this doesn't go well, I might need your help." He bolted across the trail and into the trees before they could stop him.

Murphy stared in disbelief as Jason boldly snuck up on the monster.

Chloe spun her bracelet around and around. It was a nervous, unconscious habit. "Should we follow him?" she asked, worried.

"We have to wait here," Murphy replied. "He didn't want us to go with him." He cringed, seeing her disappointment. "Hey," he added, "do you honestly think I *want* Jason to sacrifice himself as an appetizer?" Murphy looked away, feeling ashamed. "He's the one that decided to go kamikaze."

"It's moving," Chloe said, gripping Murphy's arm. The monster had raised its wings to the subtle breeze then tucked them back in to rest by its side. It appeared to be sleeping as it rocked back and forth on the branch.

Chloe sucked in her breath. Jason was too close. He held up his thumb as he approached the monster, a move that could backfire if he made the slightest noise.

Then he did something really dumb. He reached for its wing.

No, don't wake it up! Murphy pleaded silently.

Suddenly Jason seemed a million kilometres away. Even if Murphy wanted to save him, there was no chance he'd get there in time.

Jason's arm wasn't long enough, so he jumped, and as he landed, he tore off a piece of the wing. *SNAP!*

Murphy heard the appendage break and let out a cry.

Chloe made a sign of the cross.

And Jason just laughed, very loudly.

Well, if the monster was dreaming, Murphy thought, *it won't be any longer.*

Jason reached down to pick up something reflective in the dirt. He whacked the shiny object against the tree with enough force that the sound echoed throughout the woods. He whooped and hollered with excitement, tossing the item up into the monster's perch and hitting it directly. Angry that its slumber was disturbed, the monster slid down from the branch and opened its mouth, ready to take a bite.

Jason covered his head just in time and ducked out of the way. He raised his newfound prize triumphantly in the air.

"Maybe the monster snacks only on females," Murphy commented, but Chloe didn't laugh.

She was traumatized beyond words. *He's gone mad!* she thought as Jason joined them, grinning from ear to ear. Murphy was happy that he was safe, but mostly relieved that the monster hadn't followed him.

"Is it dead?" Murphy asked.

Jason laughed. Chloe made circles with her index finger on the side of her head, indicating that Jason had gone off the deep end. Murphy had to agree.

"Come on," Jason responded, putting a hand on Chloe's back and coaxing her forward. "It's easier if I just show you."

"Wait a minute," Chloe replied, slowing down, "why didn't you answer the question?" She took the flat piece of metal from Jason's other hand. "And what is this?"

Jason could hardly contain his excitement as he said, "All the answers are over there. You've got to see it for yourselves to believe it."

Murphy dragged his feet, but somehow his traitorous legs brought him to the tree. He peered up into the branches and realized what he was staring at.

It was the bow of a canoe, not a monster's gaping mouth. Upside-down, it curved into a hook that created the appearance of a massive beak that could have been attached to a great beast. And the wings were not from a killer bat, but from the shredded black material once used for gliding on the wind.

They had found Mr. Moss's aircraft.

Murphy wondered why the aircraft hadn't been destroyed by fire. *If the plane didn't crash, then why do the trees have burn marks?*

"Where is Mr. Moss, if his …" Chloe began, but her thoughts drifted to the fact that the man's skeleton could be nearby.

"The police would have found him if he was here," Jason quickly answered, knowing the question would make Murphy queasy.

"If he survived, where did he go?" Chloe wondered. "Why didn't he return home?"

It didn't make sense. *If Mr. Moss was hurt,* she assumed, *he would have received medical care. And if he had been found, people would have talked, especially in this small town. So what really happened?* Could Murphy's wild speculation be right? Could he and Mrs. Sheldon have been spies, caught by their enemies for espionage? *That would make sense, what with the cover-ups.*

"There's only one possible conclusion," Murphy commented, jolting Chloe out of her thoughts. "Alien abduction."

She smiled. "I thought we ruled that one out already."

"You never know. Maybe the bulbs will grow into little alien pods that take over our minds, making us do their evil deeds."

Jason snorted. "As if."

"Okay, maybe I've been watching too many sci-fi movies," Murphy responded.

"Just a tad," Chloe remarked, laughing.

…

It was exactly five p.m. when they arrived at the park. They could hear Gabe's voice counting out as he made the final sound check. Chloe sang to her favourite song as the band practised, while Murphy and Jason strummed their air guitars to the rhythm of the familiar beats.

"I liked your smile and your laughter too,
But lately, honey, I'm sure feelin' blue.
There was a time I believed your lies.
I was a fool, but now I've opened my eyes ..."

The band recognized them and waved as they crossed the soccer field. Paul jammed a rock solo on his guitar.

"Impressive," Jason commented. Chloe let out a shrill whistle with her index finger and thumb.

"You like that, huh?" Paul said, pleased with the compliments. "I've been workin' on it for the past two weeks."

"Cool outfits!" Gabe remarked, jumping down from the stage to get a closer look.

"Those are some fierce togs!" Ty praised, nodding his approval. "Your efforts are humbling, my pubescent chums!"

"In other words, he likes what ..." Jason started to interpret, but the rest of his words trailed off as a young woman walked toward them. Jason's eyes bulged, taking in the dazzling vision of Gabe's girlfriend, Kelly.

She sauntered over in a Grecian-style emerald dress. Her skin was covered in glitter, a shade lighter than her outfit. When she greeted everyone, her bright blue eyes sparkled too. They were rimmed in red pencil. Even her lips and nails were in hues of green. Her hair was the only thing she hadn't touched with colour. It remained dark brown and glossy, like just poured coffee. She smoothed a loose stand and placed it on top of her head, where miniature rubber snakes weaved through the curls. Wide bands of gold wrapped around her upper arms, and she wore stilettos with lacing.

"Careful boys, she just might turn you to stone," Aaron joked while he twirled his drumsticks between his fingers.

"I wouldn't do such a thing," Kelly cooed, squeezing Jason's chin. His cheeks turned pink with her touch.

Chloe nudged Murphy. "You can roll your tongue back in now."

"You're just jealous," he commented.

"Over what?" she snapped. "Kelly's costume is ridiculous! Everyone knows Medusa wouldn't wear high heels. They weren't even invented yet!"

Murphy laughed. "I wasn't referring to the shoes."

Chloe lowered her eyes, fiddling with her bracelet so she wouldn't have to see his face. "Well, he's too old for me anyhow."

"Ha! I was right!"

"Shush!" Chloe scolded, looking around to see if anyone had overheard their conversation, but they were alone. Jason had joined Gabe, Aaron and Kelly up on the stage already. "And even if you are right—which you're not—I think Kelly is just using him for popularity. He could do much better than dating the Jolly Green Giant's daughter."

Murphy pawed at her, hissing like an angry cat. "You should have dressed as a panther. Your fighting claws are out."

She pushed him, growling, "Move it, Mr. Witty. Everyone's waiting for us." He smiled when he heard her chuckling.

Chloe lifted herself up on stage and adjusted a pin that had fallen off her costume. "So, what can I help with?"

"Actually, there isn't anything left to do. We got here early, so we've already set up," Gabe replied.

"They can help us with our next tune," Aaron offered.

Gabe held out the microphone to Chloe and instructed her to chant the last words in each line of the chorus, since she was the only one that could actually sing. Jason and Murphy hung out in the back where all the stage equipment was, taking turns flashing the coloured overhead lights out to the audience, then back onto the stage to feature Kelly's dance moves.

The Deezal Weeds always played an assortment of tunes to satisfy all genres. Gabe could sing anything from reggae to rock and roll, and their debut album had it all. "It must be that time," Gabe said, raising his voice over the chatter of spectators that gathered on the grounds with blankets and lawn chairs. "Six pm., right on the dot."

Murphy, Chloe and Jason quickly joined the crowd on the grass and moved up toward centre stage. A silence fell over the audience as the mayor came out and welcomed everyone to the show. He introduced the three other groups that were competing against Gabe's for the title of best local band.

Murphy noticed that Kelly was flirting with one of the lead singers. He had a hand on the small of her back, and they looked like they were sharing a private joke. Chloe elbowed him.

"Humph. Check that out," she grumbled, following his gaze. Murphy didn't look at her. He knew if he did she'd get the satisfaction of saying, "I told you so."

It was late in the evening when the last rhythmic pulse of energy came to a close. The sky turned a deep shade of blue and the stars popped out, shining down on them like tiny spotlights. Murphy was relieved that he had the extra layer of fur to keep him warm, as the air around them dropped in temperature.

Suddenly a young lady entered the platform while Paul was finishing his last chords on his guitar, interrupting the performance.

She was petite in stature and strikingly beautiful in a pale pink sleeveless dress that hugged her form. It reminded Chloe of the garments that actresses wore in the old-fashioned movies. Her slender shoulders were draped in a sheer material that had tiny rosette clusters sewn onto the seam. She removed a cluster of flowers secured to her hair and shook her head so that her soft golden tendrils cascaded loosely around her face. Chloe watched how slowly she moved. It seemed that walking was difficult for her, as she used two wooden sticks as support. All eyes were on her now, waiting curiously for a response.

The mayor promptly introduced himself, asking her if he could be of assistance. Chloe knew just by his confusion that this was not planned.

Someone from the audience hollered, "Maybe she wants to win Best Dressed."

The comment pleased the lady, and she laughed wickedly, pushing the mayor aside to search through the crowd. She was momentarily distracted when Gabe grabbed the microphone and asked for her name.

"Be silent, like the rest of these fools!" she snarled, then turned toward the shocked spectators. "I am Aldeirah. Westfield has labelled me as a monster, a witch and a ruthless child-killer. I have never forgotten what this town has done to me. All of your pompous beliefs in the medical and judicial systems will not save you from my wrath."

The mayor signaled her to finish, but she ignored his warning and spoke to him in an unfamiliar language. Her bizarre behaviour continued, leaving the mayor no choice but to have her escorted off stage by two constables. She resisted and raised the two sticks above her head in an X formation, creating a powerful wind that swept both officers off their feet and onto their backs.

"You *will* listen to what I have to say!" she ordered, pointing one of her sticks at the mayor. "I have waited a lifetime for this opportunity, and I will not have *you* or anyone take this moment away from me!"

Stunned, the mayor remained where he was. They all watched as her sticks glowed a blinding white and then blazed with orange fire. The thought of the flames engulfing her made Chloe cringe and look away, but the heat didn't seem to affect Aldeirah.

Pop! Pop! Pop! Loud sounds shattered the air, and everyone dove for cover, fearing that the sound was coming from a loaded gun. Then they realized it was the lights over the stage. They had exploded, as if a surge of power blew them out, still sizzling and spitting with electricity.

Aldeirah spoke. "Leave this land in three days' time, or you will wish that history could start over."

Aldeirah spun around to extinguish the flames and raised the smouldering pieces of wood. They disintegrated on contact, and showered her in grey powder just as she dropped her arms. Streams of light flickered through her fingers and she threw her arms out once more. The ash hovered as the static energy pulsed and wrapped around her body like a protective shield. She slid her foot off the platform, listening to the crowd's unanimous gasp as she leaned forward into the open air and stepped onto a flat surface created by the electricity she controlled. She whirled into a blur and then stopped in front of the kids, taking them by surprise. Somehow, she had magically transformed into a ghostly old woman wearing a dress that was stained yellow.

Her face drooped on one side and her brittle hair had turned pure white. But it was her eyes that elicited fear. They were cold, translucent and focused on Chloe. Instinctively, Chloe tucked the key inside her outfit, patting it to ensure it stayed where it was. Aldeirah laughed at her defensive actions. She seemed to already know what the object was. Aldeirah mused, "*Na hiva borte tris rakwid chanool.*"

She splayed her hands out and the crowd moved back, giving her ample room as she drew three lines in the air that erupted into a triangle of flames. As she stepped into the blaze, it wavered like heat bouncing off of a paved road. "Heed my proposition," she threatened, "or pay the ultimate price …" When the flames subsided and only the smoke remained, the magical entrance vanished, blown away by the wind, along with Aldeirah and her secrets.

After her abrupt departure, all the surrounding lights blinked off, immersing the park in total darkness.

Paul flicked his lighter on and several more people copied.

The mayor carefully approached the microphone. "Let's hear it for, uh …"

"Aldeirah!" Ty yelled into the mouthpiece, and all at once, the street lamps came back on.

The crowd reacted with whoops and cheers. Apparently they'd loved the skit and started to chant her name, assuming her antics were part of the show.

Murphy had to admit that it *was* pretty cool. But his instincts told him that Aldeirah hadn't been looking for stardom. She was serious.

"Hey!" Jason said, putting an arm around Murphy's shoulder. "It looks like they're giving out the prizes. Get ready to hear your name called."

And just as predicted, Murphy accepted his prize. But to his dismay, he wasn't chosen as the winner. A man on stilts dressed in a giant praying mantis costume took first place and the electronic store voucher Murphy wanted so desperately.

"Second place—that's great!" Jason congratulated Murphy with exaggerated enthusiasm.

Murphy sighed. "Yeah, I know," he replied. He stared at the two movie tickets that he'd received as his prize. "But now I'm stuck with my beat-up boom box."

Jason shook his head remorsefully. The last time he had borrowed the music player, he had fried the speakers. "I did offer to buy you a new one. Use your tickets and I'll pay for mine. It's the least that I can do."

"Okay, enough of the sappiness," Chloe remarked. "We have at least six blocks of free candy waiting for us and those sweets are calling my name!"

"I thought Jason was the only one with an endless appetite," Murphy replied, "but you're just as bad."

"Hey!" Jason added. "Those hunger pangs are real."

Chloe laughed. "A girl's got to satisfy her need for sugar or she'll go bonkers. But cheese puffs and ketchup chips are yummy too."

"I rest my case," Murphy said.

"So, have you decided what movie we're all going to see?" Jason asked.

"What makes you so sure that I'll be taking the two of you?" Murphy asked.

"Well, as far as I know, you haven't made any other friends lately," Jason responded.

Chloe gave him a disapproving look. "That was rude. Shame on you!"

"What? We are his best buds. Do *you* want to forfeit your ticket to some newcomer trying to squeeze their way into our tight circle?"

Murphy waved his hands as a reminder. "I'm right here, guys, and I *can* speak for myself." An impish grin spread across his face and he added teasingly, "I've got one extra ticket at home. Jay's buying his, so I thought I'd ask Duncan to come along and keep Chloe company."

"Tasteless joke," Chloe replied. Clearly, she had food on her mind. Murphy waited for her to hit him, but she crossed the street instead, heading toward the nearest house and yelling out, "Trick or Treat!"

"Well, we'll never be able to forget *this* Halloween," Jason said.

"You said it. The good, the bad and the ugly."

Jason laughed. "How much time do you spend watching movies?"

"Not enough."

"Now *that's* scary!"

Murphy rolled his eyes. "Let's catch up to Chloe before she takes all the good stuff."

"That's even *scarier*!"

CHAPTER SIX

The clock read three a.m. and Murphy still couldn't fall sleep. His sheets were wrapped around him so tightly from tossing and turning that he couldn't move any longer, so he gave up and just laid there on his back, staring at the ceiling in darkness. The images of the previous day's events wouldn't go away, and like a rerun, they kept playing over and over again. To make matters worse, his mind seemed to focus on the worried look Mrs. Sheldon gave them before she vanished.

Vanished ...

A picture of the school's parking lot materialized in Murphy's mind. The scene was the same, but now there was a glowing white light that surrounded his teacher. Was this a distorted memory of what really happened? It made sense as he recalled a cloudy mass suspended above her, and convinced himself that the key and the vaporizing hole that swallowed people up were linked.

He propped himself up on his elbows and shook his head to clear it.

Could Mrs. Sheldon be working for the government? A special agent trained to protect us from an unknown force?

As he contemplated this, he heard the distant rumbling of thunder. A storm was brewing, and it was headed his way. That was his first thought—until his bed started to shake. The vibration only lasted a minute, but that was enough incentive for him to untangle his legs and plant his feet firmly on the carpet. He sat gripping the mattress and waiting for the next tremor. It came with a sudden boom followed by a screeching noise that reverberated off the window and rattled the pane.

Then there was silence.

Murphy waited, listening …

He stretched his arms and yawned, squinting with blurry eyes at the time once again. Only eleven minutes had passed. He flopped back onto his pillows, forcing himself to think of happy thoughts. His peaceful dreamland dissolved, however, when the wailing of sirens disrupted that serenity, causing his heart to beat faster. *One, two, three* … He counted five. *Wow,* he thought, *it must be a really bad car accident.*

Four hours later, he opened his eyes to a dim and gloomy room. He stumbled to the bathroom and turned on the shower. Hot water pummeled his back and he leaned against the tiled wall for the heat to penetrate his stiff neck. Then the pressure suddenly dropped, and a trickling of frigid water ran down his spine.

Of course this would have to happen when I've got shampoo in my hair.

He immediately stepped out, shivering.

As he towel-dried the mess in his hair, he peered into the mirror to see the damage.

Super! It looks like I have squirrels nesting on my head.

He rubbed his irritated eyes and turned on the sink faucet to rinse the soap out, but the pipes clanged and shuddered, letting him know that he wouldn't be getting water from that source either.

His mom knocked on the bathroom door. "Honey, when you're finished in there, call Jason right away. It seems important. He's called twice already."

When Murphy called, Jason answered the phone on the first ring.

"What's up?" Murphy asked.

"Kelly's gone!" Jason blurted out.

"Not surprised that he dumped her," Murphy remarked. "It was bound to happen."

"Huh? What?"

"They broke up, right? I saw her with Curtis last night and I thought—"

"Whoa, back up," Jason interrupted, "she was with Shaw? The singer from Broken Lyres?"

"Yup."

"So she could still be with him?"

Murphy chuckled, "Hate to break it to you, but those things can happen. You really should have paid more attention in class to—"

"Yeah, yeah, I know. The birds and the bees, I get it."

There was a long pause. "Jay, are you still there?" Murphy asked.

"Uh-huh. I'm thinking."

"Well, think fast, 'cause I'm dripping wet. Mom pretty much said that you called because of an emergency."

"It is!" Jason barked. Murphy pulled the phone away from his ear. "Sorry," Jason said in a softer tone. "when I said that Kelly's *gone*, I meant *missing*. Mrs. Grant called our house this morning saying that she hasn't returned home. Gabe didn't see her after the gig because he was too busy helping to put the equipment away."

This was normal. Kelly got bored easily and never liked sticking around while her boyfriend worked.

"Maybe you should tell Gabe what I know," Murphy suggested, feeling like a jerk for handing over bad news. He heard Jason sigh heavily.

"Okay," Jason reluctantly answered.

Murphy rummaged through his dresser drawers to find some track pants, but couldn't find any except for the dirty pair he'd thrown on the closet floor. He smelled them. The slight odour hinted at the Sloppy Joe dinner they'd had on Friday, but otherwise they seemed fine for another day.

While he threw on a long-sleeved shirt, he caught the tail end of a heated debate on the local broadcast station. It was primarily about the strange visitor at Reedman's Park the previous day and the threat that she'd imposed on the town. He descended the stairs as if his feet were made of lead. Questions weighed heavily on his mind and his stomach churned with acid from the lack of answers. He sat down on the last step, resting his head on the baluster. *I'm too young to have an ulcer,* he thought miserably.

His mother had just closed the freezer door when she gasped, dropping the breakfast sausage she had in her hands. "Honey, what's wrong?"

"Too much candy, that's what's wrong," his father replied.

Murphy ignored the comment. "I don't know. Maybe I'm just hungry."

His mother helped him up and he gave her a weak smile, hoping she'd let the little incident pass. But that never seemed to happen.

"Here," she said, handing him an instant oatmeal package. "Eat this before you get an ulcer."

"Hey, Champ," his father called out from the den, "what happened last night? It sounds to me like there was quite a ruckus."

"Nothing serious, just a crazy lady that wants everyone in town to leave or she'll punish us for staying."

"It sounds like she needs a straightjacket," his father commented.

"Speaking of jackets," his mother said, "you'd better bring yours today, just in—"

Murphy's adrenalin kicked in and he raced to grab his windbreaker. "Got it!" he hollered before she could finish. He could barely contain his excitement. They were finally planting the bulbs today.

"Dad, is there any extra rope from the trailer tarps I could use?"

"Sure is, it's hanging up in the shed."

Murphy saw the panic surfacing in his mother's eyes. "What are you doing with the rope?"

He hesitated. *Should I tell her the truth? Or should I lie to protect her from having a nervous breakdown?* He decided to tell her some and leave out all the dangerous parts. "We want to make a swing. There's an oak tree on the northwest side of ..."

"Honestly, Murphy," his mother commented. "Why can't you be like the rest of your peers and enjoy playing video games inside? They're so much safer."

He shrugged. "Because they mess with your mind and cause blindness."

His mother took a step back, seemingly horrified by the news.

"Okay," Murphy relented, "maybe not, but—"

"What if the branch breaks? Or you fall off and hit your head?"

"Jules, please stop coddling him," Murphy's father said. "Let him go out and get some fresh air."

"Well," she responded, "just be sure that you're home for dinner."

"Okay."

Murphy knew that she was watching him. Her silence was screaming. She had leaned against the doorframe with her arms folded and her eyes were on the verge of tears.

He slid down and sat in the hallway next to her. "Why are you so upset?"

Her lip quivered, but she managed to unload all the dread she was feeling about his irresponsible behaviour and his poor eating habits. He was thoroughly bored with the redundancy, having heard it a million times every week. He closed his eyes, and suddenly there was a pause.

His mother stopped. "Are you listening?" she accused.

He nodded his head. A moment later his eyes flew open "Um." He winced. "Could I skip dinner tonight? I'll be home before my curfew. Please?" he begged.

She threw her hands in the air, defeated. "I give up! Go! Have fun!"

"You're the best." Murphy hugged his mother quickly and dashed up the stairs to grab his backpack and the bulbs on his nightstand.

As he entered the kitchen again, his father was just putting his coffee mug in the sink, attempting to rinse it, but finding out that there wasn't any water. He mumbled something incoherently about getting the tank fixed and buying more lottery tickets.

"Looks like your mother will be eating alone tonight. I'm hoping to sell those two empty lots on Allen Street. There are a few potential buyers, so my day will be pretty solid."

"Good luck!" Murphy replied.

His mother unhooked the backpack from his shoulder, sighing with irritation. She opened the pantry and laid the bag next to her feet, empty-ing half the shelf into it. "It's my cooking, isn't it?" She didn't pull back the cupboard door to see a response, nor was she waiting for one. Murphy was glad she didn't. He would be lying if he said her meals were the best he'd ever tasted.

"I've packed some food for you and your friends," his mother said, plunking his backpack on the table. "So no one is going to starve today."

"Thanks, Mom."

She sat down slowly, grudgingly, as if grabbing some snacks had been too much of a burden, and poured herself a cup of tea.

"Go on now," she insisted. "You can leave. There's no need to feel sorry for your poor ol' mom just because she'll be by herself tonight."

Yessiree, she's laying on the guilt trip pretty heavily.

"It'll just be me and that fudge brownie ice cream."

"Mom, there are plenty of dinner entrees in the freezer."

"Oh, I know, honey." She grinned. "But when you're having a pity party for yourself, dessert always comes first."

Just then, the phone rang. Murphy answered. It was Chloe's mom. He held out the receiver, saying, "It's for you."

"Franny! How are you?" his mother asked, her mood suddenly changing. "Of course you can!" She hung up the phone. "Francis isn't working today, so she's coming for a visit when she drops Chloe off."

"So now you'll have an accomplice joining you for a night of junk food crimes."

Murphy's mother laughed. She ruffled his hair and then pulled away. "Yuck!" she said with revulsion, looking down at her hands. She rubbed her fingers together. "What on earth do you have in your hair?"

"It's not my fault—"

She raised her hand. "Never mind. I don't want to know." She grabbed a kitchen towel, changing the subject. "I'm so thrilled! I haven't seen Franny in ages!"

"You just saw Ms. Baker on Thursday," Murphy reminded her.

"Well, at my age, everything seems to be eons ago," she responded. "Plus, I haven't seen the new puppy yet."

"Chloe's bringing Buckles?"

"That's the plan."

A rapid tap on the door informed them that Chloe and her mother had arrived. Murphy swung the door open and a mini typhoon swept through his legs, rushing over to greet his mother. She squatted down and picked Buckles up, laughing as he wiggled and licked her face.

Chloe laughed too, but not because of her puppy's antics. She circled Murphy, inspecting the top of his head. "This is a new look. Not sure if it suits you, but I guess if you're into the punk rock scene, then go for it."

"Are you wearing *that* today?" Murphy retorted. The colouring from her overalls had casted a sickly hue of jaundice onto her dark skin. The whole ensemble was questionable, and what he really wanted to say was that it looked like someone barfed on her, but he kept that comment to himself. He was all about self-preservation.

"Sure, why not? These clothes are old." She pushed her finger through a small opening in the sleeve of her faded green cotton shirt and bent her right leg up to reveal a threadbare knee. "See? They're already worn out."

"That's not what I meant. It's the hideous colour. I don't care if your stuff is full of holes, but yellow, brown and green? You're not exactly going to blend in."

"For your information, Mr. Grump, these colours are called mustard, sienna and juniper, and they *will* camouflage me. I wore them on purpose. My top even has a leaf pattern!"

"I'd say it looks more like fish bones wrapped in balloons," Murphy replied, then laughed when Chloe stuck her tongue out.

"You're weird. You know that, right?"

An abrupt cry of "Oh my God!" startled them, and they whipped their heads in the direction of the living room.

"Was anyone hurt?" Murphy's mother asked, ignoring their approach.

"Nine were sent to the hospital with burns. Thankfully, the accident happened at night, otherwise the casualties would have been greater," Chloe's mother responded.

"I heard the crash last night," Murphy broke in, stroking Buckles' velvety muzzle.

"I'm surprised that you heard the explosion," his mother said. "The water tower is so far from here."

Ms. Baker nodded. "They're calling for an evacuation in that area. The train derailment affected at least six stores, and some are still burning. The news reports are calling it arson. It's awful. I had to shut the television off."

"Who would do such a thing?"

So this wasn't a fatal car accident. Murphy looked at Chloe. Her eyes widened as she pieced the information together. A train wreck, an explosion, a damaged water tower that incidentally caused multiple injuries … It wasn't a coincidence. It had to be …

"*Aldeirah*," Chloe whispered.

"Shouldn't we evacuate, too?" Murphy's mother asked, her voice faltering. "What if the fire spreads?"

"Don't worry so much, Jules. We're a safe distance away. We'll be fine here."

Murphy's mother stood up and Buckles jumped down with a heavy thud. She went to the closet, pulling out one of Murphy's sweatshirts and the puppy followed. "That would explain why I couldn't reach a plumber this morning," she said, handing Ms. Baker the zippered hoodie. "Every listing in the phone book had a busy signal. I guess we weren't the only ones without water today."

Ms. Baker smiled gratefully, "This is very kind of you, Murphy. Now Chloe will have some protection from the elements." She tied the sweatshirt around her daughter's waist, and then winked at Murphy, saying, "We wouldn't want her to catch pneumonia. And Chloe, you should thank Julie as well. She packed quite a smorgasbord. There's celery with cheese spread, bologna sandwiches, butter tarts, juice boxes and even roasted pumpkin seeds!"

"Compliments of our neighbourhood corner market," Murphy whispered.

Chloe giggled and hugged Murphy's mother. "Thanks, Mrs. Robinson!" Then she leaned toward Murphy. "Don't worry, I'll make sure the sweatshirt's washed before I give it back to you."

"That's good," Murphy said, "because I don't want any of *your* smells rubbing off on me." Chloe raised her elbow to sniff under her arm and shrugged. He tried to keep a straight face as he picked up his bag and was surprised to feel how heavy it was.

"Mom! How much food did you pack? We're just going out for the day. We're not *camping* there!"

Chloe lifted the flap and peeked inside. "Whoa! I think all your Halloween stash is dumped in here."

He lugged the bag over his shoulder and grunted. "No doubt. She believes that chocolate is part of the food guide.

"Well," Chloe chuckled, "maybe cocoa beans are considered part of the *legume* family." She grinned triumphantly, knowing Murphy was clueless.

The doorbell rang and Buckles ran down the hallway to greet the visitor. "I'll get it!" Chloe shouted, "I already know who it is." She scooted Buckles aside with her foot and unlatched the door.

"You're psychic, now?"

"No, I just called Jason before I left and told him to meet us here."

Mrs. Tremblay's minivan was idling as Jason held the screen door open and waved to his mom. She rolled down her window and returned the gesture as she waited for traffic to pass by before backing out of the driveway. Gabe was in the passenger's seat with his head down and his hand shading his face. He didn't look up.

"She's not at Shaw's house," Jason stated before even saying "hello." Chloe gave him a blank stare and he filled her in.

"Gabe's really worried. No one's seen Kelly since that lady vanished. Curtis thought she went home."

Murphy squeezed by Chloe to stand on the porch, "You don't think…"

"Doubt it," Jason said. "That's too coincidental. But my Mom's driving Gabe to the police station now. Mrs. Grant is there, and she needs all the support she can get."

"Maybe you should've gone with them," Chloe offered. "To support your brother."

Jason shook his head. "I tried, but he insisted that there wasn't anything I could do."

Buckles took full advantage of Chloe's distraction and maneuvered around her leg, breaking free from her hold. He darted through the gap in the door and scampered after the vehicle, wagging his tail with exuberance. Jason held his collar firmly.

"Hold on there, mister! You can't go out onto the road." He picked Buckles up and held his paw to mimic a wave goodbye as his mother drove away. The puppy's ears perked up at the sound of the horn beeping. Buckles glanced at Jason, cocking his head sideways.

"That's one person who won't get a bath from you today," Jason commented as he lowered Buckles to the ground and secured his leash. "Hey, guess what I brought?" Jason pulled his hand away just in time before the puppy saturated it with drool. He withdrew two plastic bags from the front pocket of his sweatshirt. One revealed homemade oatmeal raisin cookies. The other was beef jerky. Chloe and Murphy looked at each other and burst out laughing.

"What's so funny?"

Murphy shook his head. "Inside joke."

"Aw, come on. You know it bugs me when you two don't let me in on those things."

Instead of explaining, Murphy showed him the stuffed backpack.

"That's some serious chow." Jason whistled and felt a tug at his pocket. He slid his hand inside and it came out wet. He looked down the hallway and spotted the puppy gnawing on something that looked like rawhide. "Speaking of food, did you feed Buckles before you left home?"

"Yeah, why?"

He lifted the beef jerky bag. "This is what's left."

"Oh, no!" Chloe whined. "Now he's going to have gas all night, thanks to you."

Jason chuckled. "Gimme a break! Dogs don't fart!"

"Ha! That's what you think!"

"Are you making this a bet?" Jason offered.

"Sure," Chloe replied, amused by the challenge. She stuck her hand out. "Do we have a deal?"

"Deal," Jason replied, gripping her hand firmly. "But if *I* win, you have to promise to wash all my stinky socks for a *whole* month."

"You're goin' down!"

Jason smirked

"No, Jay," Murphy said, "she means you really *are* going to—"

Murphy wasn't able to warn him in time. Jason's leg collapsed on impact when Buckles jumped on the back of his knee. He teetered on the other before finding his balance. The remainder of the bagged smoked meat dropped to the floor and was then in the puppy's mouth as he tore it apart.

"You're not a dog, you're *a pig*!" Jason chased Buckles around the kitchen and pulled the bag from his mouth. "I don't think anyone will want these."

Chloe backed Buckles into a corner and took the jerky out of his mouth. "No, Buckles! You're going to get sick!"

"Don't push him toward *me*," Jason commented. "I don't want him barfing on my shoes!"

"It'll be your own fault if he does."

"No, it won't."

"Yes, it *will*."

"No, it won't, Twinkie," Jason teased.

"Did you just call me '*Twinkie*'?"

"Um ..." Murphy said. "Sorry to break up this quarrel, but we need to get a move on. Plus, Chloe's argument is pretty solid, Jay. You haven't got a leg to stand on."

"Call it even, then?" Jason volunteered through hiccups.

Chloe glared at Murphy. "I haven't given my demands yet."

"You can give Jason a list while we walk," Murphy said to her.

"So what's up with the 'do?" Jason asked.

Murphy smacked his forehead and looked at him. "Really? You too?"

Jason looked at Chloe for an answer, but she just shrugged and shook her head as if to say "Don't go there."

By the time they reached the vicinity of Moss Ridge, the quiet Sunday atmosphere had become a lively drone of activity. It wasn't surprising to see a few people jogging along the north side of the escarpment. The path was widely used and was the most accessible. It joined the east side to form a small level plane, where a public washroom and a dairy bar offered a place to rest. On the southwest side of Mr. Moss's home stood a large crooked oak tree in the far corner of the backyard, diagonally across from the sitting area. Its roots were like thick fingers spreading over the rising slope and grasping the rocky edge as if it was afraid of tipping over. Beside the tree was a short, dirt path trailing along the wooded area where the ground dipped and a flight of unfinished stairs descended into a dangerous drop. The trees, Chloe suggested, would provide the cover they needed from any curious bystanders.

Murphy shrugged off his bag and put it on the ground, asking his friends to wait a moment while he stretched and rubbed his shoulders.

"Here, let me take that," Jason offered. Murphy didn't object.

...

"Hey! What was that for?" Stuart grumbled, stumbling forward on the pavement.

Duncan pushed him again. "Pick up the pace, slowpoke. I don't want to lose sight of them."

"You mean *her*," Stuart corrected and stopped to turn to his cousin. "Face it, dude. You've got a thing for Chloe."

Duncan walked up so close to Stuart that he body-checked him. "So? What are you gonna do about it?"

Stuart shoulder-bumped his cousin to move him out of his way. He wasn't easily intimidated by Duncan's threats. "Just sayin'." He shrugged. "It's not like no one knows."

Duncan cocked his head and frowned. "What exactly are you saying?"

"It's no secret."

Duncan sidestepped his cousin and strode away in a huff, putting a significant distance between them. Stuart had to jog to catch up. "Why so serious? She's available, right? You know … to anyone."

Again, Duncan picked up speed, "Keep your trap shut!" he snarled, "and don't even think about it." He balled his fists as a warning.

The rest of the way, Stuart moped. He could think of a lot more fun things to do than spying on a bunch of nerds. But he followed his cousin anyhow, past the iron gate and onto Mr. Moss's porch. Duncan leaned out from the rickety railings to peer around the corner and saw Chloe bending down to pick up her dog. He snapped his head back and motioned for Stuart to move towards the garage in the opposite direction. Then he looked again.

"Hold up!" Duncan put his hand out. "What the …" He crept down the stairs and crouched beside a pillar. Stuart joined him from the back, resting his hand on his cousin's shoulder to get a better view. They both cautiously stuck their heads out to peek.

"All right, this may be fun after all." Stuart snickered.

Duncan clobbered him. "Quiet!" he hissed under his breath.

"What do ya think they're doin'? It looks to me like they're jumpin' off the ridge."

"Don't know. But we'll soon find out."

"No way. I didn't sign up for any crazy stunts."

"What are you, a wuss?"

"No," Stuart replied, backing away.

"Get back here before they spot you, loser!" Duncan growled. "It's not like they flew down, idiot. They probably have a ladder."

"Do you know how many people ladders kill each year? Especially from this high up?"

Duncan smirked. "So you're afraid of heights. Big deal. Get over it."

"Not today," Stuart replied, "I'm outta here. See you at your funeral." He ran down the driveway, not bothering to turn around.

Duncan rolled his eyes. "Yeah," he said to himself, "he's chicken."

...

They chose the crooked oak tree because of its proximity to the stairs. Its bark was scarred with ancient triangular carvings pointing up to the sky and down to the earth. It was probably one of the oldest trees in the area, and it shared its home with spruces, maples, and pines. There was no grass on the path but plenty of leaves covering the ground. The overgrown juniper shrubs had choked off most of what had grown there, and only the scant remnants of the hearty peppermint and verbena plants seemed to have survived.

Murphy wrapped the rope around the tree trunk, securing it with a running bowline, and watched it uncoil as it fell toward the ground. He had learned at a young age how to tie nautical knots. It was a passion he shared with his dad. They were both boat enthusiasts. There was just enough length to reach past the meagre plateau, and since the staircase zigzagged across the rock wall directly under the oak, it would keep them in close contact with the rope. From the ridge, it was about a twenty-five-foot drop. They'd use the rest of the rope to lower themselves down off of the last stair and onto the ground.

The rock jutted out slightly where they eased themselves over and onto the first rickety tread. The primitive steps were carved out of soil and stone and had boards secured on top to prevent slips in wet weather. The wooden slats protested under their weight with squeaks and groans. Some had split in the middle and lifted the rusty nails from the outer edge, indicating that a handrail had once been there. Weeds grew in the cracks of the rotted wood and clung to the wall of the foundation like a green tapestry. Smaller trees like birches poked out of the ground, and bushy mounds in shades of green, burgundy, purple and gold scattered vicariously across the valley. Murphy chuckled to himself. Chloe's outfit was spot on.

Buckles whined and his small frame shook all over with fright. He obviously didn't like the itinerary. Chloe wrapped the leash around her wrist and picked him up, cradling him. He barked his approval, nuzzling his wet nose in the crook of her arm.

At last, Chloe reached the final stair.

"Let me go first," Jason offered, grabbing the rope before Chloe could.

"Hey, what ever happened to ladies first?" Chloe commented.

"Technically, you're not a lady," Jason teased. "Yet." He winked at her, but she crossed her arms. "Okay, here. But don't yell at me if it breaks on you. I was trying to be a gentleman and make sure it was safe to use."

"Yeah, right," she said, tucking Buckles inside her overalls.

Murphy burst out laughing. The puppy's tail hung out on one side and his head on the other. "Now I know why Dachshunds are called *hot dogs*."

"Anyone for ketchup?" Jason chortled.

"Or relish?" Murphy jested. "She's already covered in *mustard*."

Chloe groaned. "Okay, enough of the wiener jokes. I don't want to fall."

Jason looked at Murphy and mouthed the word *wiener*, which sparked another round of uncontrolled silliness. Buckles wagged his tail and huffed, slapping Chloe in the face.

"Ugh! Stop it, guys, or I'll end up with a shiner!"

Murphy pressed his lips together, but Jason had to turn his back. He leaned into his forearm to muffle his laughter, though it didn't help.

Buckles tried to worm his way out and that unbalanced Chloe. She screamed and grabbed the rope, careening down the slope too quickly. She twisted her body to protect Buckles and slammed full-force into the wall of stone.

Murphy cringed, staring in horror.

"Ow, ow, *ow*!" Chloe let go of the rope and jumped the rest of the way, landing on her hands and knees. She sat herself up and tried to bend her right leg. "Ouch!" She grimaced.

"Are you okay?" Jason hollered, knowing she wasn't just by the way she was rubbing her ankle.

Buckles whimpered and licked Chloe's face. She unfastened one of her shoulder straps to free him. He looked up and barked.

Jason threw the backpack over the ledge, "Come on, let's see how hurt she is." He swung out in a long, fluid arc and landed on his feet. Murphy wasn't so agile, and the rope burned his hands on the way down. He blew on them, rubbing his palms together.

Jason was already kneeling beside Chloe. "I *told* you I should have gone first," he said, gently scolding her.

Murphy scurried to Chloe's other side and bent over, watching as Jason looked at her ankle. It was purple and warm to the touch.

"Is it broken?" Chloe asked.

Jason shrugged. "I don't think so, but ice would help. My dad taught me that something cold will reduce swelling, and your foot is definitely going to puff up." He gingerly held her bent leg and eased it down so that it was lying flat on the ground.

Chloe winced. "Maybe it's just bruised." She tried to stand, but the action made her wobble and Jason had to hold her steady.

"You see?" he noted. "Chivalry isn't dead."

"I'll be fine." Chloe smiled bravely, but she couldn't hide her pain. "Too bad we don't have any ice, though."

"The juice!" Murphy blurted out, remembering the frozen packages. He ran to retrieve his bag. "This should do it." He handed Chloe two so that she could put one on either side of her ankle.

Jason made a face. "Blah. I hope that's *your* drink. I don't want mine anywhere near her foot."

"Humph! So much for thinking you're a nice guy." Chloe was ready to throw the box at him, but they both convinced her that it was best to keep it on her ankle.

It took about ten minutes before the freezing took effect. "Are you able to walk a bit better now?" Jason asked. He held out his hand and pulled her up.

"I guess we'll see," Chloe said, applying some pressure. And like a trooper, she kept up with their pace.

...

Now that Stuart was gone, Duncan relaxed a little. Most times, he could tolerate his cousin's whining, but today was not one of those days. He needed a solid plan. Chloe and the others were probably already on the ground, searching for that treasure.

He took a few more minutes to make sure that they were far enough away from the ridge before he sprinted toward the oak tree. Using the trunk's bulky size to his advantage, he hid behind it and dropped to his hands and knees. Slowly, he crawled to the edge and leaned over.

Just what I need, he thought. *That dog could go and screw up everything!* He fished in his pocket and felt the candies he'd put in there that morning. They would have to do. He hoped the dog wasn't picky.

He pushed up his sleeves and made a quick guess about the distance between the last gap in the stairs and the ground. He doubted that he could jump from that height, so he'd have to use the rope, which he figured was what people used instead of a ladder anyhow.

Sweat rolled off of him and he wiped his forehead on the back of his hand. He told himself that it wasn't that warm out. Maybe it was nerves. He didn't want to get caught. He wanted to surprise them. If he could coax the dog away from the digging site and keep it busy following a trail of treats, then Chloe would have no choice but to search for her pet. And of course her little gang would do the same, leaving the treasure unsupervised.

Duncan smiled. It was a pretty good scheme.

He let out a puff of air and ran a hand over his short hair. It came away wet. It wasn't raining. *Why am I so flippin' hot?* His back felt like it was blistering from a burn, and when he turned around he saw a fireball of leaves hovering at his waist. He jumped back as it dropped to the ground; bursting into tiny glowing embers that scorched the grass as they fell. His eyes narrowed suspiciously as a figure suddenly materialized through the smoke.

A young woman no more than twenty-one stood before him. She flexed her fingers, then clenched them into a fist and flicked them open again to reveal a sparking orange flame in the palm of her hand. She said nothing while she casually walked to the tree, and watched Duncan's reaction as she grabbed the rope and squeezed, releasing the hot energy that quickly spread to the whole length and disintegrated it into a pile of ashes. The tree remained intact.

"Now that I have an audience, you may applaud," she blatantly stated.

Duncan stared at her with his mouth open.

"Well, don't just stand there! Clap for me. I'm doing you a favour." Then she added, "And a good deed always requires the recipient to give back.

Now you owe *me*."

"What kind of favour?" Duncan responded. "I didn't ask you to destroy the rope. I was gonna use it!"

"Tut, tut," she said, waving a scolding finger at him. "We'll have none of that negative talk."

Duncan folded his arms in protest but kept a wary eye on her hands. "You must be the nut job that everybody's been talking about."

The young woman grimaced. "So, you did not attend the gathering in the park." It wasn't a question. "Then let me formally introduce myself—"

"I really don't care who you are!" Duncan interrupted. "I've got things to do, and you weren't invited."

She deliberately raised her arms slowly, matching his intense glare as she opened her hands. The oak tree swayed and bent over, placing two of its branches into her palms. When she tightened her fist around them, they snapped. Duncan flinched as the tree whipped back into place with an ear-splitting shriek. The woman pointed the gnarled sticks at him, and he froze.

"It just so happens that I have a way down," she responded, "but you need to come with me."

She lowered the sticks, leaning against them as she hobbled closer to the edge. Her hair, Duncan noticed, had lost its gilded colouring, and she appeared small and frail. It was as if he was watching her body shrivel in fast-forward.

"No," Duncan said defiantly, gaining some confidence. "I'm not going anywhere with you." He planted his feet firmly on the ground.

The woman smirked, then lifted the sticks and swirled them around, mumbling incoherent words. A flash of orange suddenly flared into a flaming triangle behind him. He looked at her, then at the opening.

"Oh, I think you will," Aldeirah responded, and then shoved him through the magical doorway.

Duncan didn't have time to yell for help.

...

Murphy slowed down to talk with Chloe. "Sorry about being grouchy this morning," he commented. "I didn't sleep well."

"Neither did I," Jason stated. "I was worried about my dad. It was a wild night for pyromaniacs."

"Was there a full moon Saturday evening?" Chloe asked. "I slept, but I had the strangest dream."

"Was it about Duncan?" Jason teased.

Chloe rolled her eyes. "No, it was about my dad. I don't really remember him, but his image was so clear that I recognized him instantly. I look just like him." She plucked at the teardrop stone on her bracelet and continued, "He was warning me to be careful. He said that soon I will discover how special I am."

She had stopped, and both boys flanked her side, fascinated with her story.

"See this brownish-red line on the stone?" She held her arm up and twisted her wrist so that they could see her bracelet. "It's called *diastrum*. Now how would I know that? I've never even heard such a word before, and yet I know what it is and what it can do. Well, supposedly."

Jason lifted the stone between his fingers. "So are you going to tell us or keep us guessing?"

"It's dried blood, but it was added to a space rock when it was fresh. The combination has the power to reverse death."

Murphy's eyes bulged. "Like zombies?"

Chloe shrugged. "I don't know. That's when the explosion happened, and I woke up."

Murphy chortled. "And you think *I'm* weird?"

...

Chloe shuffled along, aware of the uneven terrain with every step. She took advantage of the spongy, decaying grass hugging the ridge and walked on it to cushion her sore foot. But the ground was damp and slippery in some areas, so she moved to a flatter surface with rock. It wasn't much better. Loose pebbles and scraggly patches of greenery made the trek hazardous. Murphy could see that she was having difficulty and let her slip an arm through his for support. He shielded his eyes as the sunlight streamed through the canopy of leaves hovering above them, and he peered up at the wall, trying to absorb the whole view from his angle.

Chloe cleared her throat, breaking the silence. "Could we stop for a moment, please? I need to rest. My ankle is throbbing." She rolled up her pant leg. Her whole bottom leg had doubled in size.

Jason threw down the backpack and handed Murphy the leash, pulling Buckles away from a fallen branch. "Hop on," he offered with his arms outstretched behind him.

"Piggyback?"

"Don't get used to this, your highness," Jason remarked.

Chloe laughed. "Remind me later to give you a big hug."

He shrugged. "You'd do it for me."

"As if!" Murphy replied. "Look at her puny little arms."

"Hey!" Chloe objected. "I'm stronger than you are and you know it!" She held onto Jason's shoulders as he picked her up. "Remember in grade two? I beat you every time in arm wrestling."

Murphy laughed, recalling the memories. "Okay, but that was a long time ago. I'm bigger and taller than you are now."

Jason found some rock smooth enough to set Chloe down and she plopped onto the tallest one with a grunt. She placed her backhand to her forehead and leaned back. "Oh, humble and gracious young man, you have saved me. How can I ever repay your kindness, sir?" she drawled in a southern accent.

Jason shook his head and smiled.

"Seriously," Chloe added, sitting up. "Thank you. I owe you one."

"Be careful what you volunteer. *I* have a witness," Jason responded, "I might take you up on your word someday."

Chloe grinned. "Bring it on."

Murphy squatted down, brushing away dried leaves. "This looks like a good place for planting." The dirt was dry. "Did you bring the trowel?" Murphy asked Jason.

Jason shook his head. "I thought you were going to."

"No, I had enough stuff to carry," Murphy replied. "Did you bring anything else?"

"Sure," Jason commented. "My charming abilities."

Chloe rolled her eyes.

"Why don't we eat first?" Jason suggested. "And then garden."

"Yeah, I always feel better once my stomach's full," Chloe remarked. "I'm starving!"

"Sounds good. Let's fuel up," Jason agreed.

"What's with you guys?" Murphy said. "Why does everything seem to revolve around food? There must be some kind of parasite growing in your bellies that feeds off of all the stuff you eat!"

Chloe had taken a bite already. "Ew! Gross!" she commented. "Now you've made me lose my appetite!" She dropped the tart onto her lap, shivering with disgust. "Thanks a lot!"

Murphy knew his harsh words were just a reflection of his impatience; he felt bad and immediately apologized. He just wanted to get the planting done.

Jason shoved a handful of potato chips into his mouth. "We're cool," he said, licking his fingers. "But you need to chill, bro. We *will* finish the job."

Buckles let out a yip, showing his support.

Murphy nodded, juggling the two bulbs in his hand. "I guess it's the curiosity that's driving me crazy."

"You've been *driving* on that path for a while now," Chloe teased, "but we like you that way."

Jason didn't comment. "What if the beast isn't an animal?" he pondered out loud.

"You mean like an evil *person* who can step through another dimension?" Murphy replied.

Jason nodded. "Yeah."

"It's possible," Chloe answered. "Aldeirah's on my list."

"Speaking of beasts," Murphy pointed out, "it looks like Buckles took the last cookie."

Jason raised his hand. "Guilty!" he admitted. "But it was for a good cause. Now he knows how to shake hands."

"Paws," Chloe corrected, and pulled the puppy away from him. "I didn't even get a chance to try one."

She let Buckles off his leash, and he immediately bounded toward the tallest weeds to relieve his overactive bladder. He returned with his muzzle covered in dirt.

"What have you been doing over there? Are you up to no good?" Chloe scratched behind his floppy ears and leaned over to brush the mess from his nose. Buckles jumped up in response and gave her a sloppy, wet kiss on her chin. She was about to wipe the slobber off with the sleeve of Murphy's sweatshirt, but thought better of it and rubbed her face dry with the back of her hand instead. Buckles barked, turning around in a circle before rushing toward Jason.

"Oh, no you don't!" Jason said, promptly covering his face. But Buckles went straight to his shoe instead and tugged at his laces. He barked again, turned and ran off in the direction he had just explored.

"I think he wants you to chase him," Murphy suggested.

Buckles turned to them and yipped, wagging his tail frantically. "He definitely wants us to follow him," Chloe replied.

They stood all at once, letting Buckles lead. He brought them to a hole he had dug up.

"There's nothing in there, you silly puppy," Chloe stated, pulling at his collar. But he resisted.

Buckles nudged Murphy's hand with his nose. He was sniffing his pocket, where Murphy carried the bulbs. Buckles sat by him and raised one ear, cocking his head sideways and panting.

"Do you want me to put the bulbs in there?" Murphy pointed to the hole and waited for a reply. *I must be crazy. I'm expecting the dog to answer me.*

Buckles padded over to the hole and huffed. Murphy shrugged. "Any objections?"

He knelt down and carefully placed the bulbs onto the bottom with their pointed sides up. Chloe covered them in dirt. Jason stomped on the pile, firmly packing it down with his weight. Buckles inspected their work, wagging his tail with approval.

They waited and waited. A quiet restlessness fell upon them as they watched and hoped for something miraculous to appear.

After ten dull minutes, Jason announced, "I guess the bulbs are duds."

Murphy wasn't surprised. His mom told him that bulbs need to be planted before the first frost. It was November and they'd already had a snow fall.

They walked away, disappointed.

Buckles stopped to sniff the air and then darted back toward the mound.

Jason and Murphy chased after him, and as they got closer to the bulbs, they heard a sound like water bubbling up to the surface.

To their astonishment, it *was* water spouting up and over the little dirt hill. Buckles lapped at the foaming liquid and sneezed. Chloe squatted down on her good leg to get a better look. She waved her hand for the boys to come closer. "Look," she whispered. "Something's moving. It's growing …"

A shiny, lime green stem pushed its way through the mud. It was sprouting right before their eyes.

"Amazing," Chloe stated.

Murphy backed up as a precaution. He didn't want to be near the flower if it exploded. *What if it's poisonous or releases a secretion of acid?* He recalled Aldeirah's face, half-melted like candle wax, and shuttered. He liked his face the way it was.

"Maybe it'll grow into a magical beanstalk where the geese lay golden eggs," Jason remarked.

"Yeah," Chloe added, "and the plates of food are piled so high that we'd have to climb the mountain of mashed potatoes just to reach the spare ribs."

"Imagine how *big* the peas would be," Jason replied.

"Sure," Murphy commented. "And the giant would use us as toothpicks to remove that food from his teeth."

Chloe gagged at the thought. "You're sick!"

"Aw, give the demented guy a break."

Chloe snorted. "You're almost as bad, Jay, believing Murphy's hypothesis that a Martian invasion would tear humanity apart."

"Hey," Murphy said. "Those alien sightings happen to be true."

"Uh-huh," Chloe responded, "just like Bigfoot was seen shopping at a Mini-Mart for party favours in the city, right?"

"It could happen," Murphy stated. "Do you think we're on the guest list?"

"Murphy!" Chloe groaned. "Oh my—"

The stem had grown twice as high in a matter of seconds, and tall, thin blades suddenly emerged like knives, piercing through the ground with deadly precision. Murphy noticed that even Jason had scrambled away from the possible danger. But Chloe had not, because she couldn't move. Buckles stood by her side, growling. She pulled her legs in closer, hugging them tight to her chest as the sharp edges slithered toward her shoes.

Jason reached under her arms and was about to drag her away when she said, "Wait!" She leaned forward and poked at the foreign object with a hesitant finger while Jason stood very still, ready to intervene.

She let out a sigh of relief. "It's just leaves," she informed them.

The bud of the flower followed, expanding to the size of a man's fist, but continued to grow in length, pushing Murphy's imagination into hyperdrive. A soft blue orb blinked in and out to the same pulse that the bloom emitted as it shook the excess water off. Then the light inside grew brighter, dispersing into thousands of twinkling dots and sliding down the flower shaft into the ground.

Buckles wagged his tail, wanting to play. He lowered his head, keeping his hind legs ready to spring, and jumped just as the blossom's tightly-knitted petals opened up. He was licking so frantically that the petals broke off at the base and fell to the ground.

"Oh, no! Buckles!" Chloe cupped her hands over her mouth. "I don't know what's gotten into him," she said, baffled by his behaviour. She pulled him away and picked him up. He wiggled in protest.

"Uh, maybe this is the reason," Jason responded. "What is *that*?"

The soil was vibrating as something clawed its way up to the surface.

They watched in awe as a pair of owl-like eyes the colour of lavender studied each one of them. The thing slowly emerged, pulling at the roots covering its head. Murphy compared its size to his Batman action figure he'd had when he was seven. It wasn't much bigger.

Jason shook his head in disbelief and the little thing mimicked his movements. He smiled and it smiled back. Its face was smooth, with delicate features.

"Maybe it's a friendly visitor from the Milky Way," Chloe jested, elbowing Murphy. But he was speechless. For all he knew, the creature could grow rapidly into a humungous carnivore.

It kind of looked like a human being, if people could shrink that small. It had silvery tufts of hair and short, fuzzy antennae curling around its ears. It stood on two legs, with bare feet, but had four identical arms with twice as many fingers and thumbs. Its skin was greyish-blue and rough, resembling tree bark. Its lower body was clothed in the same type of material the map had been made of, wrapped around its legs to create baggy-looking pants. Its chest was covered in layers of amethyst petals resembling an armoured breast plate, while its shoulders were decorated in a web of tiny gold links.

Chloe leaned in curiously, peering over the creature. There was another sound rising from the ground.

"Holy cow!" Jason remarked. "The other one just popped up!"

The second creature looked exactly like the first, except this one had periwinkle eyes and its hair was longer. A padding of the linen cloth was draped over its one shoulder and tied at the waist with gold chain as it ran down the opposite side to its knees. Violet flowers wrapped around its upper torso, poking out and curling as it flowed over its lower body like a short flared skirt. It was obvious that this one was female.

The creatures stepped forward in unison, holding each other's hands. One bowed and one curtsied as they greeted the kids in a dialect they didn't understand.

"*Tronef ki de yus!*" they choroused.

Murphy responded, "Sorry, but we only speak human language."

"Oh, that'll help them," Chloe said sarcastically. "There must be at least a hundred languages in the world."

"Hopefully there's one that includes fairies," Murphy added as he watched a thin, lacy membrane of iridescent colours sprout from the creatures' shoulder blades. They were long and narrow, like the wings of a dragonfly, extending past the creatures' height and shimmering in the sunlight as they fanned them back and forth. They giggled, somehow understanding Murphy's reply.

"Even fables are made up of some truth," Chloe whispered, quoting their teacher.

CHAPTER SEVEN

"*Tronef ki de yus*," the one with the lavender eyes said, pronouncing each word slowly.

Chloe repeated the words carefully and coaxed the creature to come closer as she sat down and crossed her legs. She cupped her hands together and laid then down in front of the creature. "It's okay, little one," Chloe reassured the creature. "I mean you no harm."

Without hesitation, it jumped into Chloe's open palms, surprising her. "Pleased to meet you," it said, shaking her thumb in a formal greeting.

"Whoa!" Jason gasped. "You can speak English?"

Buckles laid his head on Chloe's thigh, whining. His tail thumped on the ground as he waited to join the friendly salutations.

Murphy's mouth felt dry suddenly and he coughed, diverting everyone's attention to him. He cleared his throat, waving his hand to indicate he had no comment.

"We are Cromalites from the land of Quinsatheria," the long-haired creature stated. Her voice was soft and clear. "Our species are similar to what humans call sprites. We can speak in many languages, but prefer to use our own. It is called Quin, and we will teach you the basics while we journey to our home."

The female introduced herself as Que and her twin brother as Tuk. "We are honoured to be chosen as your guardians," she said. "It is our duty to keep you safe and to teach you skills that you may need during our travels."

Murphy cringed. "Why do we need protection?"

"Does this have to do with Mrs. Sheldon?" Chloe asked. "Do you know her?"

"Are we in danger right now?" Jason demanded. "Do we need weapons?"

The twins held their hands up to stop the barrage of questions. "Perhaps it will help if we start from the beginning," Tuk answered.

Chloe watched as he walked over to Buckles and rubbed his ear. The puppy started panting. "Can you please take the leash?" she asked Jason. "I don't want Buckles to think that Tuk is a chew toy."

"There's no need for your concern," Tuk chortled. "He will not harm us." He stuck his head into Buckles' open mouth, reinforcing his statement, and Chloe drew in a breath.

"We can communicate with animals telepathically," Que added.

Tuk placed his foot onto Buckles's collar and used it as a platform to hoist himself up onto the puppy's back. Buckles stood still as Tuk scooted over, allowing space for his sister to sit. Que jumped onto Buckles' tail, moving gracefully along the length as if she was a tightrope-walker.

"We should leave now," Tuk suggested. "The journey to Quinsatheria will take many hours."

"Are we travelling most of the day to get there?" Murphy asked.

"Yes," Tuk answered.

"We can't do that," Murphy blurted out. "We have curfews!"

"What time are you expected home?" Que inquired.

"8:30," Murphy replied. "We have school tomorrow."

"Then we must do what we can within those time limits."

"What do you mean by that?" Jason asked.

"Aldeirah's threats are already transpiring, and numerous attempts to sabotage her plans have failed. We need your help before she causes more destruction and trauma."

"As we speak," Tuk added, "she is having a dam built that will obstruct your town's water supply. If it runs dry …"

All of them understood. The consequences would be devastating. It would be impossible to extinguish fires, and as a result, houses and farmland would be destroyed, leaving people homeless, jobless, thirsty and dirty.

Chloe shivered at the thought, recalling this morning's disaster and first warning.

"If we don't intervene," Tuk warned, "the sanitation system will eventually fail, forcing people to abandon the area due to uninhabitable living conditions."

"She is a cruel, wicked woman," Que stated.

"But why is she doing this now?" Chloe asked. "What made her choose this year?"

"She needed time to create an empire. Aldeirah's hardships started in the late eighteen hundreds when she was wrongly accused of poisoning the children that were in her care. She lost custody of her daughter as a result. She was forced to stay in a mental institution where she was given barbaric treatments to cure her unstable behaviour. When she was released, Aldeirah wanted revenge, but her plans were delayed for almost a decade while her daughter lived in Westfield. It took six more years after Charlotte's death for Aldeirah to slowly gather a legion of servants. But now that she's prepared, she is ready to strike."

"But why demand an evacuation? Even if she's successful, she must know that we'd return to our properties at some point," Jason remarked.

"Yeah," Murphy said. "There's got to be clean-up crews that specialize in disasters."

"Most likely, but it would take months to rebuild new homes and businesses. The soil would have to be removed and replaced, which would cost money, and some insurance policies may not cover this kind of extensive damage. Westfield is mostly occupied by farmers that rely on seasonal crops, so the majority of people would have to seek employment elsewhere," Tuk replied.

"Aldeirah anticipates that the people will become desperate for money and accept her generous offer to buy their lands so they can provide for their families."

"Why does she need so much land? If she wanted to rule over the town, why couldn't she have run for mayor?" Jason asked.

"And if she has that kind of money," Chloe added, "why wouldn't she just buy a property that's for sale, build a mansion and make friends with the neighbours like normal people do. Why does she have to destroy it?"

"We do not know why Aldeirah wants to own such a large area. But we are certain that she wants Westfield to experience the same fear and despair she felt by generating the same type of atmosphere. If people lost everything that was important to them, there would be a greater sense of anxiety and hopelessness."

"But she can't blame innocent people. It's not our fault!" Murphy replied.

"She obviously doesn't see it that way," Chloe commented.

"Sound like you're defending her."

Chloe shook her head. "No, I just feel bad. It must have been terrible what she went through."

"Probably was, but that's still no excuse," Jason replied.

"I know," Chloe responded.

"Just remember," Jason added as he helped her up, "you're on our side, okay?"

Que studied the landscape and narrowed her eyes. "We should move to a more discreet area," she advised, spotting something suspicious, "before we attract unwanted attention."

Chloe was relieved that the ground began to flatten as they reached a thicket of spruce trees just beyond the far side of the wall. "So what kind of skills do we need to learn?"

"Combat," Tuk responded.

"As in fighting?" Murphy squeaked.

"In seven hours?" Jason commented. "How? Even soldiers need months of training!"

"A basic lesson on self-defence is all you'll need," Tuk said.

"What about Aldeirah?" Jason asked.

"And our parents?" Murphy worried. "My mom freaks if I'm ten minutes late. She'd call in the national guards if I didn't show up after that!"

"We will deal with Aldeirah ourselves," Tuk explained. "Your part will be to lead the prisoners out to safety once they're released. But if we are detained or occupied somehow, a few swift moves can be the difference between capture or saving yourself."

"Our kingdom holds a unique advantage to your time dilemma," Que added. "Each full day in our land is only one hour of your time."

"We actually have a week?" Chloe asked.

The twins nodded.

"What if we run into complications and we have to stay longer?" Murphy asked.

"If that should happen, the Ringos will create a hypnotic state of conscious sleep. Your families will continue with their routines in a normal and safe manner. Once you return home, the trance will break, and they will forget any previous distress," Que answered.

"Can the Ringos be trusted?" Murphy replied.

"Absolutely. They are our closest allies."

"Despite your fears," Tuk remarked, "we are confident that our mission will be successful without the aid of our friends."

"Will our bodies adjust to the different time periods?" Chloe asked.

"We are not sure why, but you will not be affected by the change," Que answered. "Perhaps it's because you are already young. It seems that the older an adult is, the more the process of aging slows down."

"So the longer they spend in Quinsatheria, the younger they become," Chloe finished.

"Like Mrs. Sheldon," Murphy stated.

"Yes," Tuk responded. "By repeating the words *eko lit ma,* she can transform into a younger version of herself anywhere in our kingdom."

"Her true age, however," Tuk continued, "remains the same. But the physiology of her blood type allows her to have more strength and agility than the average person, which is necessary to fulfill her duties."

"There is one quote, that you may find helpful," Que explained, "as it will summon a gate on command. It can only be accessed within your town and Quinsatheria, so be aware that you cannot use it elsewhere."

"You must first choose a location in Westfield by picturing it," Tuk added, "then speak these words: *Ba-neewa oc a li del see fenue far sherna eno holdyn iplis vo tris yuntay's ume.* It means 'bring us a gate so that we may enter one safe place in the county's centre.'"

"We recommend memorizing it."

"That's how Mrs. Sheldon left the parking lot so quickly," Chloe commented.

"And Aldeirah at the concert," Jason added.

Tuk nodded. "That's correct."

"Is there a shortcut to your poem?" Murphy asked. "Because there's no way we'll be able to remember what you just said."

"Hey! Speak for yourself," Chloe remarked.

"Yeah, Robinson," Jason replied.

Murphy raised his eyebrows at his best friend. "Really?"

Jason laughed. "Okay, I'm sure *one* of us can repeat it back."

They looked at Chloe.

"Ban eva otis meer …"

Jason put his hand up to stop her. "Good enough for me," he said, then turned to Murphy. "And you?"

"Yup."

"I suppose," Que laughed, "*osnow tris li*" would be easier. It is the simplified version."

"Aldeirah can speak Quin fluently," Tuk said, "so she's able to communicate with our foes, the Tri-Murids. They share our DNA and were once part of the Cromalite family. But some of their chromosomes mutated, resulting in triplet births rather than twin. They can control fire and earth in any form, just as we can with water and air. We lived in harmony for centuries, but our trust broke when Larsi, one of the older siblings, joined Aldeirah, because she wanted fewer rules and more freedom."

Que added, "Not too long after she separated, her brothers, Bot and Inek, followed. Then the whole population of Tri-Murids turned their backs on our kingdom."

Murphy leaned over and whispered to Chloe, "Do you think there'll be a pop quiz on all this stuff?"

"Shh!" Chloe scolded. "I'm trying to focus so that *one* of us will remember."

"Quinsatheria has been under attack several times this month. It is secure for the moment, but your teacher can no longer help us on her own. Aldeirah's army continues to grow. So your teacher relinquished the key in the event that if she were captured, our enemies would not find it on her."

"Therefore it is imperative," Que stressed to Chloe, "that the key remains with you."

"But why me?" Chloe asked. "How could I possibly fight and still protect the key?"

"Each warden comes from a skipped generation," Que replied. "It has been this way since the First Heirs forged the key to protect their keeper and its location. You are part of that generation, Chloe. You've been chosen because you are worthy."

"Aldeirah wants the key for herself, doesn't she?" Chloe presumed. "That's why Mrs. Sheldon had to hide. Where is she now? Is she all right?"

Tuk shook his head. "There hasn't been any word from her in two days. We believe she's been taken hostage."

Chloe cupped her hand over her mouth in shock. "Oh, no!"

"So basically, Aldeirah wants us to trade the key for Mrs. Sheldon," Jason stated.

The twins nodded.

"Aldeirah's aware that you are stronger as a team," Que informed them. "Be prepared. She might try to break up your friendship in order to retrieve *tris kusoa*."

"*Tris kusoa* means 'the key,'" Tuk clarified. "The child destined for the responsibilities as the keeper is named Key Warden of the Horn. In Quin it is *kusoa watis nef tris har-ryn*."

"For thousands of years, and twice per century, two Ezbragrytes are born. They have a gift of pure magic that comes from their horns," Que explained.

"So unicorns *are* real," Chloe responded.

"Yes, but they're depicted differently in books and named as such because humans don't know the true name of their kind," Que replied.

"Once mankind discovered that the Ezbragrytes could provide a wish, they slaughtered them for their horns."

"Whoa! Any request?" Jason asked.

Que nodded sadly. "All but bringing the departed back to the living. Greed is the reason why they're nearly extinct. Those that survived altered their appearances by shedding their horns." She continued, "There are only nineteen remaining in Quinsatheria. Regrettably, Aldeirah has taken a male and female from their sanctuary. She's hoping they will have *gurts* while they're in captivity."

Chloe looked down at the chain resting against her T-shirt and frowned. "Does the horn still work even if it's removed?"

"Yes," Tuk replied.

"What will happen if Aldeirah makes a wish?" Jason asked.

"She was granted one many years ago," Tuk admitted, "but it did not turn out well."

"Aldeirah yearned for a relationship with her daughter," Que said. "The problem was that Charlotte's adoptive parents believed Aldeirah was criminally insane, so they forbade her to have any contact. When Charlotte married, Aldeirah used her wish to mimic the appearance of the adoptive mother so that she could visit without refusal. But when Charlotte opened the door, Aldeirah didn't notice the shock on her daughter's face, she only saw a rounded belly carrying her grandchild. She tried to embrace her daughter, but Charlotte nervously backed away. The real adoptive mother suddenly stood and rushed to confront her clone, realizing who the imposter was. The fight was vicious. Both Charlotte and her adoptive mother needed treatment for electrical burns at the hospital."

"As powerful as she is, Aldeirah becomes weak when she draws voltage from her body. It's easier to battle her while her energy is drained."

Jason rubbed his forehead, contemplating whether he should mention his ordeal with the boy. "Did Aldeirah create the strange weather we had on Thursday?"

Tuk nodded. "Aldeirah discovered that the renowned child destined to obtain the key was inside the school. We lost a brave guard that day trying to keep the Tri-Murids away."

Murphy shivered, recalling the loud thud against the classroom window.

"Why haven't your kind wished for peace?" Jason asked.

Tuk sighed. "The creatures of Quinsatheria are exempt, though we have tried. But it seems after Aldeirah's incident and reckless behaviour, only children are permitted to ask. It's possible that if Aldeirah loses patience she might sacrifice one of the *gurts*, hoping to scare them into submission."

"Was Aldeirah a good person once?" Chloe asked, her voice was thick with emotion, thinking of the animals' fate.

Que nodded sadly. "She was a loving and caring provider. But those emotions are long gone now."

Chloe spun her bracelet around, and the stone flickered with light. She turned it again, watching for another reaction, but nothing happened. "Why is the key so important?"

"It has two purposes," Tuk stated. "One: it unlocks the royal thrones where the horns are kept safely hidden, and two: a warden can summon an Ezbragryte at any time." Tuk continued, "You must pull the key apart and blow into the bottom piece with the teeth pointed up. Its hollow shaft is a whistle to summon the Ezbragrytes. The pitch will be too high for your ears to hear but not for them. The top portion is used to see the animals clearly while they are hiding. Just hold the star up to one of your eyes and look through the circle. You must perform both actions simultaneously in order for the *kusoa* to work properly."

Chloe raised the key to her eyes, examining a series of words etched on the side. "What does *Tris Fim-lar Alda* mean?"

"The First Heir," Tuk replied.

The phrase sounded familiar. "Wasn't that a person who drank magical water to extend their life?" Chloe responded, remembering an article she'd read.

Que chortled. "That legend has gaps in it. We will explain the true story during your orientation,"

"Besides us, are there other humans helping you? People who aren't wardens?" Jason asked.

"There was one," Que answered, "but Eleanor Moss is a prisoner. She was taken because she can transmit her thoughts into an animal's mind by imagery, just as we can speak telepathically through dialogue. Her gift is an essential part of Aldeirah's plan. So far, Ellie has refused to cooperate, but Aldeirah has tactics that are slowly wearing her down."

"Whoa," Jason said. "She's alive and has powers too?" *This is messed up,* he thought. *What was in those butter tarts?*

Chloe rested her hand against a rotting tree stump, turning her injured foot in circles. "We can't let people and animals suffer, but how can we stop Aldeirah?"

"By using Bruce Lee's kung fu moves," Jason replied.

"I think the old lady with the sticks would whoop our butts," Murphy commented.

Jason laughed. "No way. Check this out." He spun his leg sideways, striking a branch at chest level and splitting it with the heel of his shoe. "Gabe taught me that," he remarked, then pulled the loose twig free. Murphy laughed as Jason tried to swat Chloe's rear. She squealed as she hopped around the stump, protecting her behind with both hands. But then she suddenly hunched over, blowing out a shaky breath. "Is it your ankle?" Jason asked, stopping immediately.

Chloe nodded, wincing as she took a painful step forward. "It's really sore. I need to sit." She started to crouch with her hands splayed to catch her fall.

"Wait," Jason said, but she had already plunked herself down.

Tuk hovered over Chloe's leg, analyzing her condition. "We can help heal your injury, if you'd like."

"Okay," Chloe replied, grunting as she tugged her pant leg up.

A soft blue pulse radiated from the Cromalites' centre cores and passed down through their arms into their hands as they laid them over Chloe's swollen ankle. Her foot twitched as an icy sensation trickled into her muscles. Then the twins raised theirs arms, forming a large bubble with the water that flowed from their hands. It floated for a moment before dropping, though it didn't burst open like most bubbles do when they touch a surface. It flattened out and wrapped around Chloe's ankle in a steady stream of glowing light, then slowly faded as her skin absorbed the medicinal energy.

"Wow, thank you," Chloe said, feeling relieved that the pain was gone. "How did you do that?"

"Our sacred waters have healing properties. They contain minerals that are not from this planet," Tuk explained. "We are born with a small amount in our bodies, but it's not enough to sustain you for the full journey. Once we reach Quinsatheria, your recovery will be complete."

Chloe perked up, imagining a world without affliction. "Could the sacred waters cure diseases too?"

"Possibly," Tuk replied, "but human contact outside of our kingdom is so limited that it's not likely we could remedy all illnesses around the world."

"So if you can do all these things," Murphy remarked, "why do you need us? It's not like we can perform miracles."

Que spoke up. "There is simply not enough of us, and your bloodlines connect you to the initial plight that caused this dire situation. We need your support as much as you need our security, because it's a member of Chloe's family that poses the greatest risk and puts all of you in danger."

An image of her father came to mind. "So who is it?" Chloe asked.

"It's a bit complicated without sharing an explanation about your closest relative first," Que stated. "Your great-grandmother had a child named Elizabeth. When Elizabeth married, she changed her first name to Florence in order to protect her real identity, but kept Sheldon as her surname. She gave up her daughter to the Baker family, the adoptive parents to your mother."

Chloe's mouth dropped over the shocking news.

"Mrs. Sheldon is your grandma? How cool is that!" Jason said.

"Not very, I'm afraid," Tuk responded. "Elizabeth did everything she could to keep her grandmother from finding her. Cordelia has a history of discord and aggression."

"You mean Aldeirah," Chloe added.

Tuk nodded. "Aldeirah is your great-great-grandmother's Quin name. It means 'golden gem.'"

"Actually," Chloe responded, "this might be good news."

Murphy's face twisted in confusion. "Huh?"

"What if we hosted a family reunion in Quinsatheria?"

Her suggestion was so ridiculous that Murphy burst out laughing. "Here's a nice invitation to a tea party, Aldeirah. You'll be our honourary guest."

Chloe grumbled, "If she finds out that I'm in Quinsatheria, she'll come for me anyhow. But if I could tell her who I am in person, maybe I could change her mind." *Everyone should be allowed a second chance. Even Aldeirah.*

"Absolutely not!" the twins protested. "The risk isn't worth it."

Chloe shrugged. "It was just a thought."

Buckles scampered ahead, dragging his leash through a pile of leaves. He gave a short yip, indicating his eagerness to continue. Murphy chased him in a circle before he caught the leash, noticing a temperature difference immediately as he passed the shaded tree line. He unzipped his jacket and shoved it into his backpack, realizing too late that a half-eaten butter tart had melted inside the bag.

"Aw, Chloe!" he muttered, scooping the crumbly goop out and tossing it onto the ground.

"What?" she asked, jogging up to him.

"Look at this mess!" he said, pointing down. But the only thing Chloe could see was Buckles sitting there innocently and licking his chops.

"Ugh! Never mind. He ate the evidence."

Jason was in deep conversation with Tuk as they joined Chloe and Murphy. "She sent the Tri-Murids to investigate, and when they exposed his deceptive scheme, she had the debris collected and the main frame discarded in the woods to send a message that she was aware he was alive. Larsi and her brothers found him later and took him prisoner, but not before he was able to send a message to Florence for her help."

"Are you talking about Mr. Moss?" Murphy asked.

"Yes."

That explains why Westfield police had difficulty finding proof. "How did he escape the crash?"

"He wasn't *in* the aircraft. It was all a ruse. It flew on autopilot with a mannequin sitting at the controls. He used a device to steer the plane remotely. Aldeirah heard the motor running and almost caught him. She was determined to stop his rescue attempts, and while he was supposedly in flight, she tried to destroy him."

"What is she doing with all the prisoners? Chloe asked.

"She's using them for labour to build her dam," Que replied.

"Like slaves?"

The twins nodded.

"The adults are chained and heavily sedated by a substance she puts in their drinking water. The young ones call her mother because she took them as infants. These children are called scouts and serve as her spies. Teenagers are not as easily manipulated, but the fear of pain generally keeps them obedient."

Took? Murphy thought. *Chloe's relative is the infamous Westfield baby snatcher?*

"That's abuse," Chloe remarked.

"She also uses them for her entertainment," Que said. "Two prisoners are randomly selected to play a game of survival. If they prove to be victorious in the Pit, she'll give them their freedom."

"The Pit is a deep, hollow cavern," Tuk explained, "and it is where the Nemmels live."

"These creatures will feed on your terror," Que added.

Jason grimaced. "They sound cuddly."

"Does she keep her word and release them if they win?" Chloe asked.

"No one has been successful," Tuk replied.

Murphy suddenly felt dizzy and the landscape turned sideways. Jason gripped Murphy's shoulders to prevent him from falling. "I'll be all right," Murphy remarked with a weak smile." At least Tuk had spared him the details.

Chloe was quick to change the subject. "So, what happens after we go through the gates?"

"We will reach the caves and then travel by water," Tuk replied.

"Is Quinsatheria an island?"

Tuk nodded. "The cave itself isn't dangerous," he stated, "but the exit might be. It's a nesting ground for the Waek-Lyrens."

"Are they carnivores too?" Jason asked.

Murphy cringed. He didn't think his stomach could take any more facts about monsters that lived among them.

"They eat small rodents, fish and night bugs."

"Crickets and spiders," Jason replied. "Yummy."

Tuk shook his head. "Actually, it's—"

Gross! "Please, don't say it," Murphy murmured.

"Centipedes."

Murphy's stomach churned. *There's never a bucket around when I need one.*

"Water is our only defense. They cannot swim or float on the surface."

Chloe shuddered and rubbed her arms.

"So, who's in my family tree?" Jason asked.

Murphy cupped his hands over his ears and slowed his walking to a crawl. Jason turned around. "Don't you want to know?"

"Nope."

Jason leaned on Chloe's shoulder. "He's probably related to one of the beasts."

"I heard that," Murphy responded.

"I'll find out," Chloe offered, sprinting ahead to catch up with the twins. They had stopped and were waiting for them.

"If it's too strange, let him down easy, okay?" Jason called out.

Murphy walked past him, shaking his head then felt the sting of a small object graze his neck. "Ow!" he said, rubbing the tender spot. Another one hit him—something sharp that pricked his shoulder. "Quit it!" he complained, "that actually hurts."

"Huh?"

Murphy ducked and spun around. "What did you just hit me with?"

Before Jason could respond, something struck Murphy in the forehead. He squeezed his eyes shut as the pain spread to his temples. He touched the pink welt forming with his fingertip and hissed, "I don't think those were stray acorns falling off the trees."

Jason agreed, stalking toward two large, upright boulders.

Murphy lifted his bag to shield his face and hustled over to Jason's side. "We have a follower," Jason stated, pointing to the crevice between the rocks.

"I don't see anything."

Jason inched closer.

"Wait," Murphy said, holding him back. "Let me get the twins, then we can *all* go together."

"But he'll end up taking off."

"Who will?"

"Duncan."

Murphy made a face. *Oh, goody.* "How did he find—"

Chloe jumped in from of them, her face flushed from running. "Hey guys," she panted. "Why did you stop?" She held the leash tight as Buckles lunged forward with a growl. She whispered, "What's going on?"

"Your boyfriend found us," Jason stated.

"What?" Chloe blinked in surprise. "It's not like I have a homing device attached to me."

"Where are the twins?" Murphy fretted, turning side to side. "We can't let Duncan see them."

"Shh! They're in my pocket," Chloe replied, patting the side of her pant leg. "Now excuse me while I put on my charm."

"Go for it," Jason encouraged. "I'm sure he'll like that."

Chloe rolled up her sleeves and took a deep breath. "You guys owe me *big* time!"

"Uh-uh," Jason remarked, flashing his dimples. "*You* owe *us*, remember?"

Murphy laughed as Jason tried to imitate her voice. "I'll be forever in your debt!"

Chloe sighed just as Duncan came out of hiding and clapped. "Bravo!" he shouted. "Now I know that even idiots can act."

Jason clenched his fists.

"Don't," Chloe warned. "I'll talk to him."

She strode quickly to close the distance between them, then stopped midway, tapping her toe impatiently as she gestured for Duncan to come to her. Jason and Murphy watched as she folded her arms and spoke. Duncan raised his hands, then turned and walked away.

She returned looking smug.

Murphy was impressed. "What did you say to him?"

"I told him that if he quickly went home, I'd come over later with a movie rental of Dragon Slayer."

"Seriously?"

She laughed. "No, goofball. I warned him that if he continues to stalk me, I'll inform his father."

"What about a police report?" Jason asked.

"Wouldn't need it. He's more afraid of his dad than any punishment a Detention Ward could give him."

"You are so cruel!" Jason commented, smiling.

Chloe twirled a loose curl around her finger and gave him coy look. "It runs in the family."

Que wiggled out from Chloe's pocket. "We should leave before he changes his mind."

"How did he get here in the first place?" Murphy wondered.

"I think Aldeirah helped him," Chloe replied. "He mentioned that a woman gave him three strange rocks as payment to persuade me to go back with him. She handed him a wad of cash as incentive."

Tuk narrowed his eyes. "Does he still have the seeds?"

"Seeds? I thought he said rocks." She glanced at the lump on Murphy's face. "Whatever they were, he threw them away. Why?"

"Those *strange rocks* are actually the *seeds* that create the Tri-Murids."

"This is too close for comfort," Que commented, sensing her brother's anxiety.

"That's for sure," Murphy said. "Duncan keeps popping up like a bad zit!"

Chloe laughed. "What Que meant was—"

"I know," Murphy responded. "I was trying not to think about it." He watched Jason race ahead with Buckles in tow, wishing he could be as carefree. He let out a sigh. "So, who am I a descendant of?"

"I thought you didn't want to know."

"I don't, but ..." Murphy hesitated as Chloe spun her bracelet. "It's really bad isn't it?"

Chloe pursed her lips and nodded. "Remember the doctor you met at Willow Crest?"

"Yeah."

"He's the shrink that my mom went to see for her depression."

Murphy swallowed. The experimental drugs that Ms. Baker had taken were supposed to help block her unpleasant memories but the dosage that Dr. Bradford had prescribed almost killed her.

"I didn't know he was living there, but my mom did."

"Okay," Murphy said, "but how is this related to ..."

Chloe plucked at the yellow jewel on her wrist.

"Oh, no."

"He's your great-grandpa."

Now it made sense—his mom's warning and the reason why she didn't visit her grandfather in the nursing home. She'd never forgiven him for what he did to her best friend.

"There's more," Chloe stated. "He's also the person who testified against Aldeirah in court, tortured her at the asylum and found the parents for Charlotte's adoption."

Murphy rubbed his stomach. "Super."

Chloe bent down to pet Buckles as he laid in the grass, panting, with Jason sprawled out beside him.

"Don't go over there." Jason pointed lazily to his right. "Buckles had a massive poop. Know what else is crappy?" He didn't wait for an answer, "One of my ancestors."

"Can't be worse than mine," Murphy murmured.

"Probably not, but Leonard Wheeler was the man that fired Aldeirah from her nanny position and helped to put her in the loony bin. He's Mr. Moss's grandfather, and Fred Moss is my grandpa. My mom never talked about her dad. I only knew that when she finished college, Littletown became her home and when my dad got a job at Westfield's fire station, we moved here with my Pépé Tremblay. For seven years, I had no clue that there was another grandpa in the mix."

Que's eyes darted back and forth, scanning the rocks and hilly terrain ahead for any danger. "Aldeirah isn't here," she said, relieved.

"Good," Tuk replied, "then we can proceed."

"The gate is not far from here," Que announced.

Jason slapped his hands together and rubbed them. "Let's do this!"

Chloe seized Murphy's wrist and yanked him forward, making sure he wasn't going to run. Then she dropped her hand and wiped her sweaty palm on the leg of her overalls.

Jason's brown eyes sparkled with amusement. "A little nervous?"

"A bit," Murphy responded.

Chloe giggled. Apparently the question wasn't meant for him.

CHAPTER EIGHT

Que and Tuk pointed to a gangly birch in the distance standing proudly on its own. The trunk was split and it stretched in opposite directions, as if its thin branches were defiantly pushing against the fallen rock that had piled on either side in an effort to control the boundaries.

It didn't look like a gateway to Murphy. He'd imagined something sturdier, like a steel door that opened only when someone spoke the magic words, not a tree that looked like he could blow it down. The base was no larger than his own leg.

"Why do we need to specifically enter through *that* tree?" he commented. "It looks so wimpy."

"It may appear that way, but it is very resilient and cannot be destroyed," Tuk replied.

"Aldeirah has tried," Que added. "But the trunks will instantly regrow, whether they are cut down or set on fire."

Tuk continued, "The trees with a double trunk are the only ones that have our sacred waters running through their roots, connecting our land with yours. It provides a direct passage to Quinsatheria through the caves."

As they got closer, Murphy noticed a pattern of carved notches in the bark. In fact, the symbols looked familiar. He recalled seeing similar drawings on Mr. Moss's property, particularly near the stairs that descended into the Valley. He dug out the photo of the map from his pocket and compared the markings. Indeed, the birch in front of him and the old oak tree's trunk etched with triangular shapes matched perfectly. *So that's why some of them were burnt.*

A small finger tapped the picture. "This means water," Que informed of the upside down triangle with the two lines in the middle. "It turns blue when activated. All elements have their own colours. Fire is orange, earth is green and air is white."

"Speaking of colour," Tuk announced, "the entire surface of the main cave is covered in a rainbow of gems."

"Like rubies and emeralds?" Murphy asked.

Tuk nodded. "We call it the Wall of Clairvoyance because each jewel carries a portion of the past, present and future destinies of those that seek its knowledge."

"The Tri-Murids have stolen many of the gems to prevent us from discovering Aldeirah's plans," Que added.

"Unfortunately," Tuk continued, "our time in the caves will be limited, so observing your personal experiences will be too."

"But we can show you a preview," Que offered, mirroring Tuk's actions as he extended his arms out, passing a stream of water between them. She gripped the flow tightly and pulled while Tuk unraveled the twisting current into a thin sheet, as if it were cling wrap, forming a large square with vivid swirling colours.

"The gems interlock together," Que explained, releasing her lower arms to point out how the prophetic magic worked.

Murphy was so impressed by the twins' improvised movie screen that he was tempted to ask them if they could do it at his place on the weekends. They had better reception than his TV antenna and didn't require any batteries.

Tuk poked a finger through the transparent film, creating a spout that quickly drained the pictures onto the ground and inadvertently sprayed Buckles in the face, producing a sneezing frenzy. Chloe took her sleeve and wiped his nose as Murphy shuddered, watching. He was happy it worked, but not thrilled that it was *his* sweatshirt she used as a snot rag.

He opened his palm and raised his head to the sky. Dark clouds had gathered as a cold east wind pushed at their backs. He pulled out his jacket and brushed away the sticky crumbs, shivering.

Chloe pulled the hoodie over her head and darted for the nearest cover as the rain fell, joining Murphy as he ducked under the skirt of a tall evergreen.

Jason strutted over to the tree, showing off that he wasn't wet. "You might want this," he said, handing Chloe a glowing blue stick. "Try it," he encouraged. "It works."

Chloe leaned out and lifted the stick in the air. Sparkling blue lines suddenly erupted from the narrow tip like fireworks, separating into five sections and dropping down into the shape of a dome, keeping Chloe dry.

"Do I get one?" Murphy asked, watching the water bounce off the umbrella mold.

"It'll cover you both. You just need to hold onto the handle."

Murphy slid underneath, trying to avoid hitting his head. The outline was difficult to see through the rain. As they stood side by side, the glowing lines extended out further, accommodating his space too.

Jason whirled around. "Pretty cool, eh?" He stopped abruptly and looked behind him, searching the ground. "Um, where is Buckles? I thought he was with the two of you."

Chloe's face paled. "Buckles!" she cried out, but he didn't answer.

"He *was* here a moment ago," Murphy stated.

Chloe was on the verge of tears. "We'll need to split up and retrace our steps," she replied, dashing out and dropping the stick. The filmy repellent walls instantly collapsed, absorbing into the ground.

Gloomy clouds hovered over them like a doomsday shroud and every stone seemed to have shadows lurking underneath. Something dark and small and oddly quiet moved within the gap of split boulders as Murphy approached the mound. He crouched down and extended his arm between the rock, feeling around for the puppy. "Found him!" he yelled out.

"No, I've got him!" Jason shouted back. "He's right here!"

Murphy suddenly stopped and released whatever he had grabbed, listening to the happy reunion. Warning bells blared in his head, triggering his instinct to back away.

"I guess you didn't hear me," Jason said, approaching him. "We found Buckles."

"Th-that's great," Murphy stammered. Jason clapped him on the shoulder and turned him around, walking him back toward the group. Murphy glanced back warily one more time. Thankfully, nothing came out to greet them.

Tuk was spraying down Buckles's muddy paws as Murphy and Jason returned. "I'm afraid that the boy may have buried the seeds."

"Is that a bad thing?" Chloe asked.

"It can be, if we don't remove them from the ground in time," Que answered.

"Why?"

"If you recall, we grow rapidly, and it just rained. If the seeds were covered with dirt, then chances are they—" Que gasped and her eyes widened.

Instinctively, everyone followed her anxious gaze. It led to the same place Murphy had just been. Tuk flew above their heads, observing. "We must leave, now!" he commanded. Buckles whimpered and Chloe held him tightly in her arms.

Three creatures stood boldly on top of the large slabs of rock. Their skin was the colour of bubble gum, mottled with raised patches of red and plum. The taller one had a crimson line running across its forehead and into its hairline. The two smaller ones were identical but had no markings on their faces. The taller one stepped down to the next stone. It deliberately moved slowly, waiting for a reaction as the two smaller ones hopped onto its shoulders. They squatted like gargoyles with their long fingers gripping the taller one's collar bone and smiled broadly, though the sentiment was not friendly.

Murphy stared, mesmerized by their large fuchsia and pale pink eyes. The leader he assumed was female, with winter white hair coiled into several knots resting on top of her head and fanning out like feathers. The tips flickered orange, then erupted into flames. The two smaller creatures passed their hands through the fire, igniting their own stubby hair as if it were made of candle wicks.

Murphy suddenly felt a tap on his arm, startling him. "We're waiting for you," Jason said.

"Oh!" Murphy replied. "Sorry about th—"

"Holy cow!" Jason broke in. "They just morphed together!" As one unit, the Tri-Murids stood four feet tall.

"Hurry!" Que urged. "They can't fly, but they'll catch up quickly!"

Chloe stood in front of the split tree, cradling Buckles like a baby. Que and Tuk flanked her sides, flying just above her. "Once I say the last word," Tuk explained, "the gate will open."

"Don't be afraid of the water," Que added. "It's safe to pass through without holding your breath."

"They're getting closer!" Chloe reported.

"*Osnow tris li!*" Tuk blurted out.

The space between the V-shaped tree trunk instantly formed a torrent of water churning in a triangular pattern. It flowed with bright blue energy but remained inside the border without spilling over.

"Can I go first?" Jason asked. The twins nodded and Jason stepped inside.

Chloe let Murphy go next, knowing the twins were going to follow her while they closed the gate behind them. Murphy placed a hesitant foot over the rapid water flow when Chloe suddenly screamed. She tumbled backwards, knocking him off balance and pitching them forward through the opening. He barely had time to duck as the tree branch that hit Chloe once again aimed its limb toward them, skimming the top of his hair with its leaves and glowing an eerie lime green. It thrashed against the gate as it pulled back for another assault. Que blocked the blow but the smaller, orange-spotted branches slithered in and wrapped tightly around her waist, bursting into a flaming restraint. Tuk loosened the hold but struggled to keep it wide enough for his sister to escape as it burned through her clothing.

Chloe roared in anger, throwing herself at the animated branch. She tugged so hard that she ripped it completely from the trunk, triggering a spontaneous reaction that destroyed it. The cremated remains slipped through her fingers, producing a powdery grey cloud. She tried desperately to reach the entrance, but spun like a merry-go-round with each attempt. Then she finally realized they were no longer on solid ground.

Their bodies were floating. As the gate closed, Murphy finally understood why Chloe was so distraught. A glimmer of light silhouetted a woman standing at the opening with a puppy in her arms.

He didn't have to guess who it was.

CHAPTER NINE

It was too late to save Buckles. The rush of the water crashed against the sealed door, spraying the walls with glowing droplets. It briefly illuminated the inside, exposing a funnel that flowed down into the depths. Chloe braced her palms against the smooth spiral, trying to stop her fall. "Noooo!" she shrieked, digging her heels into the water.

Murphy felt the pull as he descended into the darkness. His body twisted and turned as it plummeted down a slope faster than the luge at the winter games. Glowing lights flashed as the funnel seemed to slowly close around him. He held his breath as his heart hammered in his chest.

Jason was having fun, unlike his friends. His exhilarated cheer pierced through the silent void.

Murphy's ears suddenly popped as a shift in the current released him from its wake. "Be careful!" Jason warned them before their feet even touched the ground. "We're on a ledge." Chloe skidded past the landing and Jason threw a protective arm in front of her. She caught his hand and stopped just before she teetered over the edge. She scrambled back against the wall, drawing in a shaky breath.

"Thanks." she sniffled, wiping her cheeks. Jason turned to Murphy. *Is something wrong?* he asked, mouthing the words. Murphy nodded sadly. Jason's eyes settled upon Chloe. "Where's Buckles?"

Chloe rubbed her eyes. "Aldeirah took him."

"What? How?"

"By distraction," Tuk responded.

"She better not harm one precious hair on his sweet little body, or I swear—" Chloe ranted bitterly.

"She will not hurt Buckles," Tuk assured her. "She knows that you will come for him."

"But it'll be a trap," Murphy replied.

Jason shrugged. "Does it matter? We still have to save him."

Murphy sighed. "I know. But her prisoner list is going to get bigger."

"We will get Buckles back and safely," Que asserted with confidence.

"Promise?" Chloe asked.

"On our honour," the twins declared simultaneously.

Murphy could see Chloe swallowing slowly, digesting their words as if some part of their vow tasted wrong.

"Hey," Jason said, slinging an arm around her shoulders. "Don't be sad. Maybe Buckles will retaliate and poop in her shoes." Chloe smiled with some effort, grateful for his optimism.

Que and Tuk flew down to the water and touched it with their tiny hands. Circular impressions began to form, as if a stone had skipped upon the smooth surface. Then a rush of fluorescent light broke through the surface of the water and filled the spacious cave with a soft radiance. Priceless jewels were embedded all over the walls and ceiling, twinkling like stars. Even the twins' portrayal couldn't compare to its grandeur. It was as if they had been transported inside a billion-dollar Christmas ornament. But this decoration had artwork that moved, gliding over the rock to create authentic stories made from every gem imaginable.

Chloe stared at the blur of colours forming a scene of her father dressed in a uniform, kneeling down to press a golden flower against the bleeding gash on the side of her own face. It seemed to grow underneath his hand, transforming into thick layers of gauze that glowed as it penetrated her wound. The blood instantly clotted and disappeared, leaving four stitches in place. She touched the soft spot on her temple where a tiny puckered line existed, hidden by her hair. She couldn't recall how she had gotten hurt or why he'd used a plant to heal her, but she knew it was special. Her father picked her up in his arms, wiping off a spot of red on his crisp white collar, and that's when she noticed his unusual star-shaped pin tacked just below it.

Murphy watched as a snowman competition in the park suddenly appeared. He and Duncan had been friends back then, banding together against other local kids to win for the bragging rights of the coolest creation, wearing pyjamas and goofy footwear as the only rule. He wore woolly red socks with swimming fins while Duncan sported Kermit the Frog slippers as they molded their Land of the Lost alien masterpiece. Murphy smiled at the bittersweet memory.

Jason cocked his head to the side, peering at a familiar boy struggling to pry open a wall of thorny vines with his stiff fingers. He reached inside and yanked a small child through just before it closed up again. Then a group of wild children rushed in, surrounding the boys with handmade weapons. *Is this really happening?* He studied their faces and realized that the boy resisting capture and gesturing for the small boy to flee was the frozen kid from Mr. Moss's backyard. Jason turned toward his friends, but they were still immersed in their own episodes.

Chloe rubbed her eyes as the slideshow came to an abrupt end, reminding them that many of the jewels predicting the future were stolen.

"Is that supposed to be our boat?" Murphy asked, sizing up the strange vessel floating in the water just below the ledge.

"Sure is, *Captain* Murphy," Que replied playfully.

The hull was pearl white and shimmering in seashell colours. It looked like an enormous grain of squashed rice with its bow and stern narrowing to a flat point. The port and starboard had long indentations running along the freeboard, possibly used for propulsion, as the frame appeared to be built for speed. Its metal roof was crushed into overlapping folds, exposing half of the interior, which showed a clear waffle-textured bottom and silver wires weaving throughout. Hanging from the warped tubing was an instrument panel, damaged beyond repair by an unknown heat source.

The twins stood on the edge of the prow, cupping water in their hands. As they threw it into the air, the droplets formed a semi-circle that created a steering device and a paddle wheel to move them forward.

Jason hopped onto the boat, followed by Murphy. They extended their hands out, but Chloe hesitated.

"It's safe, see?" Jason said, jumping up and down to reassure her. Murphy gripped the roof for balance as the boat bounced with their weight, sending rolling waves splashing against the ledge.

"Maybe I should stay here—" Chloe began.

"No! It's too dangerous to be alone here," Que informed.

Chloe swung her legs over as she sat on the edge, then slid carefully onto the floor of the boat, crawling over to Murphy's side.

"Is there a motor on this thing?" Jason asked, peering through the paddle wheel.

"We'll be providing the power," Tuk responded, joining Que at the back.

They drew in a deep breath and their cheeks swelled like chipmunks pocketing too many peanuts. Then they forced the air out, rotating the paddle wheel as it dipped into the water, pushing the boat ahead. Murphy was glad that their heads shrank back to normal once the wheel started to spin on its own.

Chloe blinked as she caught movement on the wall. The gems were sliding into another scene, giving her a glimpse of a drawing her father left on his desk. She tried to understand the message he was sending regarding her bracelet, the key and his star insignia but the meanings of the words *all connect* and *Arthur Miller* scrawled hastily across the bottom of the paper were lost on her.

"Who's—" Her words were cut short as Tuk put a finger to his lips, reminding them to refrain from speaking as they entered the tunnel for fear that the Waek-Lyrens might hear them and prevent safe passage. Chloe spun her bracelet in silence, wondering.

It was dark, damp and cold as they motored silently through the winding cave. Chloe shivered, pulling the hoodie over her head and tightening the drawstring. She plugged her nose as a noxious odour of dried fish wafted toward them. Murphy almost gagged at the stench.

Tuk released a small glowing orb and pointed up to the stalactites, cautioning that they should stay seated while passing under the rocks that hung like giant fangs. The floating ball drifted further, illuminating a patch of darkness that revealed large milky sacks suspended from the ceiling, covered in a stringy substance with feathers clinging to the threads. The orb bounced, hitting one of the nests, and immediately the light extinguished. Murphy couldn't see, but squeezed his eyes shut anyhow, knowing there were creatures the size of Pteranodons huddled together inside the flexible pouches dangling above their heads. At least they were sleeping.

Until …

"AH-CHOO!" Chloe sneezed and all their heads popped up simultaneously, turning in her direction.

"Get down!" Que instructed, not bothering to whisper.

Chloe cringed, apologizing as she sneezed again and again.

A flurry of screeches and squawks rang out inside the cave.

Murphy lost his grip on the helm as the boat lunged forward at full speed. He tumbled back, falling over the edge and plunging into the water. His friends waited for him to come back up for air, searching …

Chloe pointed, shouting, "He's behind us!" The wake was dragging his body further away from them. Tuk cut the power and the boat slowed down instantly.

Jason was about to jump in when Que stopped him. "Look! He's swimming underwater toward us."

Murphy exhaled as he surfaced, hooking his arms over the side of the boat, and felt a ring of bubbles forming under his arms to help keep him afloat. Jason quickly hauled him onto the deck as Chloe draped the borrowed sweatshirt over his shoulders. She swayed, feeling the boat rock as it drifted through the passage. She dropped to her knees and scooted toward the bow, squishing her tiny frame into the narrow cavity and staring at the vacant helm. Everyone was too busy to see that no one was steering. Jason was holding up Murphy's shirt as Que absorbed the water, then twisted her bloated body to wring herself out like a sponge while Tuk sent a flow of warm air to dry Murphy's hair.

Finally, Jason noticed the wheel turning on its own and dove for it, pulling it sharply to the right. The boat swerved, scraping against the jagged rock with its back end. Four Waek-Lyrens headed toward them as they tipped sideways. Jason was able to steady the boat but fell down when one of the creature's pale yellow wings clipped his shoulder. Que raced to the front, leaving her brother to propel the boat on his own. She blasted a stream of water directly into the Waek-Lyren's face until it retreated and flew away, then hurled a slew of rain pellets at its mate. But this one wasn't going to give up so easily. It circled around, diving toward Tuk. Que saturated its wings with a thin coat of ice. It strained to keep its height as it flapped its frozen wings, creating a spray of cold fragments pelting down on them. Jason whacked it with a swing of his jacket as it dropped closer. It bellowed in rage, joining the others as they skittered across the ceiling, clawing savagely at the cracks to create a hailstorm of dust and stones.

Giant sections of rock splintered and separated, dropping into the water. The surface grew increasingly choppy as the rumbling of stones toppled and stacked into a pile that was rapidly closing the passage.

"We're blocked in!" Murphy cried out. "We'll never make it out!"

"Hold onto something!" Tuk shouted and then raised the boat vertically, squeezing the vessel through the slim gap. Chloe braced her feet, gripping the instrument panel so tightly her knuckles hurt, and watched Murphy squash Jason as they slammed into the bulkhead. Tuk finally eased the ship back onto its keel as they entered the open water.

"I'm closing this exit!" Que shouted over the flapping wings. "*Sel-clo min urden!*" The mouth of the cave collapsed in an avalanche of rock, sealing it completely.

Chloe sat up and Que patted her back. "I'm okay," Chloe assured her.

"You look a little green," Murphy commented, unconvinced. Chloe whimpered in response as something loomed overhead, creating shadows that moved across the deck.

Murphy looked up and swallowed as a group of angry survivors circled the boat, waiting for a command to attack. The dominant male screeched, raising a mohawk of rust-coloured feathers on its crown as if to show his hostile intent. He dove and the others followed, splaying their talons. Jason was cornered but he managed to pull his arm free, grateful for the defensive moves Gabe had taught him while play fighting.

The leader swooped down on Murphy, giving him an unwanted view of reptilian skin speckled with brown lumps on the inner membrane of the wings. Its slivered mouth opened, revealing a black serpentine tongue and rotten teeth worn down to the gum line. There was a telescopic appendage on its sloped forehead, splitting at the tip into two funnel shapes. It stretched out to probe the area for vibrations with its sensitive receptors.

Murphy tried to reach Chloe's cramped hideaway, but the creature landed on the roof, trapping him as it swung upside down. He dodged its claws as it swiped the air, barely missing his face. Tuk hurled a blast of water at its back but its wings deflected the assault, spreading wide to reveal hundreds of blind eyes blinking independently where the lumps had been.

It quickly took advantage of Murphy's stunned reaction, tightening its grip around his shoelaces and dragging him out in the open as he kicked and flailed. Chloe slipped her arms around Murphy's waist and pulled him back as the creature's exposed ribcage opened up, dispersing an amber mist.

"Don't breathe the vapour!" Tuk warned, witnessing the creature expel its paralyzing gas. "It's trying to attach its receptor to your eyes so that it can see."

Chloe scooted over, pressing a sleeve-covered hand against her nose and mouth. She leaned over Murphy and yanked his canvas bag onto her lap. She rummaged through the endless supply of goodies, gathering a handful. Murphy caught a chip bag that she tossed at him with his free hand. "Let's see if they like junk food!"

They scattered the snacks over the water and suddenly the boat rocked violently.

"Take cover!" Que shouted, ushering Jason to join his friends. It seemed that Chloe's idea worked, but now they had to deal with the creatures fighting amongst themselves for the last tidbits that the water hadn't swallowed up.

"We can't move forward. They are all around us," Tuk announced.

"We have more food—would that help?" Murphy offered.

He and Chloe dumped the remaining contents overboard and a shrill, squawking frenzy ensued. One of the Waek-Lyrens smashed into the prow and tumbled inside. Its wings were torn and bleeding. They heard a scrambling of claws above them as one swooped down and grabbed the injured creature with its talons, trying to pull it away, but the extra weight made it difficult to fly. Tuk brushed a wave of air, lifting them out of the boat and separating the two in flight.

The wounded creature plunged into the water, thrashing about to keep from drowning. The waves splashed aggressively against the sides of the boat, shaking the vessel like an angry fist.

Chloe dug her fingers into the bumpy flooring and whimpered. Murphy cried out too, seeing coloured lights flickering underneath Chloe's hands. Every time she moved her fingers, the silver tubing inside the padded flooring reacted. It lifted like static cling and produced tiny sparks that lit the bottom where she lay. She looked at him with frightened eyes.

Not a good sign, he thought.

"How many are there?" Que asked Tuk.

"There are four left."

"Then we'll each take two."

Before Jason could raise his head and protest, the twins were gone. He, Murphy and Chloe listened to the battle cries, the splashes of water and bodies hitting metal with a thud. It was difficult to decipher who was winning when there was so much commotion.

Then suddenly there was silence. The water went calm and their boat stopped rocking.

Jason lifted his head. "Do you think it's safe to look now?"

Murphy held his breath and listened again. There was no sound. "I don't know. I don't hear anything."

"You don't think they're … um …"

"Lunchmeat?" Murphy implied, fearing the same ending.

Chloe sat up quickly, pointing wordlessly at the stern.

A gigantic bubble emerged from the water, revealing a desperate creature wildly clawing at the impenetrable cell, trying to escape. Even its powerful wings were no match for its prison as it pushed against the lining. It slammed its body into the transparent wall, bouncing like a pinball. It roared with fury, sensing that its members were trapped inside similar confines. Ropes made of the same substance pulled them all out of the water. The twins lifted the balloon structures and spun them around, building momentum and releasing them to soar far beyond anyone's sight.

Jason threw a fist in the air, thrilled with the outcome. "That was stellar!"

Murphy had to agree, but his excitement deflated when he saw Chloe. She was trembling. Her shoulders and back were rigid, but her hands shook as she remained seated, wrapping them around a metal pole so tightly that she probably could have bent it. Murphy hadn't seen her so scared before and assumed the behaviour was simply from shock, considering she had lost her pet and been attacked by beasts that outlived the Triassic period.

"You can relax now," Jason remarked. "They're all gone."

Chloe pried an eye open. "So, we're all okay?"

Jason shrugged. "You tell me," he replied, squatting in front of her. "We can see that something else is wrong. It's not just about Buc—" He caught himself before he said the puppy's name. "Were you hurt?"

She shook her head. "You can't help with this problem. No one can."

"Well, now you're starting to sound like Murphy."

"Hey! I don't say that!"

Chloe lifted her puffy eyes to look at both of them, attempting to smile. "Actually, you do. You're the biggest worrywart we know."

"Is it so bad to worry about one of my best friends?" he commented.

"Of course not," Chloe responded. "It's just that I need to resolve this on my own. I'm sorry."

"Don't be," Jason said, plopping down beside her. "Just tell us what's bothering you."

"I don't know how to swim," she replied.

Jason rubbed his forehead. "Yeah, that could be a *huge* problem. Why didn't you tell us this before?"

"It wasn't necessary," she admitted. "Plus, I don't know anyone who has a pool that could teach me."

"Duncan's house has a nice in-ground—"

"What about a lake or an ocean?" Murphy asked, deliberately cutting Jason off.

"Nope, no beaches," she stated. "My mom works through the summer and most holidays, so I've never been on vacation."

"Bummer," Jason replied.

"I'll make sure you do," Murphy promised. "Next summer you can join me on a fishing trip with my dad. Every July we go up to Willamont Cove." Chloe's blank face showed no sign that she was familiar with the popular destination.

"It's the place that's famous for their ice cream and cotton candy. They ship their stock all over the world," Jason replied.

Chloe's eyes lit up, "Oh! You mean *Ooey-gooeys*. I know it. It has one of my favourite flavours. *Grape-a-lade*."

Murphy rolled his eyes. *Anything sugar-coated and she'll find the shops that carry it.*

Chloe grinned. "I'll be sure to remind you by June."

"She'll probably make you buy her the new fifteenth flavour," Jason commented.

Murphy gagged. "Please don't tell me you've tried all fourteen cotton candy flavours."

Chloe shrugged. "All right, I won't."

Jason laughed. Chloe was sounding a bit more like herself.

"Quinsatheria just ahead!" the twins announced.

The three of them jumped to their feet, staring out at the approaching shoreline.

They were safe—at least for now.

CHAPTER TEN

Chloe's mom, Francis, gave Julie a hug at the door. "Are you sure you'll be okay?" she asked, holding her friend at arm's length and looking her over. "I could come back after I check the apartment."

Julie desperately wanted her to stay, but knew it would be selfish to wish for more time together. She had to let her go. "I'll be fine. You've earned your wings. Besides, I'm going to page Wade to see if he can get out of work earlier."

Francis nodded, but was unsure whether to leave.

"Really," Julie said. "Now get going before I change my mind." She forced a smile. "But call me as soon as you get in."

Francis squeezed Julie's hands before letting them drop. "Promise."

Once Francis had backed out of the driveway, Julie rushed to the television and turned on the local channel. She sat on the edge of the sofa, biting her nails.

"Health Authorities have instituted a boil water advisory for residents of Westfield county that still have running tap water in their homes. After the train derailment and collapse of Westfield's water tower, emergency crews have come in from Littletown to assist with extinguishing the fires that have engulfed the whole plaza on Mercer Street. Residents in the area have been evacuated for their safety as the fire spreads. The explosion has destroyed at least eleven homes. The extent of the damage is unclear at this time, but it's estimated the cost of repairs will be close to four million dollars."

"Three seniors have been transported to Littletown's burn unit, one of whom died in the helicopter. Their names have not been released yet," a firefighter stated. "We are doing our best, but without a full water supply, it's been tough. The reserves in the hydrants have been completely emptied."

"Is it true that water trucks have been dispatched as far as Norpine Peak?" the reporter inquired.

"That's right, so it'll take a while for them to reach us," the firefighter replied. "If you'll excuse me—"

"We will be back shortly with more coverage as this scene develops. I'm Carla Simmons, reporting live from Westfield County on CHWC."

...

"Hello?"

"Hi, Karen, it's Julie."

"Oh, hi! Is everything all right?"

"I hope so. I was wondering if the kids came back to your place early."

"No, they haven't. But if you're worried about them being in the fire zone, they're well beyond that restriction point."

"That's why I'm calling. Wouldn't it be better if the kids were at home?"

"I suppose ..."

"I'd feel better if Murphy was with me. Would it be too much to ask if Gabe could round them up?"

"Not sure. He's had some traumatic issues to deal with lately."

"I heard. I'm so sorry about Kelly."

"Hello? What was this about Kelly?"

"Hi Gabe, it's Julie. I was just saying that you and your girlfriend's family are in my thoughts."

"Thanks, Mrs. Robinson ... Is Jason okay?"

"I hope so, but considering what has happened in the last twenty-four hours ..."

"You need my help?"

"I'd appreciate that. Would you mind?"

"Not at all," he replied. "I'll bring them back."

Gabe sprinted down the street, sloshing through the flooded front yards as he passed the police blockade and yellow tape. Many of the homes were still smouldering with black smoke and a few ambulances waited nearby for anyone in need. Their lights flashed against the empty carcasses of what was once a neighbourhood.

As he rounded the corner of Mr. Moss's home, he noticed a figure standing near the oak tree.

"Stuart? What are you doing here?"

Stuart turned around and raised his hands defensively. "I'm not here to make any trouble."

"I didn't say that. I asked—"

"Duncan isn't here. In fact, I don't know *where* he is. We were supposed to spy on your brother's friends, but when they went down into the Valley, I didn't wanna follow them."

Gabe gripped the back of his neck. "Whoa, they went over the ledge?"

"Yeah, but no one has come back up yet. It's like they all disapp—" Stuart held his tongue, aware that Kelly was missing. "So I've been lookin' around, and I found this." He untied the remnant of rope still attached to the trunk and handed it to Gabe. "Someone cut it."

"Or burned it," Gabe remarked, studying it. "That's strange."

"Ya know what's weirder?" Stuart pointed over to the ridge and an orange glow flickered just above the first step. "That."

Gabe cautiously took a step, watching the light pull and bend into a triangle. The space inside the shape was dark, but then it wavered, and the silhouette of a boy appeared. Gabe let out a surprised gasp when Jason climbed out and waved, coaxing them to come forward.

Stuart moved aside. "I'm not going. He's *your* brother. But if you see Duncan, can you tell him that his dad wants to talk with him?"

Gabe nodded, knowing that it was bad news. Mr. Fisher's business was located in the building that burned down.

. . .

"What is this, Jay? Some kind of fantasy game?"

Jason wouldn't look back. "Shhh ..."

Gabe lowered his voice. "Are Murphy and Chloe with you?"

141

Jason shrugged.

Gabe thought this was an odd reaction. "Why aren't you talking to me? What's going on?" He pulled at his brother's shoulder and Jason turned his head.

"Don't touch me." He scowled. "I'm trying to bring you to your people."

"Huh? People?" Gabe squeezed past his brother and jogged ahead, but couldn't see anything in the black abyss. He spun around, but needed to spread his legs out just to keep his balance, as the ground moved like air under his feet. "Why are you acting so strange?"

Jason grunted, dodging Gabe's floundering arms without making contact.

Gabe crossed his arms. "Answer me!" he ordered. But Jason refused to talk. "What happened to your voice?"

Clearly annoyed with his brother's interrogation, Jason roared, "Enough with the questions!"

Gabe stared at him in disbelief, stunned by his angry outburst. "That was uncalled for," he commented. "Your charade can end now."

Jason ignored the order, lifting his chin in defiance.

Something was wrong. Instinctively, Gabe knew this wasn't his brother, because Jason would have obeyed and laughed by now.

His hands started to tingle as a burning pressure seized his wrists to bind them together. "What the—?"

Suddenly Jason's body split into three parts, morphing into creatures that only movies can create.

...

"So, when do you get your shots?" Murphy asked Chloe to break the silence.

"Pardon?" She scrunched her nose, confused about the question.

"Your medicine," Murphy said. "The feathers on the Waek-Lyrens must have made you sneeze." He smirked. "See? I was listening to you earlier."

"Oh!" she replied, rubbing her arms absentmindedly. "I haven't made an appointment yet."

"What's this about?" Jason asked.

"I've got allergies," Chloe explained. "I've had them for as long as I can remember." She waited for him to reciprocate with a joke, but he didn't give one, so she continued. "But now, I get these itchy bumps on my arms that drive me crazy! My mom just wanted to make sure it wasn't something serious."

"Can I see?"

"There's nothing right now ... I would have to be scratching."

"Humour me," Jason replied.

Chloe pulled back her sleeves.

"Whoa!" Jason commented. "Those scrapes are nasty."

"I know, and it's not from my fingernails. They just appear on their own."

"Maybe it's scabies. You know, the bugs that tunnel under the skin."

"Gross!" Murphy scooted further away, seating himself at an angle, but then noticed something peculiar. The bumps formed a triangular pattern. "No way!" he said, grabbing Chloe's wrist and turning her forearm over. "What do these shapes remind you of?"

CHAPTER ELEVEN

Quinsatheria was purely magical. Its silvery mountains rose majestically over a lush, pastel garden, and the forest was so dense, it appeared to be made of black iron. Chloe noticed a cluster of unusual bushes growing inland. It had trumpet-sized flowers blooming in varies shades of orange with tall yellow stamens knotted in a bow. She inhaled the sweet aroma, its vanilla scent clinging to the air like a room deodorizer.

A carpeted walkway made of giant ferns called lif-ris led to the water with twinkling blue lights placed as a border. They sparkled as the glow bounced off the navy leaves rimmed in gold dust. Murphy glanced at all the sprites waiting for their arrival. Some were lining the banks, while others hid behind rocks covered in pink moss. The most curious ventured near the water, hiding behind brown, striped mushrooms they held close to their bodies as they tiptoed closer. He hoped that they were only there to greet them as their boat drifted onto the silky sand.

"*Wem-luk, derna frin-nads!*" two sprites called out.

"It's the king and queen!" the twins announced.

Jason cheered with excitement and sprung out of the boat, pulling it up onto the banks.

"Well, you can always count this as your first vacation," Murphy commented. He watched Jason scoop the sand up in his hands, letting it slowly sift through his fingers. "It's got water and—"

"Meteorite dust," the queen broke in, startling him. She approached and shook his index finger with all four of her hands. "I'm U-Dae-Yis," she said, and then turned to introduce the king.

"Nom-Lu," he replied, bowing. "But please, call me Lu." He looked back and smiled as Jason jogged over to join them.

"Feel this," he offered, dumping a pile of rust-coloured dust into Chloe's hand.

Murphy poked at the minuscule stones in her palm. "It's really soft," Chloe commented.

"Yes," Lu agreed. "This type of soil is very good for planting. It has many minerals that nourish our vegetation here."

Murphy watched as swirls of purple clouds painted the blue sky, shrouding the mountain peaks in mist. But as he lowered his eyes and followed the broad base, he discovered that they were no more than stalagmites on steroids. Then it occurred to him that they were underground. "I know that plants need sun and heat. So where does your light come from?"

"The water," U-Dae-Yis replied. "The algae growing on the bottom of this aquifer is luminescent. The glow reflects off the rock, providing a blue illusion. Depending on the depths, our sky can be a bright turquoise or a dark indigo. The clouds form from the moist, cool air of the caves, and the meteor dust controls our temperature. It absorbs heat from the sun's rays that penetrate through small cracks in the rock, then converts it into energy to create the warmth you feel."

"All year long? What about winter?"

"We only have two seasons," Lu responded. "Wet and dry."

"Just two?" Murphy commented. "We have four!"

"Then you are twice as fortunate," the queen replied.

"If you will excuse us," Lu said, "there are preparations that we must attend to before dinner is served."

...

Que and Tuk led them through a thin cluster of strange-looking trees. The bark peeled away from the trunk like a banana, revealing a shiny burgundy skin underneath. The drooping branches grew in tight bundles, forming loops with one huge leaf hanging in each circle. They were teal with royal blue veins, and cup-shaped to hold a sticky, bluish substance inside.

Tuk pointed to them. "Those are blu-sap trees, and the syrup is *tarna*. The liquid is drinkable but may cause intoxication."

Murphy chuckled, picturing all of them drunk. "I'll stick with milk," he said, then wandered toward the coastline.

Jason knelt down beside him at the water's edge to examine a plant sticking out of the meteorite dust. It reminded him of an avocado because of its pear-shaped size and dark green flesh. Tiny purple nubs covered its outer skin like polka dots, though it appeared to have rotted as the stem was black and the leaves were shriveled. Chloe leaned in. "This one looks dead," she said, "but there's more over there."

She squatted as the boys watched the shell open into four separate petals, revealing a fuzzy white grape on a stick. Each time the water washed up onto the shore, the petals closed, protecting the delicate fruit inside. When the water receded, the plants reopened again.

"This pod carries the ha-plume berry," Tuk explained, "the favoured meal of the Rinegos.

"How can they eat them when the pod is constantly opening and closing?

"They wait until evening to eat, as the pods will remain open longer while the tide is low. They lift the berries out with great care. If they draw too much air when pulling the fruit out, then the outer petals will be damaged, resulting in a smaller crop. The leaves are a natural barrier, allowing the pods to float on water even as the tides rise. But as you can see, our sacred waters have receded and they're drying out, creating weak stems that perish too quickly.

Quinsatheria was slowly being destroyed by the construction of the dam, and Chloe knew that Aldeirah was to blame.

Something dark poked its head out from the tree line, showing two small tusks on either side of a stubby trunk, then ducked back into the shadows. It moved swiftly through the bushes, rustling the leaves as it brushed against the branches.

"*Whoa!* What was *that*?" Murphy asked, backing up behind the twins. But before they could reply, he cried out as the black massive figure bounded toward them, its three-pronged toes treading lightly on the ground without any sound.

"A Rinegos," Que stated. "You can pet her. She's harmless."

It chose to sit by Jason, nudging his hand for him to lift it as it lowered its head. He laughed, assuming this was a hint to scratch behind the ears.

"Aw! She's so sweet!" Chloe cooed. She stroked the thick, leathery hide, surprised that there was no tail.

Murphy hesitantly patted the animal's hump, which was covered in the same brown and grey spots as its peculiar nose and legs. "Does she have a name?"

"I want to name her Myrtle," Jason blurted out.

Murphy chuckled. *Myrtle?*

"What's so funny?"

"I think it suits her," Chloe agreed.

Myrtle suddenly stood up, swaying back and forth. "What's the matter?" Jason asked as she made clicking noises with her tongue.

"She's hungry," Tuk responded.

Chloe looked down and stepped aside. "Oh! Sorry!" She had been blocking the berries.

They watched the tusks open, sucking air into the hollow tubes like a mini vacuum, stretching the stem to its limit until the white fluff popped off and into her mouth.

"We should go now. Our refreshments will be waiting."

...

The path they followed came to an abrupt end, replacing the dirt with polished steps of white stone. It plateaued, then separated into walkways that led to all the mountainous stalagmites, each having its own raised floor. Jason focused on the strange holes chiseled into the tapered rock. "They're Cromalite homes," Tuk pointed out. "They're also the columns that hold the ceiling in place and keep the ground above stable."

Each dwelling had an archway that opened up to a private balcony, but there were no doors to lock. Murphy frowned, wondering how they could feel safe knowing their homes weren't properly secured.

Que sensed Murphy's concern. "You'll notice that all the entrances are out of reach," she explained. "That's purposely done to ensure access is difficult to obtain."

Tuk added, "We do have ladders, though."

"Why, when you could just fly up?"

"We can, but our former family members and friends can't," Que replied.

"It's also necessary when our wet season approaches," Tuk added. "The waters can rise quite high, flooding this area for months."

Que flew in front of Jason. "Be careful," she warned, holding up her hands to stop him from stepping onto a circular disk lining the edge of the platform.

The staggered rows of embedded metal began to howl as a rush of air forced its way up, pushing jets of swirling water through the holes to create a wall of treacherous geysers.

"For security," Tuk said, raising his voice. "They're placed along the entire perimeter of our village." Que joined her brother as he completely submerged himself into the watery tornadoes.

Beyond the water shimmered a pillar that rose slowly from the floor, turning clockwise to reveal an opening. Then suddenly, the water in front of that passage solidified into ice crystals, forming a bridge. As the twins emerged, the remaining waterspouts drained back into the disks. Murphy finally let his breath out when they waved for them to come forward.

"It will be safe to enter now. The waters have identified us as guardians. We have been granted passage."

Murphy looked up at the towering cylindrical doorway, wondering what would have happened if the waters hadn't recognized them.

"Ow!" Chloe remarked as he bumped into her. She bent down and rubbed the arch of her injured foot, noticing gold lettering underneath her. "What is this?" She raised her eyes to see more of the unusual script on the curved walls.

"It's our burial site," Que responded. "The paint is mixed with the ashes of our ancestors. We honour them by writing their names on the pillar's interior.

"It's their spirits that allow entry," Tuk added.

Murphy was the first to exit the tunnel. "Where is everyone?"

"They're down by the water, setting up for the party."

Murphy was relieved. At least they hadn't been abducted.

...

"Where are you taking me?" Gabe demanded as he used his weight to resist the hands that were pushing him toward a set of stairs carved from the same rock that surrounded them.

"Keep going," a young boy responded. Gabe felt a sharp point prodding his back.

"Mother will be very pleased with us," another child boasted.

Gabe couldn't believe what he was hearing. He whirled around, surprising his captors with his quick movement. He gasped, taking in the shocking scene of five kids no older than ten years old carrying weapons in their hands. And they were aimed at him.

"Mother?" he asked. "What kind of sick game are you playing?"

"It's no game. You're our prisoner." All of them leaned forward, ready to attack. He tried to raise his hands to show he wasn't going to challenge them, but the restraints around his wrists flared up again and so he dropped them.

They led him past a number of sealed archways that were covered in thick leaves and thorns before shoving him into an opening that looked similar to the others. As soon as he stumbled through the entry, the fiery binding around his wrists extinguished and left his skin red and blistered. He threw himself at the opening, but before he could reach it, thick vines swiftly grew from the ground up to the ceiling. He slammed his palms on the greenery, gripping and tugging, but the vines were too strong and would not budge. Gabe pulled away, hissing in pain as he turned his hands over to find little drops of blood. He watched helplessly as the vines threaded their branches and sprouted thorns the size of needles to enclose the entire opening.

In frustration, he kicked the growing mass with his heel but fell onto his side when his shoe got punctured and stuck. As he landed, he felt something move from under his shoulder. It let out a yelp. Gabe instantly scrambled to his feet in a defensive position, listening for further movement.

The cell was faintly lit, but he thought he saw what looked like an animal cowering in the corner. He stepped closer but stopped when he heard a growl.

"Hey!" Gabe called. "I didn't mean to hurt you." The animal turned its head toward the friendly voice and panted. That's when Gabe knew it was a dog.

He crouched so he wouldn't intimidate it and put out his hand. "Come on," he said, coaxing the small dog out. It stood and stretched but remained in the hidden shadows, reluctant to leave its space. Gabe thought of the three creatures that could magically transform into a human resembling anyone and figured the animal was just spooked. Finally, the dog sniffed his outstretched hand and wagged its tail. Gabe flipped over the orange tag on its collar and read "Buckles."

Gabe stood as close to the prickly wall as possible, pulling his shoe off and ramming his foot inside. "What have you done with my brother?" He yelled. "Where are they? Where are Murphy and Chloe?"

"Gabe? Is that you?" a desperate voice called out.

"Kelly?"

Gabe heard feet shuffling nearby. "Yes!" she cried out, relieved. "It's me!" She squeezed her arm through the thick greenery, not caring about the scratches that marked her skin. She waved. "Can you see me?"

"No, where are you?"

"Where are *you*? I thought you were here to get us out."

Us? "Who's with you?"

"Mrs. Sheldon, but there are a bunch of teenagers in the other holding cell. They tricked me, Gabe. I thought those *things* were you."

"I know," he answered sadly.

"Gabriel, listen to me," Mrs. Sheldon advised. "We must—" Suddenly there was a commotion at the end of the corridor and Buckles started barking.

"It's your lucky day," a female voice taunted.

"No, no it's not! Pick someone else!" a young male pleaded.

"Oh, we will. We need two of you to make it fair." Gabe could hear the boy being dragged away.

"This is madness! Where am I?"

"It's called the Pit," Mrs. Sheldon said. "We're underground. And I'm afraid that Kelly could be chosen next."

"For what? Why?"

"My, my ..." the female stranger said. "You ask a lot of questions."

"Just answer his questions, Larsi, so the dog can shut up!"

Larsi turned to her brother. "Don't tell me what to do. When I'm ready, I will tell him." .

"Tell me what?" Gabe asked.

"Your girlfriend was just bait. She is expendable now that you're here."

"What do you want from me? I'll do it! Just release Kelly and Mrs. Sheldon."

"Elizabeth will stay with us!" Larsi replied.

Gabe was confused. Wasn't Mrs. Sheldon's name Florence?

"What if I offer a deal?" Mrs. Sheldon suggested.

"What kind?" the brothers asked.

"No deal!" Larsi warned.

Mrs. Sheldon ignored her. "What if *I* battle the Nemmels on my own? Surely *that* would entertain Aldeirah. What do you have to lose?"

"Everything," Larsi replied coldly.

"Wait—" Gabe cut in. "Aldeirah? As in the crazy woman that jumped up on stage yesterday?" He rubbed the side of his face. *This is getting stranger by the minute.*

CHAPTER TWELVE

It occurred to Murphy, as he rested his feet on a stool and slouched down into a big padded chair, that the furniture was designed for humans. He recalled thinking that Quinsatheria would be the size of a mini-putt golf course. "Why is everything made to fit *our* size instead of yours?"

"The furnishings were built by the Xaldorians. They lived in Quinsatheria for centuries."

"What are Xaldorians?" he asked.

"You mean *who* are the Xaldorians," Tuk answered. "They're an ancient race that travelled from another galaxy to make a home here on Earth."

"Martians?" Murphy squeaked, his voice pitching to a higher octave. He turned to Chloe. "See? I *told* you they were living among us! What do they look like? Are they green with bug eyes?"

"Murphy!" Chloe scolded.

"Well, so far my guesses have been pretty close."

"The Xaldorians have the same physical traits as humans but possess higher than average intelligence," Que answered.

"So, basically they're the same," Jason replied, "just smarter."

"With one exception," Tuk continued. "They can manipulate the elements."

"Are those the symbols you showed us on the map?" Jason asked.

The twins nodded.

"Will we get to meet them?"

Que shook her head. "Unfortunately they avoid this area for fear of being discovered. In the past, there were threats to annihilate their kind."

"Why?" Jason asked. "Did they do something awful?"

"No," Tuk replied. "Unless you consider falling in love to be against the law. Then, I suppose …"

Chloe crossed her arms. "What would be so bad about that?"

Que sighed. "As you're aware, Chloe, there are still people out there that are not willing to accept mixed-race relationships. Similarly, Xaldorians believe that infants born from earth and stars are very different and jeopardize the purity of their ancestry."

"But if they look and act the same, what makes them so *different* that humans or Xaldorians would want to destroy innocent lives?" Chloe remarked with a huff. "Why can't everyone just get along?"

Murphy wasn't surprised by her outburst, as she was no stranger to discrimination. "Is it because they're from another planet?" Jason asked. "Or because they have special powers?"

"It's both, actually," Tuk responded. "Their special abilities make them stand out."

"How?"

"When they use any of the four elements to its full potential, their bodies become transparent."

"Like invisible?"

The twins nodded.

"So how does it work?" Jason asked.

"Their power is activated through their forearms," Tuk answered. "Each triangular shape that's exposed on their skin has the ability to draw from a particular element."

Murphy's eyes bulged and Jason quickly turned his attention to Chloe's arms. She looked at them with panic in her eyes.

Jason took her arm. "Take a look at this," he said, pushing her sleeve up to her elbow. "These marks look just like what you described."

Chloe bit her lip, waiting for their reply.

"We're not surprised." Tuk commented. "There's so much more that you need to learn about your family's history, Chloe. Knowing who your grandmother is has been the starting point."

"Is Chloe an alien?" Murphy blurted out.

She snorted. "I was born by Caesarean, not some Martian egg."

"But your mom was unconscious during surgery, so how would she know if you were switched?"

Que covered her mouth to hide a smile. "Unfortunately, we do not have the time to dwell on your past, but Murphy has pointed out something that you and your mother should know."

"You have a twin brother," Tuk stated. "The two of you were separated at birth. A trustworthy nurse placed him in your father's care for safety."

"My dad?" Chloe commented with disgust.

"Despite your disapproval, he is a good father, Chloe."

"Good?" she countered, blinking back tears. "He dumped my mom! He hasn't come around once to see how we're holding up and he's never introduced … whatever his name is."

"It's Zareb," Que quietly offered. "He's wanted to, but exposing your location is risky."

"What is he? A criminal? Is that why you mentioned that love could be against the law?"

"We know you are hurt over this, but please understand that he has had no choice in the matter. Attempting to make any contact would be putting you in harm's way."

"Okay, I get it. For whatever reason, *I'm* the child that needs to be protected. Fine." Chloe splayed out her arms. "Do you have any idea what he put my mom through?"

Chloe wasn't just upset, she was angry. Murphy stepped back to give her more room. He certainly didn't want to step on her foot again.

"Why did he abandon us?" she demanded.

"To save your life. There are repercussions to mating with humans. It can result in the death of them and their children, especially if the human has blood of the First Heirs running through their veins. The power becomes greater if twins are born, becoming a double threat for a proud race that's dying out."

Chloe lowered her eyes and spun her bracelet. "My dad's Xaldorian, isn't he?" The twins nodded, but somehow Chloe already knew.

"Cool! We've got a superhero on our side." Jason cheered.

Chloe sniffled, giving him a weak smile.

Que patted Chloe's shoulder. "It's time for dinner. You'll receive more information at the table."

That's good, Murphy thought. He was curious about the nurse that had intervened, and about Chloe's potential alien powers. Most of all, he wondered if the twins regretted telling her the truth.

...

The table was built from the same iridescent white rock as the security platforms. It was low to the ground and shaped in a continual S pattern, with each indentation having a braided rug made from the leaves of the navy ferns. Each place setting included a gold platter and a metal tool with a pointed end on one side and a flat, hollowed out piece on the other. There were countless dishes in all sorts of sizes steaming with the promise of hot food. Jason's stomach started rumbling.

Murphy noticed that there was a wider gap in the middle accommodating two matching chairs that were molded together like an open book. Chloe's eyes travelled over the complex patterns chiseled into the tall backs.

Que explained that the Ezbragryte's horns were located inside the thrones. "Once the puzzle is completed correctly," she stated, "a lock will appear for the warden's key." Murphy squinted at all the horizontal and vertical lines. It looked impossible to solve. "There's no chance for error," Que continued, "the warden must press their index finger onto the starting position, which will trigger a stream of liquidated silver that will follow the finger's direction. The warden cannot lift their finger or stop moving as they trace an outline. If they succeed, the metal will be absorbed back into the rock, revealing a keyhole. But any misguided turn and the silver will overflow, filling in the maze with an impenetrable casing."

"Shall I begin?" Lu asked, raising his voice to get everyone's attention. The kids quickly found an empty spot on the sand.

There was a definite distinction in the royal wardrobe compared to that of their subjects. All the Cromalites were dressed in simple fashion with tree bark and linen cloths. But the king's garments were made of a silky material, dyed in ink that looked the colour of a night sky. He wore pants and a matching tunic with a high collar made of sage leaves. The queen's attire had more of a fairy look. Her bodice was woven from thin, pliable branches of the pussy willow tree, intricately designed so it knitted together to form a furry layer that covered her from the collarbone to her midriff. Her shoulders were draped in white, lacy foliage, and her full skirt was adorned in blue flower petals that overlapped one another.

Among the unusual garments she wore, her crown was the most unique. It was made of spun gold and shaped into thousands of tiny stars, then molded into one large blooming flower resting on top of her head with its leaves hugging the back of her ears. Her hair was pulled through the middle, rolled into cones and decorated with smooth, coloured stones that came from Xaldorn U-Rion, the doomed planet of the Xaldorians.

Before taking her portion of the feast, U-Dae-Yis stood, closed her eyes and was immediately bathed in a shower of sparkling gold powder that the Cromalites blew on her as a blessing. It was an old ritual using the stamen of the Cromalisum flower because of its ties to their creation. Her skin gleamed in the light, and the gems that dotted the bridge of her nose sparkled too. Nom-Lu didn't have a fancy crown, but he did look every bit as regal with an equal share of gems placed along his cheekbones. He even had the same stones weaved into his gold mesh sleeves, forming stars along the length of his arms.

"Trona," the queen said, extending her arms out, "*joisen tris moplenta dek en-quay ibaz nat.*"

Jason lifted his utensil and hesitated. Tuk gestured to go ahead. "Have as much as you'd like."

"This is really good," Murphy said, popping another stuffed apricot into his mouth. "What is it filled with?"

Lu chuckled. "You speak as if you're surprised to find our food edible."

"I am," Murphy replied. "I thought maybe you ate flies."

Chloe was appalled. "Don't be so rude," she scolded in a hushed voice.

Murphy winced. "Sorry."

Lu waved his hand, dismissing the statement. "No need to be," he remarked. "The paste inside is a mixture of ground almonds and dried cherries."

"What are the brownish bits in these little squares?" Jason asked. He pinched the soft dough, pulling out the unknown ingredient with his fingers and savouring the sweet taste. "They're delicious."

"That's protein," Tuk replied with a mischievous grin.

Jason chewed slowly, waiting for Tuk to elaborate. "These aren't chocolate chips, are they?"

Tuk shook his head. "They're crickets."

Jason opened his mouth, letting the mush roll off his tongue and into his hand.

Que clapped in delight. "It seems my brother has a sense of humour," she chortled, handing him a cloth. "But in all seriousness, we do not eat bugs. That dessert was made from honeyed dates." Jason looked clueless. "They're like giant raisins," she offered.

Tuk erupted into a laugh that created a chain reaction throughout the table. Chloe was the only one silent and lost in thought as she stared at her empty plate.

Jason reached over, heaping a mound of jelly onto a wafer. He plunked it down in front of her. "In case you're hungry, I thought I'd show you how to use this thing."

She rolled her eyes. "Thanks, I think I can man—" She stopped, realizing it had quieted down. A soft humming sound filled the air.

They watched as the sprites formed a line to take part in dumping the contents of their cups into a flute partially filled with a cloudy liquid. U-Dae-Yis slid the glass toward her and the humming ceased. She dipped a finger in the fluid, swirling it around until a torrent of sparkling lights appeared. "*Cheyla!*" she announced, lifting the flute to her lips and emptying the contents in one large gulp. Her whole body began to glow like a beacon, and as she raised her arms, a golden mist circled around her. It formed into a young woman that looked a lot like Chloe would if she were older. The apparition floated toward Chloe and kissed her on the cheek, whispering her name. Then she broke into beams of light. Each sprite withdrew a blue orb from the magical rays and placed it on their heart, where it was immediately absorbed.

Murphy lifted his cup and sniffed at the liquid inside. Was it safe to drink? He wasn't sure, considering what he just witnessed.

"U-Dae-Yis, our mother," the Cromalites chanted in harmony. "We

157

are one with you. For you alone have the gift to bestow life and provide knowledge at our birth, we honour your secrets and promise to fulfill our destinies with skills that keep our survival strong. Forevermore you will be queen, until fate of your departure claims you."

They bowed their heads and slid their crossed fingers across their hearts in an X.

The queen smiled. "We are Cromalites," she announced proudly, "guardians of the horn. Xaldorian blood flows within us, as well as the First Heirs', just as our sacred waters do. All of these components are vital to our survival. We rely on the rich minerals to keep us strong. But the levels are depleting day by day and we will not permit this precious resource to dry up, nor will we be passive in our fight to abolish the evil deeds that Aldeirah has set forth. Today, we will celebrate a new beginning where we rise together and win this battle."

A roar of cheers followed and many Cromalites were eager to share their stories. There was one tale in particular that was quite interesting. It was about the First Heirs, and it started two thousand years ago when the Xaldorians occupied Earth.

"In the beginning, a gathering of humans witnessed a massive rock plummeting from the sky," a sprite named Mitra revealed. "It produced lightning that crackled upon the land with blue light and flames. They watched in fear as strange white capsules hidden in the depths of the meteor suddenly emerged, gliding on the wind with transparent wings that shimmered in the sun. The Xaldorians chose the bottom of Lily Valley to disembark and found themselves greeted by a clan of native people that believed the space travelers were gods. They worshipped the Xaldorians and gave them many gifts, including diamonds, which were used for their carbon to make fuel for their ships.

"For their gratitude, they in turn offered plants and animals from their planet, Xaldorn U-Rion, which flourished and grew on the favourable grounds. This peaceful union continued for centuries until the Ezbragrytes' secret was uncovered. Fearful of their magical steeds becoming extinct, an elder named Sygus Tanu looked to science as a solution and worked endlessly in a lab to produce a new species that could assist with protection. In a fluke experiment, he mixed DNA from the Cromalisum, a flower that possesses mutating cells that can change its structure to fit any environment, and added his own blood.

"At first, the cells multiplied, giving him hope that he had found a solution. But then, the cells shrank and parted, leaving the two different molecules separated. He suspected that in order to graft them together, he needed DNA from an outside source, like human blood. So Sygus Tanu approached the clan leader of the humans and asked if she would give her blood to him for the purpose of creating life. She agreed, but misunderstood when he asked for only a few drops. She ended her life, giving all her blood as a sacrifice."

"Couldn't they have stopped her?" Chloe asked.

"No," Lu replied. "It was too late."

Seeing the shock on their faces, Mitra gave them a reassuring smile. "This is the best part," she replied. "In honour of her selfless act, Sygus Tanu drew blood from his own palm and rested it upon her chest, healing the open wound. To his relief, the woman did not die. Her body had grown a second heart, an exact replica of his. It thrummed in the lower cavity of her ribs, pumping the life back into her human heart. She not only was given a second chance, but his blood gifted her with powers to manipulate all four of the elements. Lay-E-Fenya became the first warden. She is the contributor to our existence and a revered hero. A polished stone commemorates the historical event. It's made from the planetary crystals of Xaldorn U-Rion and the blood of both our ancestors."

Que glanced at Chloe knowingly.

"Is that why you have powers too?" Jason asked.

Mitra nodded. "Yes, but we can only control wind and water. The Tri-Murids have earth and fire."

"I'm confused," Chloe commented, tightening her fist around the key. "Am I warden because I'm partly Xaldorian, or is it because I have First Heir blood in me?"

"Both," the queen answered. "The Wall of Clairvoyance has shown that there is a saviour amongst your family. One who will triumph and—"

"That can't be me, I'm still just a kid!"

The royal couple smiled. "True," Lu agreed, "but you are a powerful one."

CHAPTER THIRTEEN

Duncan felt someone shake him. "Wakey, wakey," they said. He opened one eye and peered up at a child gripping a wooden rod and poking his foot with it. "Get up!" the boy ordered. Duncan lifted his head, but the nauseating rush made him flop back down again. The child groaned in frustration and smacked Duncan's back with the blunt end of the stick. "Move!" he said.

"Shut up and go back to your mommy," Duncan growled. He slowly shifted his weight to one side, leaning heavily on his elbow to prop himself up. His eyes were still closed as he shook his head to clear the dizziness.

"He told you to stand, now do it," an older voice commanded.

Duncan's eyes flew open as a shocking jolt of pain vibrated through his ribs. He rolled onto his feet and quickly grabbed the weapon, pulling the shaft and the child toward him. The handle was curved and wrapped in leather strips, and the tip had two mechanical fingers with wire threaded between them. The boy pulled on a hidden lever beneath his hand, triggering a spark, and the pinchers sizzled to life with electricity. Duncan let go, pushing the child away from him. The boy stumbled sideways, but someone had raised their arm to stop his fall. Duncan peered at the dark silhouette, straining his neck to look down, and was surprised to see Jason's brother kneeling on the ground. He was loosening the vines that were binding his ankles. "Gabe? What are *you* doing here?"

"I could be asking you the same question, but I don't really care. We need to get out of here and find my brother and his friends."

Duncan stepped out of his restraints and kicked then aside. "Why should I help? They're probably the ones that put me here."

Gabe shook his head. "Trust me, they're innocent."

Duncan folded his arms, jerking his chin toward the boy. "Is he with you?"

Gabe nodded. "But there are others, including Kelly and Mrs. Sheldon, who are still locked in their cells."

"Your girlfriend and my teacher are here? What about Chloe, is she a prisoner too?"

"No, but her puppy was in my cell. She's with Jason and Murphy somewhere on this island."

"Did you just say *island*, or am I hearing things?"

Gabe let out a frustrated sigh. "Yes, you heard correctly."

"How did you get out?"

Gabe paused, searching for words that wouldn't sound ridiculous. "Someone created a diversion with fire, I crawled out, using the smoke to conceal my escape."

Duncan was still suspicious. "Where's the dog?"

"He's with Mrs. Sheldon. I didn't want Buckles to give away my location by barking. When I backed up, I bumped into the kid."

"Her magic will protect him," the little warrior commented.

"Whose?" Duncan asked.

"Mrs. Sheldon's," Gabe answered.

"Wha—?"

The boy interrupted, "There's no ti—"

"Hey, whatever your name is," Duncan responded, "don't—"

"He can't remember his name," Gabe replied. "He was only three when Aldeirah kidnapped him."

"Those stories are true?" Duncan rubbed the tender spot on the back of his neck. "That looney bin must've knocked me out and hauled me in here."

"Tell him what you told me," Gabe encouraged, "about the Pit and her slaves."

Duncan swallowed as the boy described the horrors of child labour and deadly games.

"We have to hurry!" the boy pleaded, looking anxiously past the opening. "You need to warn your friends, or we'll all end up captured again."

The thought of being stuck in this place crossed Duncan's mind as he judged the boy's age. He had to be at least seven, which meant he'd spent at least four years of his life surviving in a cave. "Okay, I'm in," he stated.

...

"Prepare the cages," Aldeirah instructed. "And I want the Nemmels to be ready."

"Shall I increase the guards on all exits?" Inek asked.

Aldeirah smirked. "No, let them think they have a chance of getting away. My boy will lead them straight to me."

Inek smiled. "A trap."

"Once our guests are secured, Elizabeth will be furious! She'll try everything in her power to free them."

"But Elizabeth is weak. She had already used her energy to open Gabe's cell."

"Precisely, so there's no need to fret over her interference. She'll be too exhausted to leave after Kelly is freed."

"Then she will search for Gabe," Inek speculated.

"And he will find his brother and friends, making it easy for us to catch them altogether."

"You are very clever, Golden Gem," Inek marvelled.

Aldeirah agreed. Everything was working out just fine.

...

The prison was a labyrinth of polished stone hallways, one corridor connecting to another until they reached a brightly-lit cavern with a domed ceiling. There were heavy chains wrapped around a winch and secured to the wall across from them, holding up a boxed structure made of netting and splintered wood. It looked like a shipping crate.

Gabe surveyed the vast open area that separated them from the other side. The ledge dropped to a dangerous fifty feet or more, curving to a flat bottom made of a strange, orange-coloured sand. There was a mound of rocks placed in the centre and Gabe figured it was there to be pulled out from the makeshift quarry using the lifting device and storage unit.

"That looks like our cells over there," Gabe murmured.

"It is," the boy answered. "We had to go around. Aldeirah purposely blocked the other entrance, so this is the only way in or out."

"Is that the Pit?" Gabe wondered.

Duncan snorted. "Well, unless this is the movie set for Raiders of the lost Ark, then yeah, I'd say it is."

"Don't get smart with me," Gabe warned.

Duncan threw his hands in the air. "Just sayin', it's kinda obvious."

Gabe rolled his eyes.

The boy tapped his foot. "Are you guys done blabbing?"

Gabe chuckled. "Totally."

"Then come on." He waved impatiently. "Violet's waiting for us at the bottom of these steps."

Duncan looked at Gabe for clarification, but he just shrugged. The woman was a mystery to him too.

The boy went first, cautiously looking in both directions. Satisfied that there were no scouts lurking close by, he splayed his hands out to touch the wall for support and shimmied his way along the rock to a hidden staircase. Duncan and Gabe followed, quickly descending the stairs.

The boy slid an enormous bolt from its latch, unlocking a steel grate. He swung it open and warm rays of light greeted them. A woman dressed in beige garments lingered not far from the opening. She was leaning against a burgundy tree with her back facing them. Something about her long golden hair made Gabe's steps falter, and as she turned around, he immediately recognized her.

Gabe grabbed Duncan's shirt from behind, pulling him into the shadows before she saw him. "Wait," he whispered, "it's a trap. That's Ald—"

"No," the boy interrupted, "it's Violet."

Duncan shoved the boy against the wall, pinning his shoulders. He dropped his weapon as Gabe loomed over him, "Tell us what you know," he demanded, "and why you're so eager to hand us over to that woman."

"She's a nurse and she's really nice, I swear!" the boy replied.

Gabe squinted through the murky light, scrutinizing the women's physical appearance. Her entire form was identical to Aldeirah's, proving it difficult to believe the boy. "Go and tell her that you've changed your mind. Let her still think that we're prisoners."

Duncan released his hold and pushed the boy toward the exit. The child turned. "Are you sure you want me to say that?"

He exchanged a short dialogue with the woman, then ran back with the woman trailing behind. "I need to get to those cells!" she said, worried. "Elizabeth is counting on me."

"What if you don't find them?" the boy asked, speaking loud enough for Gabe and Duncan to hear.

"Then she'll need to find another way to get them out."

Gabe had heard enough. He stepped out from the darkness holding the boy's weapon and confronted the woman. Duncan flanked him, gripping a rock in his hand.

The woman was genuinely surprised to find them on the pathway and gasped.

"I'm Violet. You must be Gabe," she stated. "And Duncan. But where is Kelly? She was supposed to be with you."

The boy explained that they'd used their time to pry a hole in Elizabeth's cell for a friend's puppy to fit through, otherwise he would have been left in Gabe's cell alone. Before they could widen it further for the girl to pass through, the scouts had come to douse the flames. "Mrs. Sheldon said a smaller group would be easier to protect anyhow."

"You have done a great job, Jesse," Violet praised.

"That's not my name," the boy said, whirling around to face her.

"It is, and your last name is Malone. I've been searching through health records to find your mother. She is living in—"

"That's super and all," Duncan interrupted, "but we need to get outta here, like now. Or *Jesse* will never get back home. And I personally would like to leave this place sooner rather than later."

"Will Kelly be safe with Mrs. Sheldon?"

"She will. Elizabeth is a powerful woman."

"Yeah, that's an understatement," Gabe admitted. "Can we trust you? I'm assuming you're related to— "

"Aldeirah," Violet revealed, "is my twin sister."

Gabe noticed that Violet walked with a limp, and he was able to quickly move ahead of her. "You didn't answer my question," he responded, motioning to Duncan to block the entrance.

Violet pinched the bridge of her nose. "Of course you can! I've been helping Elizabeth for years."

"Do you have some kind of secret meeting place?" Duncan wondered.

"At Moss Ridge," she answered. "Quite often, my sister would go out into the woods in the evening. She loves when it rains because she can practise her powers without being noticed. But we knew. Lightning comes from the sky, not the earth. If Elizabeth sees anything unusual, she contacts me. Together we've been trying to stop her." She turned sideways, looking in both directions. "What more can I say to change your minds?"

Duncan shrugged.

"How about something personal?" Gabe offered. "Mrs. Sheldon must have filled you in on all our backgrounds, or you wouldn't have known who we were."

"Fair enough," Violet responded. "I know that Duncan's parents are divorced and he lives with his father."

"Big deal," Duncan snorted. "Anyone could've guessed that."

"Your father," she added, "comes from a long line of judges."

"So?"

"One of your ancestors, Russel Burke, became an enemy of my sister. He accepted a bribe that ultimately ruined her life."

"What does this have to do with me?"

"Revenge."

"Why?" Duncan asked.

"Cordelia suffered tremendously because of your great-great-uncle's greed. Her curse involves the bloodline of all family members connected to her past imprisonment, including you."

"But your sister is crazy. She should be locked up."

"I'll admit that I don't agree with her criminal acts. But her reasons are personal, and they make sense to her. She is not well, but this is not her fault. So don't presume that she's always been this way," Violet replied, reigning in her anger.

"So, who's going to protect us from her? You?" Duncan snapped. "'Cause you kinda suck at it."

Jesse backhanded him in the arm. "Stop complaining!" he remarked, then slipped behind Gabe to hide. "She's doing the best she can."

Duncan rolled his eyes. "How come your sister didn't swipe me as kid?" he asked. "Why now, when I'm older?"

"She only wants firstborn children. Your mother had a miscarriage and it took several years before your parents chose to have a second child. When Aldeirah found out, she did attempt—"

"Mum never got over it," Duncan revealed. "She'd rather cradle a bottle of alcohol in her arms now."

"You may have forgotten," Violet responded, "but Elizabeth saved you from being Aldeirah's next victim."

"What happened?"

"There was a parade that day. Your mother was upset because she had to drop off the signed divorce papers at your father's workplace. She held your hand and dragged you through the festival streets, not paying attention to the people around you. Aldeirah pushed her and she released her grip. You quickly got away, squeezing through the crowd and stepping off of the curb right into the path of an oncoming float. Your mother couldn't reach you in time before the platform knocked you down. Elizabeth dove toward the wheels just before it crushed you. She scooped you up and rolled away to safety. Since then, your father—"

"Yeah, I know my own history," Duncan remarked. "My mum is a drunk. Always has been, always will be."

"That's harsh," Gabe commented.

"Don't care."

"Anyhow," Violet said, "I think the information I just gave you is enough to prove I am a friend of Elizabeth's. In fact, that's where I'm heading now. We agreed to meet here, but only the three of you showed up." She walked to the entrance, peered out and returned with a frown. "Something's wrong. She and Kelly should have been here by now." She faced the tunnel, "Jesse can show you out. He knows the way."

Gabe put a hand on Violet's arm to stop her. "You're not going without me," he declared. "That's my girlfriend you're talking about."

"Seriously?" Duncan remarked as they left him standing near the archway. "Don't I get a choice?"

"Sure. It's either me or Aldeirah. Either way, I can't guarantee what will happen."

"Then I'll take my chances," Duncan replied.

"Good, then let's go," Jesse said.

"No," Duncan remarked. "I meant with them."

Jesse stuck his tongue out. "Suit yourself. I'm outta here."

"If I'm following them," Duncan cautioned, jabbing a finger into Jesse's chest, "then you're comin' too."

The boy's shoulders sagged.

"Plus," Duncan added, "you're stating to grow on me, little dweeb."

Jesse spun around, smiling from ear to ear.

...

"You should try and eat more than a pear slice, Chloe. You need to build your strength," U-Dae-Yis remarked.

"I know, but I'm not hungry. I just want to find Buckles and my grandma, then go home."

Tuk looked up at her as she stood. "We'll leave soon to free Elizabeth and your *yuderhund*," he said sincerely.

"When?" Chloe replied, raising her foot to twirl her ankle in circles. "I know we need to learn, but time is slipping away."

Her shadow stretched across the table, then disappeared as she bent down to rub her leg. She was still hunched over when it reappeared, its dark outline spreading into the shape of wings. Chloe rubbed her eyes and sat back down.

The image was gone. No one seemed to have noticed anything different.

"I'm not crying, if that's what you're thinking."

Murphy shrugged, "I wasn't."

"*Ah-choo!*" Chloe looked around. "What's making me sneeze?"

Suddenly, everyone looked up and scrambled away from the table. Four Waek-Lyrens descended upon them from all directions.

"Run to the water!" the queen commanded. "Submerse yourselves as much as ..." Her voice trailed off. One of the creatures had U-Dae-Yis in its grasp. It made three short trumpeting sounds, calling out to the others.

Murphy didn't have to witness what happened next to know that the queen had met her demise. He heard a crunch, then a roar of anguish coming from Lu. For such a little guy, he had a good set of lungs.

Chaos erupted. Jason bolted onto the table, sliding across it to join his friends. "Come on!" he shouted above the noise, pulling Chloe up.

She wrapped her arms around her friends' shoulders, hopping as fast as she could. "Stay here," Jason said, releasing his grip. "I have to help the twins. I think the queen is dead!" He met Murphy's eyes, and for the first time, he looked scared. Then he turned and ran toward the centre of all the fighting.

Murphy shook his head in disbelief. *What is he doing?*

Jason broke one of the tree branches and returned to the area where the twins were battling two of the monsters. He whipped the branch in the air, colliding with one of the wings. It shrieked and circled higher. Jason jumped but couldn't reach it. Murphy cringed as Jason gestured for him to risk wading deeper into the water. Chloe was already feeling uneasy about the depth as the level rose above her waist, and he feared that he'd be unable to keep her afloat.

Jason opened his mouth and yelled something, but a rush of wind drowned it out.

A pair of monstrous wings swooped down and pulled Chloe up as she kicked and screamed. The creature's clawed hands drew her toward its skeletal chest and its ribcage opened, emitting a yellow substance that surrounded her head. All at once, her struggling stopped, and her body went limp.

Murphy *had* to do something. So he rushed to the shore, searching for rocks, but all he found were tiny, smooth stones. He plucked them out of the sandy soil and a feeling that he'd done this before tugged at his memory until his nightmare came into focus. If he was able to successfully blind an evil monster in a dream, then what could prevent him from trying while he was awake? *Actually, there are many possible things*, he thought, but couldn't afford to dwell on them.

The massive wings deflected every pitch he made as its chest cavity encompassed Chloe like a Venus flytrap catching a bug. Thankfully, he saw that Que was coming to his aid.

"*Ma my-ana ki stonis!*" she shouted, skidding across the water with her hands skimming the surface. Droplets of water clung to her arms like magnets, and when she blew on them, they rolled off, turning into snowballs. "Take them," Que offered. "They'll harden as you throw them. Do it now!"

Murphy flung them with all his might, managing to dislodge the nasty appendage that had attached itself to Chloe's eyes for it to see. He hurled another assault—a direct hit to the chest. *Bingo!* The impact jolted the creature and it released Chloe, dropping her into the water below.

"You get Chloe, I'll handle this one," Que ordered.

Murphy dove into the water, pulling Chloe's unconscious body back to shore. "She's not responding!" he wailed, panicking. He sat her up, leaning her body over his shoulder and pounded her back. There was no reaction. "How do I save her?"

"Lay her down and put your ear close to her nose and mouth. Do you feel her breath?"

Murphy shuddered with relief. "I can hear her breathing!"

"Look," Que pointed out, "she has the crescent marks above her brows. The Waek-Lyren must have used her sight to search for the king. Unfortunately, it had time to absorb Chloe's fears. The outcome will have her believing the frightful scenes in her mind are real. We must be ready to comfort her when she awakes.

Super. "How do I—"

Chloe's screaming cut off Murphy's question. She tossed and turned, flailing her arms in front of her. "Don't hurt him!" she pleaded. "Please, I beg you!" Her hands frantically grabbed at something they couldn't see. "Don't you dare come near me!" she hissed, nearly slapping the side of his face.

"Dunk her, Murphy. Hurry!"

"What?"

"Put her head underwater. It's the only way to wake her from the terrors she's having."

Chloe fought him all the way to the water with fists of fury, pummeling his forearms as if he was the bad guy.

"I hope this works," he said, cradling her head in one hand and avoiding her punches with the other.

Chloe's back arched, then relaxed. She sat up, coughing and gagging. "Why am I all wet?"

"Th-the ... creature, it ..." Murphy stammered. "I ... th-thought you were ..."

Chloe hugged him fiercely, whispering, "Thank you. Where are Jason and Tuk?" she asked, twisting the bottom of her shirt to wring it out.

"Tuk is defending the king and Jason is helping him," Que pointed out. "There is only one creature left." Her voice trembled as she continued. "We mustn't lose any more family members."

The kids nodded, understanding her sad predicament. With the queen gone, there would no longer be any Cromalite births. U-Dae-Yis was the only one with the power to create their species.

Chloe gasped. "Fire!"

A small patch of shrubs was burning in the distance. Then a herd of black objects stormed the shore in one large mass.

"The Rinegos!" Murphy muttered.

"They're moving like a shield!" Chloe stated. The Rinegos stood in a row, shaking back and forth like a dog drying off. Their greyish-brown, rope-like tresses began to rise straight up. "And all the Cromalites are behind them."

Que agreed. "Yes, their long hair is covered in tiny hooks, and when they feel threatened, the swirling barbed wire can be quite effective as a barrier."

"Except Jason," Murphy responded, frowning. "He's not covered." Some of the smoke had cleared, revealing a troubling scene. Jason's brother appeared out of nowhere, and it looked like they weren't having the best conversation. In fact, Jason pushed him and darted away, running toward Murphy and Chloe.

"Run!" Jason yelled. "That's not Gabe! It's the Tri-Murids!"

He swerved into the defense line and came back out with one of the animals following, breaking away from the pack. Jason grabbed its hair and pulled himself up, straddling its hump like a camel jockey. But before he could reach them, a tree root lifted from the ground, tripping the animal.

Jason went down with it, pinned underneath. The twins arrived just as the Rinegos got up. The Tri-Murids had trapped them in a ring of fire.

There was a single trumpet sound, and the relentless winged monster opened its talons to grip the hair on the Rinegos. Up and up it went.

"Myrtle!" Jason cried.

The animal's weight was making it difficult to fly and so the monster dropped her. The Rinegos hit the ground with a heavy thud. Chloe clamped her hand over her mouth to stop a scream. "We need to get Jason out," she said, her eyes still fixed on the motionless beast.

"How?" Murphy asked, desperate to find a way. "We're losing the battle."

"Don't you want to help your friend?" the Tri-Murid named Bot taunted.

"Stay where you are!" Jason cautioned. He got down on his knees, grunting with effort. "This is what Aldeirah wants. If we're all together, then she'll win."

"Find Elizabeth," Que urged, keeping her voice low. "Travel through the trees. It's a shorter route to reach the other side of the island."

"What about Myrtle?" Chloe worried. She watched as Jason rested his head against her thick neck, gently stroking her stubby trunk.

Que looked over at the silent heap. "She will heal. I'll personally attend to her. Then I'll join you."

"Shouldn't we wait for Tuk?"

Que shook her head. "He'll stay with Jason. He needs to—"

The fire abruptly went out. Tuk emerged with Mitra and several other Cromalites that had helped to extinguish the flames. Chloe rushed toward him, stepping over the charred ring. "Are you okay?"

Jason stumbled toward her, but Bot threw out his hand, saying something in Quin. They ducked as he flung pieces of bark ripped from the trunks of the blu-sap trees toward them. Mitra blocked Murphy from the onslaught of deadly splinters with a clap of her hands. But the wind she created pushed her further back, leaving him exposed. Bot switched his position, angry that she'd foiled his attack. Chloe tucked her head between her elbows for protection as wood chips pelted her back. Jason slipped in behind her, trying to take the brunt of the painful strike.

"Watch out!" Tuk said, blasting water in Bot's direction. There were too many pieces of wood flying about for him to stop all of them at once.

Jason didn't have time to react as the bark wrapped around his neck like a collar. Tuk braced his legs on Jason's chest and both of them tried to break the hold, but it wouldn't budge. Bot's brother Inek, gathered the discarded bark, and while his adversaries were preoccupied, he immobilized Jason's legs with a fabricated tube made of wood particles.

Que and Tuk charged at the siblings with enough wind to blow down the trees, but the Tri-Murids anticipated their move and lifted the soil to create a whirling mass of orange-coloured dust. The diversion gave Larsi enough time to bind a tree root around Jason's waist. Its tendrils crept up his chest, winding its way around his left arm. Larsi yanked him forward and Jason had no choice but to hop toward her.

Chloe's fists balled up. "You jerks!" she yelled. "Leave him alone!"

Tuk intervened as she stomped forward. "I'll handle this," he replied, shooting blasts of water toward the two brothers. Again, Bot and Inek countered the blow with heat and the water vaporized into steam.

"The female is getting away!" Chloe shouted.

The surviving Waek-Lyren followed her, and as it lunged for its victim, the sky lit up with a red glow as Larsi propelled a glowing rock toward it. It fell into the water, flames and smoke trailing in a spiral decent.

"Mitra!" Lu called out. "Go after her!" She nodded and flew away.

"No, you won't!" Inek informed. "Or I will burn this human alive." He proved his point by making the root surrounding Jason's waist flicker with sparks. Jason struggled against the restraints, but the more he moved, the tighter Inek made them. He winced as the root dug deeper into his stomach and his neck began to turn crimson. He pulled at the collar with his free arm, gasping for air as it choked him. "*Flit-wik,*" Inek said with a sneer as flames sprouted from the root. Jason let go and deliberately tipped to the side, falling to the ground and rolling over to smother the fire. He hissed in pain as his right hand touched the tender skin under his singed shirt.

"Stop it!" Chloe screamed. "Aldeirah wants me, not him. Take me instead!" she demanded.

"Now look what you did!" Bot scolded his brother. "If the boy is damaged, the Golden Gem will not be pleased."

"Chloe isn't going anywhere with the two of you," Jason remarked. "It's just me or no one at all."

"We're not here to negotiate," Bot responded, "all three of you must come with us. We will inform Aldeirah—"

"I don't think so," Jason growled.

Soon after he boldly objected, Que returned with Myrtle. Resting on her back was Larsi, frozen with a surprised expression on her face. Que winked at her brother.

"Your efforts are noble," Inek quipped, "but they're all in vain."

Tuk raised an eyebrow, and before he could react, Inek lifted the soil from underneath Myrtle's feet. The Rinegos teetered as she tried to gain her balance and the block of ice that incased Larsi slid off her back. Inek and Bot blasted their frozen sibling with heat, melting the ice in a matter of seconds before she even touched the ground.

Chloe rushed toward Bot, but he quickly moved out of her grasp. "I dare you," he mocked as she got closer. A globe of fire ignited in his hand and he threw it up in the air, catching it in his palm as if it were a ball. He threw it in Jason's direction.

Murphy's legs wobbled as he watched the glow of flames hover in front of Jason, waiting to finish the task of lighting his friend up like a matchstick. Chloe bellowed, ignoring Bot's threat, and charged sideways into him. She knocked him back, but he quickly recovered.

"It seems the great-great-granddaughter has a mean temper."

"You haven't seen anything yet," Chloe snarled, lunging for Larsi.

"No!" Murphy yelled out, trying to grab her. But he let go when Chloe's forearms radiated a brilliant light. "*Flit-wik* or *my-ana?*"

"Huh?"

"Fire or water?" she repeated impatiently.

"I don't know!"

"Just pick one!"

"Ah, water, I guess!"

Chloe focused all her strength on the leader.

Larsi started to back up into the charred circle. "Now, you don't want to try that," she warned.

"Why not?" Chloe responded. Her arms were shaking. Flashes of orange and blue were pulsating underneath her skin like traffic lights. "Are you scared that I might kick your butt?"

"On the contrary," Larsi smirked. "You've just proven what you're capable of, but your weakness is not knowing how to control it. The Golden Gem had hoped for this." She turned her back, drawing a triangle in the air, uttering "*Osnow eno nef tris lis.*" The shape erupted into flames. She and her brothers picked Jason up and hurled him into the magical gate. Tuk followed without being noticed.

Then *poof!* They were gone.

"*Sel-clo min li,*" Que whispered sadly. "I have failed the queen, your friend and my brother. *Na omat del sawa.*"

"It's not your fault," Chloe and Murphy replied in unison.

CHAPTER FOURTEEN

Chloe sat on top of Myrtle, patting her side. "Come on, Murphy. Just pull yourself up."

"What if she bites me? I could get rabies and—"

Chloe rolled her eyes. "Unless an eyeball pops out from the lump on your forehead," she replied, "I'm not too concerned."

"Gee, I'm so glad you care," Murphy said, swinging a leg over the backside. It wasn't the most graceful mount, but he managed.

Que giggled. "Need help?"

Chloe twisted around to see that Murphy had positioned himself backwards. She laughed. "You'd never make it as a cowboy, that's for sure."

Myrtle's head suddenly retreated inside her body like a turtle's, then emerged facing Murphy's direction. "Hey!" Chloe objected. "No fair!"

"Whoa! This gives a whole new meaning to *butthead*," Murphy commented.

Que chuckled. "Their limbs are double-jointed as well," she described, "which enables them to reposition without the need to physically turn around."

Murphy smiled, imagining the surprise on an enemy's face.

"May I try to open a gate?" Chloe asked.

Que nodded. "Focus your attention on the spot you wish to enter, say

175

the words and draw the gate. You will feel a prickling as the power flows to your arms. Concentrate on the element you choose, and that energy will obey."

"*Osnow tris li*," Chloe uttered, picturing the farthest stalagmite peeking above the trees from the opposite side of the island. She drew two connecting lines from the ground to accommodate Myrtle's size. Blu-sap leaves immediately sprouted from the green illumination and formed a triangle with its interlacing stems.

Murphy's mouth dropped open.

"Impressive," Que remarked. "Your grandmother will be proud."

"Then let's go rescue her and show Aldeirah what I'm made of."

"Yay," Murphy responded, stepping through the gate Chloe had made.

···

Jason tumbled out of the gate and rolled to a stop at Aldeirah's feet. "I see that you did not come alone," she said.

"Where do you want me to stick this pest?" Bot asked, holding out an iron cage. Tuk's hands rattled the bars but he was unable to pull them apart.

"Along the wall, and make sure there's enough *tarna* to glue his wings to the rock. I will not be happy if he pries himself loose and goes free.

"*Reta-vem tris bae-yads*," she said, stepping away as the bark that securely bound Jason crumbled to wood pulp. He tried to swallow but coughed instead, sending a wrath of searing pain to his dry throat. He sat back on his haunches, glaring at his captors in silent fury.

···

"Are we getting close?" Duncan asked as they were nearing a bend. "Or are we just going in circles?"

Violet ignored his complaints.

"Shhh!" Gabe responded. "I hear someone."

Violet held her hand up, motioning them to stay where they were. She slid along the wall, glancing out as it became an opening, then quickly retracted her head and raced back to the boys with her heart pounding.

"What did you see?" Gabe asked.

"Aldeirah and the triplets," she said. "She has your—"

"Why don't you pick on someone your own size!" a boy demanded. His speech was hoarse.

"I know that voice," Duncan announced.

"So do I—that's my brother!"

Gabe rushed past Violet.

"No! Wait!" she pleaded, reaching out, but her fingers only skimmed his jacket.

"Uh-oh," Jesse murmured. "We're in big trouble now."

Gabe ran out into a brightly-lit open space. He recognized it immediately as the floor of the Pit. He whirled around anxiously, searching for Jason. Narrow stone ledges jutted out from the holes that were chiseled into the rock. Each one had thorny vines strewn across its opening like iron bars. He peered up, knowing that those prison cells held Kelly, Mrs. Sheldon and countless other victims, including Jason and his friends.

"Jason!" he shouted, not caring about his own safety.

Jason's face appeared over a flat plateau. He was on his hands and knees. "Gabe? Is that really you?"

"Yeah, it's me! What's going on here?"

"Why don't you come over and find out!" piped Larsi.

"Indeed," Aldeirah remarked, extending her arms out, "You are welcome to stay here in my game room." Gabe suddenly felt the rust-coloured stones shifting under his feet as he sank knee deep into the soil. It was swallowing him like quicksand. "In fact," she said, "I insist."

Violet came out of hiding. "Stop, Cordelia!" she yelled. "This young man has nothing to do with your past!" She gripped Gabe's hands and pulled him out.

"I beg to differ," Aldeirah responded. "But I will let him leave … on one condition."

"Name it," Gabe replied.

Violet shook her head. "Don't give in to her demands."

Gabe gritted his teeth. "What should I do then?"

"Suggest that *if* you win, she must release Jason as well."

"*If*? Are you telling me that I could lose this game?"

"I'm hoping you won't, with my help, but there's always a slight chance that—"

"Hey!" Duncan interrupted, waving his arms in the air. "I'm not with these people!" He walked across to the other side and stood below the plateau, looking up. "If you've got a beef with them, fine. I don't want to get involved. Just let me go, or—"

"Or what?" Larsi's eyes widened with interest.

"Let him finish!" Aldeirah snapped.

"Or I'll have my dad … sue you for …" His words faltered. He couldn't think of anything to threaten her with. "He'll put you in jail," he finally blurted out.

"Well," Aldeirah laughed, "that certainly would be a déjà vu."

"I think we should make *him* go first," Larsi suggested.

"I agree," Aldeirah answered. "Inek, did you prepare the cage?"

"Yes."

Duncan turned side to side, watching as the sand gathered beneath his feet and raised him up to Aldeirah's level.

Violet dropped her head and closed her eyes. She inhaled a deep breath, slowly blowing it out as she focused her energy on Duncan's back. Gabe shuffled to the side as Violet's skin began to glow white. She lowered her hands, then lifted them high above her and swiftly brought them down to her sides, creating flight. Violet was in the air, balancing perfectly on a jet stream that Gabe couldn't see. She landed near the crate, thrusting her hands out to stop Aldeirah from throwing Duncan inside. The crate, Gabe realized, was not for loading cargo. It was meant to be a cage.

Duncan hunched forward as his clothes whipped behind him from the force of wind that Violet was creating through her fingers. She slashed back and forth, attempting to penetrate the barrier Aldeirah had made by pulling rock from the wall.

Jesse was watching from a safe distance. He still kept to the shadows because he'd be punished if Aldeirah found him with the enemy. But when he saw that she could stack rock so easily and it stayed in place, he wondered why she made all of the older kids work so hard to build her a dam. He slammed the side of his fist against the wall. *She is so mean!*

Then he heard a scream. He backed away from the shadows and looked up at the battle taking place. Violet was tearing the rocks away piece by piece with shots of water. But her skin was becoming transparent, and

Jesse could only guess that this wasn't a good sign as Aldeirah countered the blows with her own wind power. The cage behind Violet rocked violently back and forth, jostling the occupant inside until the side barrier broke and a boy slid out. He dangled precariously upside down with his leg caught in a wooden slat.

Jesse's face paled. *That's Brandon!* He left the security of the tunnels and joined Gabe, pointing out his friend. "Can you save him?" he begged. "He helped me."

Gabe shook his head sadly, seeing Jesse's desperation. "I'm sorry, but I can't fly."

...

Chloe broke the silence as they trotted through the gate. "Thanks for pulling me out of the water. You actually saved my life!"

"You're welcome," Murphy replied. "I'm just glad that I didn't have to kiss you."

"What?" Chloe asked, intrigued.

"You know, the mouth-to-mouth rescue thing."

Chloe chuckled. "That's called CPR, not smooching. You've got to tilt the head back, pinch the nose and blow a puff of air into the lungs."

"How do you know all this? Been practising on someone?" he teased.

Chloe rolled her eyes. "No, goofball. I learned from Mr. Tremblay."

"Huh. Where was I?"

Chloe shrugged. "Probably hiding."

Yeah, Murphy thought, *that sounds about right.*

...

"Can you run fast?" Jesse asked.

"I suppose," Gabe responded. "Why?"

"I can get you up there," Jesse said, jerking his chin toward the prison cells, "but you have to promise that you'll rescue Brandon."

"I can't promise," Gabe replied, watching the cage swing like an amusement ride, "but I'll try." He recognized that Brandon was the unwilling participant pulled from his cell.

Taking the steps two at a time, Gabe reached the plateau and dove for the handle that operated the winch. He had to use two hands to turn it, but the cage finally came to a halt, leveling off at the plateau. Brandon's unconscious body sprawled across the smooth floor. Gabe untangled his leg from the boards and pulled him down.

"Thank you." Jesse wept, hugging Gabe.

"Take him out of here and hide," Gabe instructed. Then he darted away before Jesse had a chance to warn him that a mob of children were rushing up the stairs. He had no choice but to stay where he was. He couldn't drag his friend down the steps when the only way out was blocked.

"About time!" Bot complained, jumping down from the cage and surprising Jesse. "Take the prisoners to their cells," he ordered, dismissing all them but Duncan. "Except this one."

"Me?" Duncan pointed to himself, suspicious of the decision. "Why not choose one of them?" he asked, jerking his chin toward the young boys.

Gabe strode toward him, annoyed.

"You aren't as useful to us as they are," Inek responded. "Once your friends show up—"

"What friends?"

Gabe chuckled. "Exactly. He has no friends, so they won't come around to look for him. Let Duncan go. Murphy and Chloe will come for us."

Duncan grumbled but didn't argue.

"Jason would be a fitting match for the smart-mouthed kid," Inek suggested.

"And a good replacement for Brandon," Bot added.

"True," Aldeirah responded, "but I'm afraid he will rebel and forfeit the game by refusing to play."

"Then he will lose and die. Isn't that what you want?" Bot asked.

"No," Aldeirah replied. "I need him alive. At least until my great-great-granddaughter arrives."

"Mother!" a young girl shouted, breaking through the crowd of kids. "They're here!" She panted. "Chloe is with Que and her friend."

"Splendid," Aldeirah said, stroking the child's hair fondly. "I will see to it that they have a proper welcome."

...

"Ahhh! Where is Elizabeth?" Larsi screamed, searching her cell. "Where are *all* the prisoners?"

"They can't be far," Inek responded, looking at the charred remains of the thorny vines. They were still smoking. "Her cell is still hot."

"Spread out and find them. I'll deal with her personally." Larsi stormed off, leaving Bot and Inek with the job of restraining Gabe, Jesse and Brandon by any means necessary.

"Why does she keep leaving us to finish all the work?" Bot asked.

Inek shrugged. "Your guess is as good as mine."

Gabe roared with anger, but the long blades of grass wrapped tightly around his mouth muffled his voice. The binding covered his body, leaving only his nose exposed as he thrashed on the floor to try and loosen the cocoon-like casing. Jesse's eyes welled up with tears, pleading for mercy while Bot formed cuffs around his small wrists. He and Brandon were bound together with the same thorny vines, and each time either one of them moved, the binding would dig painfully into their skin. Inek made sure that no one would be able to shout for help, let alone whimper. They too had their voices muzzled.

"Done," Bot said, satisfied. "Now let's catch up with Larsi."

Inek shook his head. "I'm not wasting my time looking for her. Go if you'd like, but I'm heading to the games."

"Wise choice, brother. I think I will join you. Larsi is much better at hunting anyhow."

Inek smiled. "Larsi isn't the only one with brains in the family."

...

"Is it just me, or is the sky getting darker?" Murphy asked.

Chloe raised her eyes to the ceiling, frowning. "Looks like it. And it's getting warmer too. That's strange."

"True, but it's not impossible," Que replied, flying higher and searching the immediate area. "We haven't had weather changes since ..." She paused a moment as the cloudy grey mist rumbled like thunder. "Since Cordelia first made a home here."

Chloe saw a flash of light passing through the dense foliage. "Was that lightning?"

"Aldeirah must be close." Que nodded. "She knows we are here."

"But how?"

"Her scouts."

"Jason's somewhere in that compound, isn't he?" Murphy commented, looking toward the clearing that revealed a collection of black, mirrored domes resting on top of one another like a stack of inverted bowls. "And that's where you're taking us."

"Yes," Que said, "but we must go on foot from here as Myrtle's size is too noticeable."

Chloe slid off the beast first, hugging her. "You'll be safer here," she said, rubbing the Rinegos's neck. Myrtle hummed, swaying from foot to foot. Murphy jumped off, smacking both of his hands onto the unforgiving hard ground.

"She senses that someone is near. Go to the dam and hide!"

They ran to the wall made of stones and mortar. It towered over them, providing some protection at the base where the darkness lingered. They crouched down into the shadows, waiting for further instruction.

"Maybe, Myrtle's wrong," Murphy remarked. "No one seems to be out here."

"I don't think so. Animals have better—"

"Hearing?" Larsi offered, looking down at them from the top of the dam. She smiled. "Gotcha!"

They scrambled away from the wall, but she split into two and grew taller, blocking their escape.

"Now why would the guests of honour try to run away?" Larsi said, tapping Chloe on the nose.

Chloe swiped her hand away. "Where is my puppy?" she demanded, stepping closer to challenge one of Larsi's doubles.

"The *yuderhund*?" Larsi asked, backing up. "Oh, he's with your grandmother."

Chloe's fists balled up. "Take me to them!"

Larsi's duplicate images disappeared. "I can't," she replied.

"Why not?" Chloe insisted.

"Watch out!" Que warned.

A green glow suddenly appeared, forming a vertical line on top of the wall. It stretched out as Elizabeth slid through. "Because Larsi didn't know where I was."

Que relaxed, lowering her arms.

"Grandma?"

"Mrs. Sheldon? You escaped?"

"Buckles!" Chloe screeched, scooping up the dog from their teacher's arms. He growled as she turned to face the Tri-Murid.

"Keep that beast away from me!" Larsi warned, wiggling her fingers to create sparks. "He bit me!"

"You probably deserved it."

"Where is Jason?" Elizabeth asked.

"In the Pit, and Gabe is in one of the holding cells," Larsi answered.

"Gabe is here?" Chloe asked, confused.

Larsi nodded. "And so was his girlfriend."

"Kelly?" Murphy blurted out. "What do you mean by *was*?"

"She's gone back home," Elizabeth replied. "Larsi helped her escape."

Whoa, didn't see that coming, Murphy thought.

Chloe looked puzzled, "Why?"

Larsi shrugged. "Because I'm tired of serving the Golden Gem. She is not who I believed her to be, so I'm trying to help mend all her wrong deeds."

"Larsi is a good actress," Elizabeth said. "Even her brothers aren't aware she's a renegade."

Murphy nodded. "Very convincing."

"When we first met Cordelia Miller," Larsi explained, as Chloe's eyes lit up recognizing the surname, "she understood how it felt to be shunned and judged unfairly. Our queen doesn't consider us to be Cromalites because we're born genetically altered. We wanted change because *we* were changing, but she refuses to modify the old ways. So, my species joined Cordelia, making up our own rules and honouring her with the title of Aldeirah, the Golden Gem. She was supposed to be our mentor, the hero that would bring all species together for a greater purpose. But it didn't last. Vengeance is only thing she cares about now. The Tri-Murids are just as much slaves to her cause as the children she imprisons."

"She's mentally ill," Mrs. Sheldon added.

"Isn't that hereditary?" Murphy chortled as Chloe shoved him away.

Elizabeth was about to respond when she caught movement further down the tree line. "What are they doing out here?"

"Who?" Chloe and Murphy asked in unison.

"Nemmels."

Larsi pulled herself up onto the dam, watching Myrtle's hair spike into a defensive shield. "They aren't supposed to be out; they hate the bright ..." She realized the sky had darkened "Light ... Oh ..."

Murphy held his breath as Myrtle galloped toward the albino monsters that crept out of the woods. Buckles wiggled in Chloe's arms, barking.

"Get behind us," Larsi instructed as she used her index finger to draw several flaming cylinders. The lanterns formed a protective arc, hovering on the wind that Elizabeth provided. The Nemmels approached but did not cross the fiery barrier.

"There's more!" Chloe shouted, pointing at the wall. "Look!"

Que flew past them with her cheeks fully expanded and met the slew of Nemmels crawling over the ledge with a blast of cold air. They slipped on the thin ice and fell back into the water contained by the dam.

"Hurry!" Que said, waving the kids over. "Larsi, use your—"

"I'm on it," she finished, blasting a ray of heat across the top of the wall.

Elizabeth clasped her hands together, creating a pocket. "Put your foot in here and I'll boost you up."

Chloe took Murphy's hand, and as he pulled her over, Buckles growled. "It's only me," he said, patting the dog.

Chloe's eyes widened and she shook her head slowly. Murphy turned just as black claws reached out and clutched a fistful of his hair. The Nemmel dragged him closer and seized his neck in a death grip. Chloe set Buckles down and he lunged for the Nemmel's ankle, gnawing at the wiry hairs covering its skinny leg, allowing Murphy to breathe again as it bent over to pry Buckles off with both hands.

"*Lif-ris!*" Chloe ordered, recalling the name of the dark blue fern as she summoned her powers. She wove a circle of leaves around its eyes, giving Buckles time to jump away while it was blinded. Murphy swung his leg out, replicating the branch-cutting high kick that Jason demonstrated in the valley and it stumbled backwards, toppling on its side.

"We're surrounded!" Chloe cried out, looking in both directions as Que and Larsi battled the creatures on either side. Elizabeth hurdled over the fallen Nemmel, reaching them in one giant leap. She grabbed their arms. "Hold on tight," she advised, then ran right off the ledge.

Murphy didn't have time to scream as they plunged into the deep, dark water.

...

Kelly moved slowly, holding onto one child and leading thirteen others through a flooded street littered with debris. Her legs were scratched, and her feet were aching from walking barefoot. She didn't want to think about the sewage they were wading in and what infections it would cause later. She just wanted to go home. But first, she had to drop off the children at the police station. It was a promise she'd made to Mrs. Sheldon.

There was shouting in the streets, looting and more fires. She picked up her pace, swinging the young girl onto her back. "We need to hurry," she called out. "There are only two more blocks to go. Then you'll be safe."

The children followed without complaint.

She ripped at the tattered bottom of her dress, tying the strips around the children's noses and mouths as clouds of smoke hung in the air. One block to go.

She coughed and squinted through her dirty contacts, trying to focus on something dark that moved along the side wall of the Justice Department. She could have sworn the shadow was as large as a hippo, but disregarded it as exhaustion set in.

As she tugged open the automatic door, a rush of heat overwhelmed her. The building inside was a carcass of smouldering embers. Kelly whimpered as three pink creatures greeted her, claiming they were newborns and introducing themselves as Teja, Vymus and Zubi.

The Tri-Murids left her on the steps crying as they gleefully morphed into one being and ran away.

An older child tapped her on the shoulder, pointing to the shadow that she'd seen just a moment ago. Kelly gasped as it came out of hiding and headed toward them.

"Helper," the child said as the Rinegos approached with caution.

...

Jason gripped the bottom wooden plank as the cage tilted up once again. He was getting irritated by Duncan's nervous pacing each time he left his side. "Would you *please* stay in one spot? You're making this contraption unbalanced."

"Can't help it. I'm thinking," Duncan replied.

"Well, do your thinking over there."

Duncan sat in the corner, scowling. "Are we gonna die?"

"I don't plan to," Jason responded, waving to Mitra as she motioned him to get ready.

"What are you doin'?"

"Bracing for impact."

"What?"

Mitra whistled. Its shrill sound echoed throughout the cave. The kids guarding the winch stood up, searching in every direction for the cause of the noise.

"Over here!" she hinted. The two children left their post to investigate, peering over the edge of the plateau. Mitra popped up suddenly with a mocking grin, startling both of them. She pinched her nose. "You two stink," she said.

They looked at her, baffled.

"Time for a shower!" She opened her palms, releasing a spray of water that drenched the kids in a cascade of glowing blues. Mitra quickly froze the winch's handle and chains into one solid piece, then proceeded to pull Tuk free. He pushed against the sticky *tarna*, stretching it thin as Mitra tugged. But his wings were saturated in the syrup and they tore from his back when he fell away, losing his ability to fly. He had no choice but to flee on foot, hoping to find help through a gate that had not been used in years.

"Great, now we're stuck up here," Duncan complained, watching the children scurry away to search for something else to do. The whole mechanism was useless now.

"Just wait," Jason replied. "They're coming back."

Sure enough, the kids returned with tools to chip away the ice. Once the handle was exposed, they tried turning it. It groaned in protest, snapping in half and unravelling the chains. The cage hit the ground with such force that the side tore open, ejecting Duncan two meters before he landed. He moaned as he rolled onto his knees, crawling over to Jason. He shook his shoulder. Blood oozed from Jason's ear. "Tremblay?"

Jason didn't move.

...

"Cordelia ..."

"You called?" Aldeirah asked, striding over to her sister, who was shackled to the wall with metal clasps. They crisscrossed over her shoulder and under her arms, leaving her feet to dangle freely. Aldeirah smiled broadly, knowing Violet could not escape but struggled against the iron anyhow. It was clever of her to use the natural magnetic field that the rocks emitted, as it seemed to have a negative effect on her sister's energy.

"Stop this idea that vengeance will give you peace of mind," Violet reasoned. "It won't. You know I'm right, because no matter how many terrible deeds you've done, Charlotte is still gone, and your misery remains. We've lived a longer life—"

Suddenly Aldeirah was in Violet's face, snarling. "Don't you dare try and downplay my misery!" she hissed.

"Wh-what are you doing?"

"Something I should have finished years ago."

"Cordelia, *please*! This is madness! Can't you see that?"

Aldeirah ignored her as she piled sticks beneath Violet's feet. "Now," she declared, seething in anger, "you can be the witch on trial and suffer with agonizing pain." She formed a cup with her hands, letting the ball of fire roll off her fingers.

...

Murphy held his breath as they were sucked into an invisible vacuum. A blur of grey swirled all around him as Nemmels dove into the whirlpool to pursue them. His lungs were about to burst when suddenly the water stopped, dropping him, Chloe and Buckles in a free fall where they collapsed on top of two Nemmels that had survived the torrent plunge. They hissed and squirmed under their weight.

Chloe heaved herself off of Murphy, letting Buckles jump down on his own.

Murphy took a ragged breath, watching the creatures fail in their attempts to turn over. "How did—?"

"Air bubble," she answered. Buckles's tail wagged proudly.

"Something's burning," Elizabeth remarked from the opposite corridor. She jogged the last few meters to join them, passing by the Nemmels while freezing their extremities to the floor. Her face had paled from the exertion and she leaned against the wall as a white aura wavered around her.

Chloe worried, *She's using too much energy.*

"Keep low to the ground," Elizabeth instructed, "and follow my lead." She crept along the wall and listened as a muffled voice grew louder and more terrified. She sprinted ahead and gasped at the scene. Violet was trapped, pleading for help.

Orange flames had consumed most of the twigs that were stacked underneath her. She had her legs tucked to her chest and her face was slick from perspiring. She strained against the metal bindings, but the heat made it unbearable to touch.

Elizabeth blasted the metal with ice, weakening the prison bars. Then she created a thick wooden pole, swinging it with enough force that it smashed through the iron. She dropped her battering ram and extinguished the fire.

"Thank you," Violet choked as her great niece tore her gag off. Elizabeth cooled the restraints and pulled. The clamps sizzled beneath her fingers. She let go, frustrated and tired.

"Chloe, I need your help."

Elizabeth had turned ghostly white. Chloe trembled as her grandmother took her hand, covered it with her own and placed both of theirs on top of Violet's.

"*Eko lit ma,*" she uttered, and Violet repeated the words over and over again until her body glowed and rippled with four distinct colours. She began to shrink, or rather transform into a little girl. Her small arms slipped through the claps easily and Elizabeth caught her as she fell.

"I'm Violet, Cordelia's twin sister," she revealed, dusting the soot off her pant legs. She murmured something in Quin and the rainbow faded from her skin as she changed back into an adult.

"Are you well enough to walk?" Elizabeth asked, feeling much better after Chloe's energy had pulsed through her.

Violet nodded. "I may be old, but I still can outrun you," she joked, but then her tone turned serious. "I've found the Ezbragrytes. They're in a pen not too far from here." There was a silent exchange before she continued. "It may be our only way to end this battle."

One by one they followed Violet through the maze. Murphy shivered as an eerie feeling came over him. It seemed he had been down this path before.

"Through here," Violet urged, pushing against a crack in the wall. The stone screeched as she slid it open. The stench hit Murphy with a walloping punch as a warm breeze carried the scent of feces and dead grass. *Ah, the wonderful aroma of farmland.*

Chloe squeezed through, wanting to be the first to see them. "It looks empty," she announced. "Where did they go?"

Violet chuckled. "Look harder. They're along the metal fence." She pointed to a heap of tan and yellow lumps.

"Still don't see them," Murphy stated, walking further into the mucky enclosure. He nudged one of the hay piles then flinched when it bleated and stood up. "Holy cow! They *really* blend in."

Elizabeth agreed. "They have full camouflage protection. The stripes enable them to hide unnoticed in any environment."

"Like a chameleon," Chloe replied. Their long ears twitched as she squatted to their level. She gently touched one underneath its beard and began scratching its chin.

Murphy approached one of the goat-sized animals and patted the bristly fur on its head, noticing an indent on the crown. *This must be where its horn was.* Murphy stepped back as it shyly pulled away. Its slender tail vibrated, indicating its anxiety as the tuft of fur at the end shook.

"Where's Buckles?" he asked, suddenly panicked.

"I have him," Elizabeth said. "I'm keeping watch out here."

Violet dug her hand into the soil, grimacing as she yanked a thick, gnarly root out of the ground and wrapped it around an iron post. She raised her arms, lifting the spidery network of tree growth above her head. The fence toppled like dominoes as the posts were ripped from the foundation, dangling on the roots like loose teeth.

Thankfully, the Ezbragrytes didn't waste any time escaping through the gap, and then the fence came crashing down. A group of Tri-Murids gathered on the other side, surprising Violet. Elizabeth placed Buckles between her feet and then raised both arms. But before she could react, a slew of children marched from the wooded area with weapons and joined the triplet brigade.

"You don't want to hurt *them,* do you?" the female Tri-Murid taunted.

Chloe glared at her, feeling foolish that she had fallen for a traitor's lies. But as the female hopped over the broken pen, Chloe could see that it wasn't Larsi. She remembered that this Tri-Murid had distinctive markings. She was the one that had fought the twins at the gate in Lily Valley. *Where is Larsi, anyhow?*

"Surrender! There is no es—"

Elizabeth broke in: "Are the boys safe?"

"For now," Teja replied.

"Gather them together and take us to them. I want to judge for myself."

Chloe protested, "But—"

Elizabeth turned to her granddaughter and tapped her temple. "You know what to use when the time is right."

The infamous key. Right.

"Does that include Jason, Gabe *and* Larsi?"

"All of them," Violet insisted, "including Jesse, Brandon and Duncan."

Murphy's mouth fell open. *Say what?*

CHAPTER FIFTEEN

Buckles whined as Chloe looped a vine around his collar. She tugged at the leash, but he resisted, splaying all four paws out in a stubborn show of defiance. His tail wagged excitedly as he sniffed the air, sensing that Que was hovering behind Murphy.

Que whispered in Murphy's ear. "Can you make a diversion?" He nodded and she flew back into the shadows.

"Hey Chloe!" he shouted. "Do you still have the magical key?"

Chloe spun around. "I don't know what you're talking about," she responded, shushing him.

"You know," Murphy said, raising his voice, "the one that grants wishes?"

That did it. Their line suddenly stopped, and Chloe's irritation rose. "Are you insane?" she hissed.

"Must be," he said, grabbing the chain around her neck and breaking it. "Who wants their dreams to—"

"Me!" a child hollered.

"No, *me!*" a few others yelled. Soon after, a fight broke out in the corridor.

Murphy unthreaded the key from the chain. "Here, take it!" He threw it as far as he could. "Good luck!"

Chloe screamed and punched him square in the jaw. "Ow!" He rubbed his chin, then opened his palm, showing her that he still had the heirloom.

"My mom is going to flip when she finds out I lost the house key."

Chloe bit her lip. "Sorry about that."

Buckles barked again and Que flew into focus. "*Osnow tris li!*" The end of the tunnel lit up and a blue haze painted the walls. Murphy grabbed Chloe's wrist, but she gently pried his hand off. "We can't leave without our friends."

Murphy wasn't sure if he felt ill because of guilt or dread, but she was right again.

Elizabeth stormed up to them. "What in the world—"

Murphy held up the *kusoa*, "I gave them a fake." Her shoulders sagged with relief.

"They're getting away!" Vymus announced, seeing a blue triangle open beyond their reach.

"No, they won't!" a child remarked. "I have the key!"

Murphy looked at Chloe. "Uh-oh."

The young boy squeezed his eyes shut, then opened them. "It worked!" he squealed. "The gate is closing!"

"Is that all you wanted?" Zubi said, swiping the key from the child's hand. "Let me show you what this can do."

Suddenly the walls crackled with ice as a blast of frigid air pushed its way toward them. A small iron cage with Mitra inside glided through the dense mist, followed by Gabe, two young boys and Aldeirah.

Violet looked both ways. They were trapped.

"Bonus," the Tri-Murid remarked.

...

"Where is my brother?" Que demanded.

"He's left this world," Aldeirah responded, waving goodbye.

Que fell to her knees.

"You witch!" Chloe snarled.

"I've been called worse."

"You murderer, you ... you ..." Elizabeth hugged Que as tears rolled down her cheek.

Aldeirah showed no emotion as electrical currents wove through her fingers, motivating them to move on.

The area she'd shoved Murphy into looked like a stadium made of rock with rounded chambers high above, covered in greenery. A group of children had gathered to sit on the ledge that wrapped around the entire dome, watching them as if they were circus performers.

Aldeirah stood on a platform with her servants.

She aimed a spear directly at Murphy. "The game will begin with you," she announced, tossing it onto a rock pile.

Murphy had no choice but to climb up and retrieve the weapon. He tiptoed toward a crate lying on its side, hoping there wasn't a monster waiting to pounce on him. He glanced quickly through the slats and saw that Duncan was inside, kneeling over Jason's lifeless body. His sleeves were rolled up and his hands were covered in blood. "I didn't do this," he commented as Murphy's face paled from the sight. Duncan stood abruptly and slammed Murphy against the slats, splintering the wood further. "This is all *your* fault!"

Murphy pushed him away, looking at Jason's head wound. "How is this *my* fault?"

Duncan grabbed Murphy's shirt. "Because—"

Suddenly, the torches providing light from above extinguished, plunging them into darkness. Duncan shoved Murphy through the opening. "Go see what's happening."

A circle of light glimmered on the upper level. It sparked with electricity as lines rippled over the space where the prisoner's sat, connecting together to create a dome of deadly current. It was Aldeirah's reminder that she was in control, and that lives were at stake if they chose to not play by her rules.

It was so quiet that Murphy could hear his own mind screaming ... or was that Duncan?

A Nemmel was dragging Duncan to one of the lower cells. Murphy whacked its arm with the blunt side of the spear, and it howled, releasing its hold. Duncan shuffled over, trying to find the momentum to stand, when its hand lashed out to grasp his ankle and he fell forward onto his knees. Murphy swiftly scooped his arms under Duncan's and pulled. He hollered in pain as his leg stretched in a tug of war. Finally, the Nemmel let go, and they could hear the disappointment from the young crowd.

"Robinson, to your left!" Duncan threw the spear to Murphy just as a Nemmel slipped behind him.

"Which left?" Murphy asked, swinging the weapon like a bat.

He barely missed Duncan's head as he approached from the side, taking the spear out of his hands.

"This one!" Duncan replied. He jabbed to the right, hitting the creature in the chest as it stood up from a crouching position. It hissed, backing away.

Murphy reached for his weapon. "Give it," he demanded.

"No way! You're dangerous with this thing!"

"I'm supposed to be!"

Duncan pushed him. "Not so dangerous now."

"Said the coward hiding behind the weapon," Murphy murmured.

"I heard that," Duncan growled, tackling him to the ground. He pinned Murphy's shoulder and swung, but Murphy blocked the punch and returned the hit. Duncan's head snapped back from the blow and Murphy had to shake out his hand. Duncan pushed off Murphy's chest and picked up the spear in one fluid move. He rose it above his head as if it was a victory prize. "This is mine now," he taunted.

"No, it's not!" Murphy dove for the weapon, but Duncan reacted with a kick to his stomach. Murphy bent over, hugging his waist, and vomited while Duncan laughed.

Until a Nemmel sprung onto his back.

Murphy had a strong desire to let the ugly thing chomp on Duncan's neck as he spun around, trying to throw it off, but something grabbed the back of his hoodie and pulled him away before he could make that decision.

"You boys need to get your priorities straight," a man scolded, then chased after Duncan with a tool similar to a violin bow in his hands. The man stopped at the base of the rock pile, trying to catch Duncan's attention as he pitched stones at the Nemmel climbing up the slope. "Come down on this side," the man encouraged. He retrieved a square metal pick from his pocket and rested the instrument on his hip. "Cover your ears," he warned as Duncan jumped from the lowest boulder. He scraped the pick across a metal cord, producing such a racket that the creature scurried away.

Murphy recovered the spear and hustled back, following the man closely as he led them to an empty cell. Murphy looked back at the crate, feeling helpless. He squeezed his eyes shut, bumping accidentally into the man and poking his back with the sharp end of the weapon. "This is not a toy," the man remarked, turning around and taking the spear, "and it won't keep you safe."

Murphy recognized him immediately.

It was Mr. Moss.

"But these will," Mr. Moss said. He handed them each a flashlight. "The Nemmels will stay away so long as the batteries last."

Duncan pressed the button and swept the beam across the wall. About a dozen crimson eyes shone in the dark as the light passed over them. They scattered back, shielding their faces until one boldly climbed down to the opening. It stretched its elongated neck and hissed with its mouth open, showing a gap of missing teeth. "Thirsty," it spat, arching its skeletal back. Mr. Moss backed up slowly as more of the pale creatures came out of hiding.

"Move!" he ordered, and Murphy sped out of there like he was doing laps in the Indy 500, rushing by a human blur. He skidded to a stop.

A tall, thin woman dressed in rags held Jason in her arms. The Nemmels kept to the shadows, watching and waiting. She headed toward them.

"No!" Murphy cried out, running back.

She laid Jason in front of them, offering the creatures small bundles of folded blu-sap leaves. They tore them open, sucking up the sweet syrup greedily. She clicked her tongue and their heads rose. They responded with clacking noises.

"I see you've met my wife," Mr. Moss said, smiling.

"Can she really talk to them?" Duncan asked.

He nodded. "They were trapped down here before we arrived. Aldeirah sealed their exit. This used to be their home, a place where they gathered during the wet season to stay warm and dry. Many of them have families still outside that they haven't seen in months. They're angry and have difficulty trusting humans. But Ellie has been gaining their respect, so most of them leave us alone.

"Until there's no more food to give," Duncan said.

"There's plenty of preserved food that had been stored prior to Aldeirah's takeover. Finding something to drink is the problem. So we compromised. They would share their rations if we provided a source of water."

"But if you can leave to get water, why not escape?"

"The same reason Elizabeth and Violet won't."

"The children," Murphy stated.

Mr. Moss nodded. "It's not that simple though. We *can't* leave. There is only one way in or out. But we've been tearing down the rubble that's blocking the Nemmels' cell and have successfully opened a hole that Ellie's hand can fit through. She's been communicating with the Ringos, and they in turn have informed the Cromalites. That's how we receive our water and syrup."

"Why couldn't they help to get you out?"

"The rocks," Mr. Moss explained. "They're too heavy to lift."

"You need Mrs. Sheldon's power."

"I can arrange that."

Murphy whirled around. "Lu! How—"

...

Buckles stood trembling while Larsi sat between his legs, stroking his paw while keeping watch with Mitra. Even she couldn't stay calm knowing the risks Elizabeth, Violet and Chloe were taking as they combined their energy to dig through the rock. Que's voice faltered as she tried to maintain a song that would disguise the noise.

"Stop that singing!" one of the scouts complained. "It's so annoying!"

"We're almost there. Keep it up," Violet encouraged, lowering her voice.

The boy hadn't said anything about howling.

Buckles belted out a serenade that could make alley cats seeking a mate jealous.

The boy came over but had no weapons. Apparently, Aldeirah was wise enough to know that anyone touching metal to the prisoner's dome would not take kindly to the shock it would give.

"Mother!" the boy yelled. "Your prisoners have disappeared!"

...

"Be prepared!" Mr. Moss interrupted, directing their attention to the chaos above. "Sounds like Aldeirah's rounding up everyone for a battle."

"It's not the scouts," Nom-Lu declared, "it's the Rinegos pushing through. We've found a weak spot in the barricade."

"Scouts!" Aldeirah shouted. "Close the exit!"

Two older boys pulled out a heavy iron door from a gap between the walls, struggling to secure the bolt wedged inside the door jamb. They backed up, giving Aldeirah plenty of room. She raised both her hands and the door hummed to life.

So much for that exit, Murphy thought.

"Look!" Ellie cheered. The cell brightened, and large shadows came trotting through.

"Myrtle!" Murphy cried out. She was leading the pack with a tree trunk in her mouth.

"Fools!" Aldeirah screamed, wobbling on her feet. The prison dome flickered and went dark.

Murphy thought the rumbling under his feet was from the heavy treads of the Rinegos entering the grounds, but recalled that Myrtle was silent when she moved. He raised his head and saw that the platform was crumbling.

"Ellie!" Mr. Moss yelled. "The level above is about to collapse. The cell below is the supporting structure!"

Oh no.

All the young spectators hustled down the steps and gathered at the bottom, reluctant to join them for fear of how they'd be greeted. The Nemmels crowded on the other side, just as scared and suspicious, but the Rinegos quickly brought them together, herding them like sheep and moving them to the middle of the floor where it was safer.

"Freedom!" a Nemmel said, pointing its long black fingers toward the crude hole at the end of their cell's tunnel. They swarmed the area, and in a matter of minutes, the creatures finally got their wish.

Is *that* our only way out?" Murphy asked.

"It is now," Mr. Moss responded.

"Hurry," Nom-Lu ordered, looking up at the deserted platform. "We need to get everyone through before that ceiling drops."

"What about Chloe and the others?" Duncan asked.

Huh. He really does care, Murphy thought.

"We're here!" Chloe replied, descending the stairs. Buckles sprinted over to Myrtle. She was rolling Jason over with her muzzle, huffing and rocking back and forth. "He'll be okay," Murphy lied to her, wondering if that was more for his benefit. Gabe caught up and helped Murphy lift his brother onto Myrtle's back.

"I didn't say that the game had ended," Aldeirah shouted, finding her balance on the ledge.

"No one is losing today!" Chloe shouted back.

"That's where you're wrong, child." She lashed out and a vine wrapped around Elizabeth's wrists and the cage that held Que and Mitra.

Chloe gasped.

"Now, how can I make this more fun," she pondered. "Ah, yes ..." She swung her arm out and grabbed the vine as it lifted them into the air, then sent a line of electrical current inching its way toward Elizabeth's hands.

"Anyone want to try—"

"Lu!" Elizabeth called out. "Use the water!"

No, Murphy thought in horror. *She'll be electrocuted.*

"*Stonis!*" Chloe commanded. He turned to her in shock.

She gave it her all, spraying a sheet of ice around her grandma's wrists. The electricity sputtered as the ice expanded and the vine slipped off. Elizabeth tucked the cage under her arms as she fell, but Chloe continued to mold a capsule of ice around them, rotating her arm in a wide circle. Violet eased them down, using her wind to cushion the fall.

"Go!" Violet advised when she heard another rumble.

Aldeirah paced, mumbling and unaware that the last child climbed through the hole. Then a few stones dropped from the ceiling, and suddenly the whole cell came crashing down, bringing Aldeirah and the ledge into a tumbling heap of rubble.

Murphy covered his eyes. Their exit was gone, but so was Aldeirah.

"Where is Cordelia?" Violet asked.

"She's under there," Mr. Moss replied, jerking his head to the pile of rocks.

"Good riddance," Duncan remarked, and Violet shot him an angry look.

"Help me?" she pleaded, looking around at all the faces her sister had hurt.

Larsi folded her arms. "Why should we?"

Eleanor volunteered first. "Because it's the right thing to do."

One by one they cleared the stones, using the Rinegos' size to clear the heavy debris. "I see her!" Violet cried, kneeling down to brush away the dirt from her sister's mangled arm. Mr. Moss lifted Violet out of the way as Elizabeth used her wind to roll the remaining stones off of Cordelia's chest. She tried to sit up, wheezing from the effort, but her broken body wouldn't obey. She closed her eyes, taking small breaths to ease the pain.

Violet crawled to her side and picked up her limp hand.

"Why?" Aldeirah choked.

"Because we are family."

Tears rolled down Cordelia's face as she stared at the ceiling. Then she gasped and her eyes widened.

"The foundation," Ellie shouted, "it's cracking!"

Violet used her sleeve to wipe the blood from Cordelia's torn mouth. She looked at the adults and gave a slight nod. Their eyes were wet and glistening. "Go, now. Before it's too late."

Violet made the choice to stay.

Duncan slid on his stomach, using his forearms to propel him through the narrow tunnel. "The opening's too small. Myrtle won't be able to squeeze by."

"I have an idea," Elizabeth announced, digging into the sandy soil. She focused her wind and threw the rust-coloured particles in the air, creating a mini tornado. "Chloe, Larsi," she directed, "use your fire and blast the sand."

Orange and brown pebbles twirled inside the opening as the intense heat penetrated the funnel, turning it to glass as it melted along the walls. There was enough space now to park a tank.

"Cool," Duncan praised.

Elizabeth ran to end of the passage, noticing that the exit walls had not changed. The heat hadn't reached this far, which meant she'd be unable to smash through the opening as she had hoped.

She stepped back and rubbed her eyes, thinking of a solution, when a muffled voice called from outside.

"Elizabeth, is everyone with you?"

"Yes," she answered, relieved. "Over here!" She waved her hand through the small hole.

"Clear the entrance. We're coming in," the man ordered as the roar of an engine started up. "This is going to get messy."

An explosive boom vibrated under her feet as she ran, followed by a wail of scraping metal against rock. Elizabeth had just enough time to dive through the opening before a rainfall of glass came crashing down. The nose of an aircraft pitched forward, skidding over the loose debris. It reached the top of the pile, then slid back down to rest on its side.

It looked like a replica of the boat Murphy, Chloe and Jason had taken, except this had triangular symbols on its side and iridescent wings rippling in the element colours.

The cockpit lifted and out popped a boy about the same age as Chloe and her friends.

"Are they ready, Dad?" he asked. There was no doubt that this was Chloe's twin brother. He looked just like her.

"I believe they are, Zareb," a man in his early thirties said, approaching Chloe with half a smile. She stood very still as he lifted her chin and whispered, "You have your mother's beautiful eyes."

Then she fainted.

"Well, that wasn't quite the reaction I was hoping for," Khalon chuckled.

Duncan squatted next to Chloe, shaking her gently, but she didn't respond. Khalon pulled her up onto his lap and cradled her head, giving her time to recover. Gabe called out her name as he held her hand and squeezed, sending a flutter of butterflies straight to her stomach.

"Maybe I can help," Tuk offered. He flittered out of the aircraft with a pair of new wings similar to the aircraft's, ready to summon water, when Chloe's eyes flew open at the sound of his voice. She blushed, secretly disappointed that Gabe released his grip when she sat up.

"Tuk!" Larsi cheered. Que and Mitra jumped with joy, throwing themselves against the bars to embrace him. Nom-Lu was behind him, grasping a tiny hollow tube in his hand. "Violet gave me this," he stated, pushing it through a set of loops to unlock the cage door.

Mr. Moss cleared his throat. "I hate to interrupt the reunion, but—"

Chunks of rock fell in heavy thuds from the ceiling as cracks in the foundation spread across the dome. Elizabeth wove nets of greenery to help keep the massive stones from dropping, and the sprites assisted Larsi to create pillars from the fallen rock, hoping to provide some stability.

Zareb hopped into the cockpit and started up the engine to reverse the ship, when all of them screamed, "STOP!" The vessel was keeping the inner tunnel from collapsing and just about everyone was inside. Chloe stood at the entrance, terrified, as Murphy tried to inch his way under a huge boulder that teetered over him. Elizabeth turned, thrusting out her transparent arm to push the rock back up the slippery slope, but her power failed.

Murphy carefully took the key from his pocket and threw it in Chloe's direction. The boulder slid further down, and he crouched to avoid being hit, praying for the first time.

Chloe wiped her sweaty hands on her overalls and separated the key. "I can't remember the words!" she uttered, panic-stricken.

Tears brimmed Murphy's eyes. "Hurry!" he urged. Larsi molded a rim around the rock with her fire, temporarily holding the rock in place as he scrambled inside.

"*Eko lit ma!*"

"No, Chloe!" Que responded. "That's the wrong phrase!"

But Chloe hadn't blown into the top portion as expected. She'd placed the star shape onto her bracelet, connecting the two layers together to form the Az-Yen fleet insignia her father wore as a pin. She started to grow taller and shapelier as she aged. Her hair flowed beyond her shoulders as her clothes morphed into a bodysuit of armoured gold.

"That can't be," Elizabeth remarked, "she shouldn't be affected by the phrase."

"Unless *she* is the true Golden Gem," Larsi said.

And she was golden. Her skin shimmered like a sunset on the water. It radiated out of her and covered the entire opening. Murphy's watch buzzed, flashing zeros, then stopped. Chloe had halted time. She spun around in her new body, lighting up the tunnel with a sparkling display of wings. She was gorgeous.

"Do you know what this means?" Nom-Lu remarked, flipping in the air.

"Chloe holds the legendary powers of life. She has the Cromalisum DNA to transform and create! Our species can be saved!"

Chloe accelerated into multiple shapes until she found the smaller body she wanted. She trotted over to Myrtle. "I think she wants to heal Jason," Murphy suggested as she lifted up her front legs to reach Jason's temple with her curly horn.

A mass of golden particles swirled in the air, hovering over Jason as a woman's head emerged. Lay-E-Fenya's face stretched over to kiss Chloe on her forehead. "I am proud of you, Aldeirah."

Chloe backed away, transforming into a teenager. "I don't want to be called that."

"I understand," she replied, vaporizing into a golden mist that streamed into Jason's nostrils. His chest rose as he inhaled a deep breath.

"Called what?" he asked, taking a second look at her and grinning. "I like Twinkie better."

Murphy turned to Duncan. "If Chloe looks like that when we're in high school, *you* will have some serious competition."

Chloe morphed again, knowing that her wish would decide the fate of everyone around her. She closed her eyes, concentrating on the wedding band Cordelia wore and the name Arthur Miller.

Duncan chortled. "Yeah, I'd ask her out, but I'll pass on dating a goat."

Chloe kicked him with her hoof, bleating. "Ezbragryte," Duncan corrected, almost peeing his pants from laughing.

Chloe leaned her little body against the wall, panting. Violet waved goodbye, mouthing the words *thank you* as she lay beside her sister. Violet and Cordelia's skin began to dry and shrivel, exposing their skeletal frames, and then they disintegrated into dust.

Suddenly Murphy's watch beeped.

CRACK!

The boulder crashed to the ground, surrounding them in darkness.

...

Murphy opened his eyes to true sunlight. It was cold, but it still felt good. Chloe, Jason and Gabe were talking to Zareb and laughing. Khalon showed the children some magic tricks with Mitra and Buckles's help, while Duncan, Larsi and Nom-Lu showed off their dancing skills. Murphy propped himself up on his elbows.

"How are you feeling?" Que asked as Tuk brought him water.

"*Glavik*," Tuk stated, holding it out. "It means—"

"I know. *Glass.*" Murphy replied.

Tuk winked. "You're learning."

Murphy decided to join Jason and the gang when Duncan waved him over. "Robinson, over here."

Duncan noticed Murphy staring at his ripped pant leg. "It's from the Nemmel," he answered, smoothing his hand over the rough blisters that had formed on his ankle. "I refused treatment because it's the only evidence I have to prove I'm not nuts."

Murphy nodded. "Just so long as it doesn't get infected."

"Aw, didn't know you cared," Duncan remarked, holding up a blu-sap leaf to his lips.

"Well, if your leg falls off and you grow a bug appendage, don't come crying to me." Murphy backed away, laughing at Duncan's baffled expression.

"So ...?" Murphy said as he approached Jason and Chloe.

Chloe shrugged. "I'm able to grant my own wishes." She smiled, taking in the happy gathering.

"It all worked out, didn't it?"

She nodded, recalling her father's message on the cave wall, "I realized that if Cordelia's husband survived his illness, she'd be able to stay home and raise Charlotte without the need to work as a nanny. No court, no suffering and no cause for revenge or destruction."

"What happened to the doctor?"

"Jail. He attempted to murder one of my ancestors and the court found him guilty."

"Huh. That's why Joel wanted the key. He knew he could change history with it. So Westfield is saved and the children that Cordelia abducted are back with their families as if nothing happened. Sweet justice!"

"Helen was found too. Mr. Moss is thrilled to have his sister back."

"My hero," Murphy said, giving her a nudge. "Just don't let it go to your head. You're pretty without resembling Que's mouth full of water."

Chloe hugged him. "Promise."

"Your mom will be so proud."

"Yip," she hiccupped.

"Are you drinking the *tarna*? Because Duncan looks like he's had his share."

"Maybe a little," Chloe giggled, taking Duncan's hand.

Murphy laughed, watching her hop away to the rhythm of the Conga line.

EPILOGUE

"Did you bring the popcorn?"

"Check," Chloe replied.

"Did *you* bring the pop?"

"Yup."

They turned to Jason. "What?" he remarked defensively, "I brought something too."

"And?"

"My marvelousness."

Chloe rolled her eyes. "Is that even a word?"

"In Quin it is," he stated.

Chloe knew better, but it was Jason's dimple that betrayed him, proving he was holding in a grin.

"Okay," he admitted. "I brought pizza."

"Where?" Murphy asked. "And please don't say it's in your pocket."

Jason chuckled. "No. I set it out already, but a few slices are missing." He stopped rubbing his stomach when he saw their disappointment. "Aw, come on guys. It's Hawaiian!"

They sat together with their legs hanging over the ledge, watching with excitement as the coloured gems slid across the walls, creating fragmented stories of their future, allowing them to fill in the gaps. It was literally history in the making.

"We should write a book about our adventures," Jason suggested. "It would be legendary!"

"Why?" Murphy responded. "We're already watching the movie."

Jason sniffed the air. "Hey, did you let one rip?"

Murphy waved his hand in front of his nose. "Not me."

"Well, it wasn't ..." Chloe leaned over Murphy. "Jason!" She pointed at Buckles, lying beside him, chewing on all the discarded pizza crusts that just happened to fall conveniently on the ground.

"Busted," Murphy whispered with amusement.

"Huh," Jason, commented. "I guess dogs really *do* fart."

GLOSSARY

A
A - a
Alda - heir
Aldeirah - Golden Gem

B
Ba-neewa - bring
Blu-sap - trees found on Quinsatheria Island
Borte - found
Bae-yad(s) - bond(s)

C
Chanool - child
Chey-la - Cheers!
Cromalisum Flower - Xaldorian plant used to create Cromalites
Cromalites - hybrid species of sprites

D
De - meet
Dek - your
Del - so
Derna - dear
Diastrum - magical liquid formed by blood and alien rock properties

E
Eko - aquire
Eno - one
En-Quay - Earth

Ezbragryte - animal that grants wishes

F
Far - may
Fenue - we
Fim-lar - first
Flit-wik - fire
Frin-nads - friends

G
Glavik - glass
Gurt(s) - newborn Ezbragrytes

H
Ha-Plume berries - favoured food of the Rinegos
Har-ryn - horn
Hiva - have
Holdyn - safe

I
Ibaz - has
Iplis - place

J
Joisen - enjoy

K
Ki - to
Kusoa - key

L
Li(s) - gate(s)
Lif-ris – leaves of royalty
Lit - new

M
Ma - form
Mican-dul - instrument used to turn jewels into fuel
Min - this
Moplenta - meal
My-ana - water

N
Na - I
Nat - made
Nef - of
Nemmels - Creatures of the Pit
Nom-Lu - King of Quinsatheria

O
Oc - us
Omat - am
Osnow - open

Q
Quin - Quinsatheria's official language
Quinsatheria - Island of the Cromalites

R
Rakwid - chosen
Reta-vem - remove
Rinegos - allies to the Cromalites

S
Sawa - sorry
See - that
Sel-clo - close
Sheenu - share
Sherna - enter
Stonis - ice

T
Tarna - drinkable substance from the blu-sap tree
Tris- the
Tri-Murids - enemies of the Cromalites
Trona - please
Tronef - pleased

U
U-Dae-Yis - queen of Quinsatheria
Ume - center
Urden - exit

V
Vo - in

W
Waek-Lyrens - winged monsters that produce nightmares
Watis - warden
Wem-Luk - welcome

X
Xaldorian - humanoid alien species
Xaldorn U-Rion - former planet of the aliens

Y
Yuderhund - puppy/dog
Yuntay - county
Yus - you

Z
Zar - our

ABOUT THE AUTHOR

SIMONE E. OWS is a personal support worker and holds a diploma in Child and Youth Work. The inspiration for The Legends of Moss Ridge came to her in a dream so compelling that she was driven to write it down. After many years of development, it is now her debut novel. Born in Windsor, Ontario, Simone lives in Niagara Falls with her husband, Wally, and her cat, Milo.

CPSIA information can be obtained
at www.ICGtesting.com
Printed in the USA
BVHW030032101021
618619BV00001B/3

9 781525 586194